Alfred Austin

The Human Tragedy

Alfred Austin

The Human Tragedy

ISBN/EAN: 9783337361969

Printed in Europe, USA, Canada, Australia, Japan

Cover: Foto ©Andreas Hilbeck / pixelio.de

More available books at **www.hansebooks.com**

THE HUMAN TRAGEDY

BY

ALFRED AUSTIN

FOURTH EDITION

𝔏𝔬𝔫𝔡𝔬𝔫

MACMILLAN AND CO.

AND NEW YORK

1891

DEDICATION

TO

THE EDITION OF 1876

TO H. J. A.

THREE graces still attend me, since the day
Your step across my graceless threshold came:
Reverence, and Gratitude, and Love, their name.
Reverence, whose gaze fears from the ground to stray,
And bows its head, and sues to you to lay
Your foot thereon, and keep my base self down:
Next, Gratitude, that, bolder, by degrees
Creeps up the folds of wedlock's rescuing gown,
To make a circling fondness round your knees ;
And lastly, Love, which from that low perch sees
Chaste lips, and tender eyes, and tresses brown,
And, darting upward, finds a home with these.
So stand we level in that high embrace,
And I have all your glory on my face.

ACT I

ACT I

PERSONAGES:

OLIVE—GODFRID—GILBERT.

PROTAGONIST:

LOVE.

PLACE:

ENGLAND.

TIME:

JUNE—NOVEMBER 1857.

THE HUMAN TRAGEDY

ACT I

I

Love! all-creating Love, primordial Power,
By whom the Heavens, from whom the stars had birth,
Fountain and force of air, light, season, shower,
Growth, and the green apparel of the Earth,
Source of the seed and secret of the flower,
Parent of all our woe and all our worth,
Thine too the fervent tenderness that gives
Breath unto Song, whereby it, quickening, lives.

II

Therefore this earthy strain, wherein are blent
Peace and unrest, meetings and partings dire,
Joy that consumes and never can content,
Passion and pain, despondency, desire,
And hope that weaves its own pale cerëment,
Do Thou with heavenly harmony inspire;
So that it steal within the heart, and be
A cherished sadness, even like to Thee.

III

But not of these alone, of yearnings blind,
Swift raptures and slow penalties, I sing.
I must be lifted by a fiercer wind,
And whirled and wafted on a wider wing,
Still as Religion, Country, or Mankind,
Wakes in the shell and wails along the string.
For Faith, Hope, Charity, whereby we be
Noblest, enact The Human Tragedy.

IV

Rude Winter, violating neutral plain
Of March, through April's territory sallied,
Scoured with his snowy plume its fair domain,
Then, down encamping, made his daring valid.
Nor till May, mustering all her gallant train
Of phalanxed spears Spring's cowering levies rallied,
Did the usurper from the realm of sleet
Fold his white tents, and shriek a wild retreat.

V

Then, all at once, the land laughed into bloom,
Feeling its alien fetters were undone ;
Rushed into frolic ecstasies ; the plume
The courtly lilac tosses i' the sun,
Laburnum tassels dripping faint perfume,
Hawthorn and chestnut, showed, not one by one,
But all in rival pomp and joint array,
Blent with green leaves as long delayed as they.

VI

The dog-rose, simplest, sweetest of its kind,
Brocaded brake and hedgerow ere as yet,
In grassy hollow screened from sun and wind,
The primrose paled and perished.   The violet
Closed not blue eyes, to early doom resigned,
Ere it beheld the clambering woodbine wet
With honey self-distilled, and knew that earth
Would, at its death, be sweet as at its birth.

VII

And to its woodland grave with hasteful feet
Came the anemone, and o'er it flung,
In love but scarce in sorrow, such a sheet
Of pink-white petals as befits the young
Whose fair false hopes the kindly gods defeat:
While, following swift, the hyacinth upsprung
From the soft sod, and through the sylvan shells
Thrust his bold stalk, and shook his scented bells.

VIII

The cuckoo, babbling egotist, from tree
To tree as with short restless wing he flew,
Called his own name, doubling the word for glee:
The stockdove meditated, all day through,
Its one deep note of perched felicity;
And the sweet bird to one sad memory true,
Finding the day for its laments too brief,
Charmed listening night with its melodious grief.

IX

No longer cowering by the fleecy screen
Of their warm dams or bleating at the ills
Of unkind life and norland tempests' spleen,
Huddled the helpless lambs,—but skipped like rills
Among the dykes and mounds of pastures green,
And orchards sunned by golden daffodils;
Frisked like young Loves, in ever-shifting ring,
Round the old boles, flushed with the wine of Spring.

X

A subtle glory crept from mead to mead,
Till they were burnished saffron to behold,
And, from their wintry byres and dark sheds freed,
The musing kine lay couched on cloth of gold.
Abetted by the Spring, the humblest weed
Wore its own coronal, and gaily bold
Waved jewelled sceptre.   Stirred by some strange power,
The very walls seemed breaking into flower.

XI

And all throughout the air there reigned a sense
Of deep smooth dream with odorous music laden,
Of life too conscious made and too intense
By sudden advent of excessive Aiden:
Bewilderment of beauty's affluence,
Such as delights, though dangerous, man and maiden.
And then it was, by Love's despotic grace,
Godfrid first gazed on Olive's form and face.

XII

She was no goddess of majestic mould,
That draws the gaze and homage of the crowd,
Mere marble flesh, voluptuously cold, ·
Bait for the rich and chattel of the proud;
One of those splendid idols, gorged with gold,
And surfeited on flattery's scented cloud,
Within whose hollow bosom fashion dwells,
False priest, and thence emits its oracles.

XIII

She was an English maiden, unexiled
From that true Paradise, an English home,
Where fair Eve's fairer daughters, unbeguiled
By tree or subtle serpent, still may roam.
Evil and good she knew but as a child
Knoweth, when reading in some ancient tome
Of gruesome deeds, it sheddeth transient tears
For wrong it neither understands nor fears.

XIV

She had been cradled amid loveliest things,
And rocked to sweetest music.   Scent of flowers,
Long dreamy lawns, and birds on happy wings,
Keeping their homes in never-rifled bowers,
Cool fountains filling with their murmurings
The sunny silence 'twixt the chiming hours,
Kind looks, and gentle voices,—these had made
The even world in which she lived and strayed.

XV

Harsh word or cold she never heard nor spake,
But simple homage with frank smile repaid,
And they who served her, served her for the sake
Of being near so fair and kind a maid.
E'en in brute breasts her coming seemed to wake
A human instinct : loud the stables neighed,
Hearing her footfall ; and the herds that fed,
Felt her afar, and trooped to greet her tread.

XVI

Until she rose it did not seem the dawn.
The shaggy deerhound none could yet decoy
From where he lay long-stretched upon the lawn,
When she came forth, bounded and bayed for joy,
Then followed on her gaze ; the orphan fawn,
To every other voice and summons coy,
Came trotting through the dew at her command,
And laid its head beneath her lily hand.

XVII

Fancy, to find her likeness, earth and skies
Would vainly sweep ; all paragons must fail.
For unto what would it compare her eyes ?
Not unto violets ; for violets pale.
Her hair to golden daylight ?   Daylight dies.
And, for her face, how would the rose avail
When the rose hangs its head and bends its stem ?—
Compare fair things to her, not her to them.

XVIII

Such, and so guarded by benignant stars,
Was Olive, when that unknown factor, Fate,
Who every earthly calculation mars,
Made Godfrid guest within her father's gate:
After May, marching with her shimmering cars,
Had driven Winter from the plains where late
He overawed the Spring and had unfurled
His hoary usurpation o'er the world.

XIX

Who says the Seasons change, nor haply knows
That to each change man's heart is still replying?
That sweet shy Spring whose colour comes and goes,
That Summer in a golden languor lying,
Half-stifled by the smell of the musk-rose,
That Autumn of her hectic beauty dying,
And even Winter blowing through his hands
To thaw his veins, rule us with unseen bands?

XX

Had Godfrid first that peaceful threshold crossed
What time the robin pecks against the pane,
When dripping boughs beweep their beauty lost,
And furrowed fields lament the rifled grain,
Or e'en when curled by crisp October's frost,
The shivering leaves are blown aslant like rain,
He might have come and gone and left no trace
In Olive's heart, no shade on Olive's face.

XXI

Winter is ruled by male Divinities;
But Summer, gentle Summer, owns the sway
Of that coequal sex whose mild decrees
All understanding souls love and obey.
And so it happed that ere by tame degrees
Of trite acquaintance broadening day by day,
Which disenchant the sense, till all seems known,
Godfrid and Olive walked the woods alone.

XXII

And who amid June's world of fair and sweet,
Eglantined hedgerow, woodbine-scented air,
To guide his novel footsteps was so meet
As Olive, queen of all things sweet and fair?
Who knew so well the foxglove's cool retreat,
In what moist crevice hid the maidenhair,
Where piped the throstle loudest, or the sound
Of runnel rippled silveriest underground?

XXIII

Distinguished she a flower, he plucked it straight;
And if she spied a rounded nest half hid
In forkëd spray, from which the fluttered mate
Had flown as they drew nigh, though still amid
Yet denser boughs its love-lord piped elate,
He, while she half abetted and half chid,
The curtain drew aside, for her to peep
Upon the warm close-nestled eggs, asleep.

XXIV

Then, as she held her breath, and crosswise laid
An arrowy finger on a bow-shaped lip,
The leafy covering, careful, he remade,
Just as before, then soft away would slip.
When hark ! the cuckoo called !   Anew they stayed
Their steps, more deeply of the sound to sip,
And gazed at one another with mute ken,
Until it should repeat the note again ;

XXV

And then walked on, still hearing in their heart
Echo on echo of that joyous strain,
Which hath a sense of moisture, and seems part
Of childlike April's laughter-rippled rain ;
Which makes the soul to bud, the pulse to start,
The hackneyed heart youth's wonderland regain,
When, ere by passion parched, by grief turned sere,
Life gleams with smile or shimmers through a tear.

XXVI

Then would a freshet runnel cross their track,
Low-purling to itself for secret bliss,
Now pattering onward, now half-turning back,
To give the smooth round pebbles one more kiss :
Here travelling straight as haste, there, with changed tack,
Meandering on in utter waywardness.
Now diving under tangled grass, and then
With frolic laugh bubbling to sight again.

XXVII

Whereat they stopped afresh, for him to say :
"Shall we not hearken to its musings bland ?
For Nature hath a gift of tongues, which they
Alone who heed the Spirit understand.
Sometimes I hope I am not wholly clay,
And you, meseems, are of the chosen band."
Attentive then they drank its teachings clear,
Seeming to listen with the selfsame ear.

XXVIII

But what it spake, neither nor said nor asked,
But on a seat, under a blossoming thorn,
One bunch of whiteness, that had vainly tasked
The painter's hand and put his art to scorn,
Olive the guide, they sate them down and basked
In shaded sunshine of the mounting morn,
And knew, by silence dropped on bush and brake,
'Twas noon, when birds their wise siesta take.

XXIX

And they grew silent too, till with a smile
He turned and said : "Now, do not laugh nor scoff!
But will you graciously sit here awhile,
And let me stand a little farther off?"
He spoke so simply, so exempt from guile,
She, guileless, did his will.   "And, pray you, doff
That churlish hat, and leave your forehead bare,
So that the shadows fall upon your hair.

XXX

"Yes, yes, like that!   Now, on my word, you make
A monstrous pretty picture, thorn and you!
Wherein we see full many a hanging flake
Of Winter living within Summer's hue.
How strange it seems the thorn should neither shake
Its snowy plumage down and o'er you strew
A white cold sheet, nor in the radiant glare
You shed should melt, leaving its branches bare!"

XXXI

Then to the rustic seat beneath the thorn,
Which overhung them with its bleachëd hood,
Returning: "They are right, though sophists scorn,
Who say that Beauty is the chiefest good.
For Truth still leaves its votaries forlorn,
And Virtue hides within a tangled wood,
Which, as one pushes on, yet denser grows.
Beauty alone hath wisdom and repose."

XXXII

"O no!" she said, "it is a little thing,
And to be strong and manful is the best:
Beauty is queen, but Valour still is king,
Mere consort she, but he the lord confessed.
Her wisdom and repose from this but spring,—
She waits his bidding; but his large unrest
Life's arduous height still climbs, nor ever stops,
Like the young sun shouldering the mountain tops."

XXXIII

"Yours sounds the nobler doctrine," he replied,
"And fits you well, though mine saves honour too.
But words for ever of the mark fly wide,
And language makes that false which thought left true."
"Then let us call wise silence to our side,"
With laughing lids she said, "to find the clue
To that agreeing ground where creeds that jar
Upon the lips, the mind's twin-brothers are."

XXXIV

"Nay, if you thus discourse, I would have you talk
Till the declining sun shall yield the sky
To the mild lustre of the milky walk."
Whereat the laughter faded from her eye;
And, like two flowers upon a single stalk,
Fed by one hidden root, they secretly
Drank the same thoughts, same feelings, and same air,
And, without looking, knew each other there.

XXXV

He was of open mien and virile guise,
In manhood fully blossomed, as are those,
Reared by the tarrying Northland's seasoning skies,
When their fifth lustre draweth just to close.
Of that hard-wooded stock time checks and tries,
Whose fibre slowly unto ripeness grows,
But, once matured, withstands the storms and drouth
That stunt the hastier saplings of the South.

XXXVI

Unto the ancient Faith his folk had clung,
When reason chimed with passion to unbind
The folds in which, while yet its limbs were young,
Fond nurse Authority had swathed mankind.
Withal 'twas whispered by the curious tongue
He had, himself, of late unserfed his mind,
But, out of courtesy, and since the goal
Uncertain seems, in peace possessed his soul.

XXXVII

To him was woman's loveliness the sum
Of heavenly intimations from earth's dome.
The smell of tasselled larch-woods, and the hum
Of happy bee bearing its honey home,
The cascade's plash, the breezes crisp that come
From unguessed lands on backs of bounding foam ;
These, to his sense, but scattered fragments were
Of central beauty, perfected in Her.

XXXVIII

And when his eyes the radiance did perceive
Of such, it moved him like a dewy star
That tingles on the high calm brow of eve,
It would be far too gross to wish less far ;
And with whose peace we but aspire to weave
The thoughts and feelings which the deepest are
In the unfathomable soul, and do
Alone feed hope that we are heavenly too.

XXXIX

And now it was as though June ne'er before
Had filled her lap with roses ; as though now
Did merle first sing and skylark rippling soar,
And wren and blackcap glance from bough to bough.
The daisy's frill a wondrous newness wore,
And childlike marvel puckered up their brow,
When from deep banks, with tangled tussocks heaped,
The roguish periwinkle, laughing, peeped.

XL

When with staid mothers' milk and sunshine warmed,
The pasture's frisky innocents bucked up,
Flush from the ground, or, on smooth hillock swarmed,
With hornless fronts each other 'gan to tup,
That frolic sight their eyes as freshly charmed,
As though ne'er carved on many an antique cup,
Nor time on time, when men and Gods were young,
By the pastoral Muse of the sweet Sicilian sung.

XLI

But them, whom morning had together brought
And knit with links of Nature's subtle art,
By no third breath divided or distraught,
The eve unkindly worse than thrust apart ;
Conjoining with them tongues, disowned, unsought,
Whose foreign accents jar the home-sick heart,
Making it inly fretful, and but yearn
The shy secluded hours would swift return.

XLII

And these returned, when on the hawthorn spray
The covert nightingale unceasing sang
Sweet trouble that but fitful broke by day,
− And every copse with argute anguish rang.
The moon came up and took her trackless way,
Pale as when first she heard the love-bird's pang,
Pale with a sorrow of her own untold,—
Found it a voice, perchance were half consoled.

XLIII

Then, with no other nigh them or between,
And over them the night's resplendent vault,
Olive and Godfrid in the dewy sheen
Stepped forth, unmindful of fair Eden's fault.
Beneath a flowering chestnut's moonlit screen,
At a white gateway leaning, made they halt,
By currents drawn of pleasurable pain
Onward to Love's immeasurable main.

XLIV

But they were still among the fresh sweet rills
That feed Love's brackish ocean ; and the call
Of nightingale to nightingale in trills
That lived upon each other, like a tall
And many-plashing fountain that refills
Its silvery jets with silvery jets that fall,
Seemed to speak all their thinking, and impart
What was yet inarticulate in their heart.

C

XLV

Thus in the leafy moonshine hushed they stood,
Their entranced souls surrendered to the night,
Deep drinking of unmoralisëd good
From the clear founts of beauty and delight.
And when some throat its wistful treble would
Prolong, it seemed, beyond even music's might,
They listened with eyes that met, till the slow strain
Quick quavered down the sharp descents of pain.

XLVI

Thus steeped in luscious sadness, unexpressed
Save by joint silence, back they turned, alas!
Home from the shrubbery's many a tuneful nest,
By twinkling gravel skirting shimmering grass.
Then Olive, folded to her father's breast
An instant, like an image from a glass,
Vanished,—and all seemed blank : though Godfrid's host
With kindly converse filled the vacant post.

XLVII

He could not vaunt, bequeathed to him from yore,
, A knightly name, in sooth a dubious boast
Now when the knightly scutcheon glows no more,
And knightly honour stalks a nerveless ghost.
His sires had wrung from ransacked sea and shore
The guerdon modern glory covets most,
Wealth, with wealth's crowning symbol, once the spoil
Of faithful swords, a hold upon the soil.

XLVIII

Among his sylvan acres, loosed from care,
He led the free and philosophic life
Denied to those poor straws of fate, who share
The Court's mean pomp or Senate's frothy strife ; ·
Constant at covert, Sessions, house of prayer,
To that true household god, a helpful wife,
Left gracious hearth and hospitable board,
In his own home adoring and adored.

XLIX

For Olive's was a heart which back to love
Turns as a flower will turn to warmth and light ;
And on the perch of home, even as a dove
Upon one bough, with never a thought of flight,
Heedless of all beyond it or above,
Will sit and coo from morning unto night,
So stayed contented, happy,—unaware
That earth held ought or larger or more fair.

L

But as there lies a deep and dewy cell
In the most open flower, which yields the sweet,
Stored in its virgin coy receptacle,
Neither to parent sun nor fostering heat,
But guards it close, till on the fragrant bell
Some child of air, with wandering wings and feet,
Settling to sip, down to its heart doth press,
And boldly rifles its last lusciousness ;

LI

So in the heart of most ingenuous maid
That ever nestled at a father's knee,
Hearkened a mother's precepts unafraid,
And slept unweaned from home felicity,
Dwells a dim nook not parents' feet invade,
No tongue may violate, no eye can see,
Till some strange wanderer, sent by Heaven, shall dive,
And suck the secret of that honeyed hive.

LII

And thus within fair Olive's filial breast
There was another Olive, unallowed
To outer gaze, and by herself but guessed
Dimly, as by deep lake a fleecy cloud :
Olive that trembled, yet to none confessed
That she had trembled, when her lids were bowed
Over some poet's page which freshly told
The old, old story, that is never old.

LIII

But at no other than the rainbow tale
Which tearful fancy weaves, had Olive yet
Felt the pulse quicken and the cheek grow pale ;
No voice had heard, to mesh her like a net,
No touch had known, to thrill her like a wail,
No face had seen, impossible to forget ;
But only thought, when bent the page above,
How sweet, for others, it must be to love.

LIV

But when, that night, she, left alone with sleep,
Dimpled the pillow with her golden head,
Did stealthy dream o'er trustful slumber creep,
Now come, now gone, now clear, now vanishëd,
Of one whose words could thrill, whose voice could weep,
Whose silence more than others' language said,
Manlier than men, gentler than women are,
Bright as a sun, but quiet as a star.

LV

And gentleness-in-strength wins those that are,
Not strong, but gentle only; and when dawn
With glittering prow burst o'er the Eastern bar,
And gossamer-veiled mead and dew-faced lawn
Seemed waves of rippling sunshine scanned afar,
The waking thoughts of Olive back were drawn
Unto sweet yesterday, with half-owned hope
To-day, afresh, to tread love's gradual slope.

LVI

But from that pleasant pathway fitful Fate,
Who bridles with delay the human heart
Only to speed it to the goal more straight,
All the long morn, with many a spurious start,
Withheld their fretful footsteps,—trifles, prate,
Which, themselves worthless, let prized time depart.
Nor till the dark elm shadows nigh had grown
Long as the trunks, roved they once more alone.

LVII

Then over silent sward, and underneath
Pendulous trees, and onward to the sweeter,
Path-thridden woods, whose arching branches wreathe
For the heart's communings a refuge meeter,
Where even the thoughtless winds forbear to breathe,
But the fleet hours pass pitilessly fleeter;
Or where, half-sadly warbling as it went,
Like a boy-poet's happy discontent,

LVIII

Moss-bedded runnel anxious music made,
Eager for broader future; and along
The freër streamlet, till the rash cascade
Bounded adown the cataract, would-be strong;
Thence by the lake's mild margin that delayed
Its froward petulance, and by the song
Of river blithe with its enfranchisement,
Olive and Godfrid solitary went.

LIX

The world was all shut out, and Eden's gate
Upon its golden hinges back was rolled.
Death, deluge, tongues' confusion, sorrow, hate,
Seemed but a tale, to please sweet sadness told;
Such as some minstrel, welcomed by the great,
Strenuous would wring from simple harp of old,
Waking live echoes in the long-dead years,
And melting happy hearts to happier tears.

LX

No such, no kindred thoughts, as yet perplexed
These two young souls, on moving to their fate.
Cheeks nearer drawn by some magnetic text,
Hand at a rural stile or churlish gate
Held out for courteous aid, but till the next
For more than courtesy retained, and prate
Which dipped into the inner life, were all
That proved them heritors of Adam's Fall.

LXI

But summer days, like happiest fairy story
That e'er of love and love's crowned longings breathed,
Sadden to close, and slowly-fading glory
Of dell, and glade, and runnel meadow-sheathed,
And breadth of bracken green round beeches hoary,
Dies, and to memory only is bequeathed;
And tight-linked hands, at parting's leaden knell,
Relax, and wave irresolute farewell.

LXII

And by the porch impatient horses paw,
And nearer sound admonitory feet.
Spurred by the desperate hour, released from awe
By sudden sense of parting, rashly meet,
But strangers hitherto, their lips, to draw
A draught of joy so novel, so complete,
They feel that, voided of the common air,
That kiss must linger, fixed for ever there !

LXIII

A moment only : but such moments are
Beyond time's count, aye, or eternity's.
Closer the feet ; upon the door ajar
Intrusive hand.   From just-discovered bliss
Themselves they wrench asunder.   Faint and far
O'er gravel drive, o'er harder highway, is
Prolonged the fragile link of sounding wheel.
Then, hush.   Then twilight.   Then Night's silent seal.

LXIV

And swiftly borne along through winding lanes,
Belted by thickets in whose cloistered deeps
Nature's recluses sang late vesper strains,
Godfrid, like one who now half wakes half sleeps,
Dropping on dreamy consciousness the reins
Till o'er the will an opiate slumber creeps,
His soul surrendered to that mystic bliss
Which memory keeps from a departed kiss.

LXV

Kiss, because flown for ever, ne'er forgot,
Since unfulfilled, with freshness still besprent,
Love's baptism of dew, love's tightest knot,
Of all love's rites the holiest sacrament :
A never full-ripe fruit, that cannot rot,
An unplucked flower which ne'er will shed its scent ;
Perfect imperfect, nought can mar or mend,
A fair beginning, still uncursed by end.

LXVI

And when the gloaming, faded from the sky,
Left dim the outlines of each winding lane,
He still was wandering where the sun rode high,
By glade and stream, grave wood and florid plain,
With one whose soul was stationed in her eye,
Fresh as June's grass, golden as Autumn's grain,
Whose voice was passion's undertone, whose mouth
Sweet as warm showers blown up from the soft South.

LXVII

Nor till he marked the melancholy gleam
Of huddled homes, and with a shock of pain
Heard the Promethean monster's strident scream,
Vanished calm rapture's visionary reign.
Then, like to one who starts from a deep dream,
And but beholds the darkness, so in vain
He strove with fancy's eye once more to see,
Lying awake with black reality.

LXVIII

And as on roaring adamantine feet
Further and further ever was he whirled
From the closed gates of Eden's vanished seat,
Beneath dun domes in rolling vapour furled,
Or by white banks of moonlit meadowsweet,
From dreamland's height yet lower was he hurled,
Till, hemmed in between past and future years,
Turning, he stood, like quarry girt with spears.

LXIX

"Can this be Love? Love no such question asks.
Love never yet was yoked with sluggish doubt ;
And while tame Fancy in the sunshine basks,
And purrs and blinks, wild passion roams about,
Intent upon its predatory tasks.
Who questions if love's fire be in or out?
The moment 'tis alight, it shines so clear,
Nought then is seen but its own atmosphere.

LXX

"This is not love : 'tis fancy's newest born ;
A bastard to be strangled in its crib ;
A misbegotten harbinger of scorn,
Quick from the sight for ever to be hid.
Yet,—yet how fair, under the flaky thorn
She looked ! how fresh, the vocal woods amid !
And when the nightingales sang fast and clear,
How more than fresh or fair ! How close ! How dear !

LXXI

"Could hers be love, though mine but fancy were?
Are not maids caught in springes manhood breaks?
That which I doubt may be deep truth to her,
And she thirst more from draught that my thirst slakes.
Yet were I base as any garbage cur,
If I could sleep when such a bosom wakes,
Or could I call out love's name loud and clear,
Then let its echo die upon her ear.

LXXII

"Love's name!   Doth love thus readily reply?
And can her heart, chaste as yon dewy moon
That lo! once more comes gliding up the sky,
From mine have taken fire,—so soon, so soon!
From mine?   Presumptuous thought!   Why, what am I?
An instrument unused, so out of tune,
That, did I sound it, who would care to sing
To its discordant note and slackened string?

LXXIII

"Who cannot see it all?   Assume the best:
Let self-love brood upon the fervid hope
That I could force the chamber of her breast;
'Twould swiftly swarm with foes with whom to cope,
I all unarmed, were madness manifest.
What are your means?   Enough to buy a rope.
Buy it, before the world, indignant grown,
Dangles you from a gibbet of its own!

LXXIV

"So, better that that kiss should seal the past,
Than we should journey on from stage to stage
Of lengthening bliss to a bare goal at last,
And be but heart-sore for the pilgrimage!
Farewell, sweet lips!   I will not break my fast,
Nor at your fount youth's selfish thirst assuage.
Forgive—forget—that one deep breathless draught:
You, the pure wave; 'twas I alone that quaffed.

LXXV

" And you may go upon your maiden way,
Careless and free as never-stopping brook,
By which the drouthy hind, at close of day,
Halting, and laying on the ground his crook,
Lies prone and dips to drink its sparkling spray ;
Whilst it, nor robbed nor soiled by what he took,
But laughs and trips along, elusive elf,
Singing its happy secret to itself."

LXXVI

Thus with a sigh, such as will ofttimes heave
Pathetic fancy in a gentle breast,
Not, not those gasps of passionate pain that leave
No room in the heart for any wiser guest,
And hence with ear attentive to receive
The hints of reason, friend of what is best,
Spurning soft pleasure for right's harder sake,
Godfrid relinquished what he scarce could take.

LXXVII

"I send," he wrote, "the book of Tuscan lays,
You said 'twould give you pleasure to possess,
In poor return for those two happy days
I owe to your abounding graciousness ;
Such as a grateful bankrupt debtor pays,
Who cannot pay, but would his debt confess.
How I enjoyed them never can I tell :
To such as I, they come not twice.   Farewell."

LXXVIII

"I thank you," she replied, "for your kind note,
And for the Tuscan songs you send with it.
Already I know some of them by rote.
Others transcend my feeble woman's wit.
The best, I think, are those I heard you quote ;
And once or twice I wished that you could sit
Beside me as I read them, and explain
The passages that puzzle my dull brain.

LXXIX

"You recognise a debt that is not due,
And readily could pay whate'er were owed.
You have a world of wealth amassed by few,
Which was on me too lavishly bestowed.
I did enjoy our strolls as much as you,
And there are walks beside the ones I showed,
That lovelier grow with the advancing year.
Be sure you always will be welcome here."

LXXX

He wrote again, still striving to combine
Homage to her rare winsomeness and worth
With hinted grief that he must needs resign
His dream, and own his servitude to earth ;
Hoping that she would read between each line
He was uprooting fondness at its birth,
Only because he knew, if left to grow,
The flower would be but bane, the fruit but woe.

LXXXI

But there are hearts in whom love's subtle seeds
So promptly germinate, so swiftly spread,
That ere the careless hand which dropped them heeds,
'Tis all too late to tear them from the bed.
And Olive, wandering slow through woods and meads,
Haunted by one dear voice, one echoing tread,
Felt she could never the remembrance smother
Of that one kiss, excepting with another!

LXXXII

He was not near to give it.   In its place
Came letters, loveless, lacking warmth and life,
Which, changing vague delight to keen disgrace,
Self setting with intenser self at strife,
Deepened the sense of that too close embrace,
Such as transforms to all but wedded wife
The bosom truly maiden ; uncompleted,
Leaves a reproach behind, profoundly seated.

LXXXIII

O purity of women who are pure !
To praise it is to soil it.   Sudden pledge,
At moment when no surety can be sure,
Had she bestowed by treacherous parting's ledge.
Should that betrothal hasty not endure !
Would she were lying underneath the sedge
Strolled past with him, whom she, unkissed before,
Too much had given, should she give no more.

LXXXIV

And stronger waxed within her trembling soul
This demon horror, till, whene'er she walked
By grassy undulation, tufted knoll,
Concealing hedgerow where the slender-stalked
Convolvulus peeped out, or past the bole
Of weathered ash where she had sate and talked
With him the afternoon away, it stepped
Close to her side, till, terrified, she wept.

LXXXV

And when lone night from its dark loosened tresses
Did o'er the earth invisible spices shake,
What time its subtle sister, slumber, presses
Consenting lids, would Olive, still awake,
Bent o'er his letters, with unstable guesses
At their fixed meaning, aggravate her ache,
Then lean out at her casement, with moist eyes
Raised to the stars, unanswering in the skies.

LXXXVI

But when the hush was very deep, and o'er
The drowsy world the slumberous film had floated,
The trouble in her breast would rise and pour
Out melody, low, brief, and broken-throated,
As to sick babe a nurse of simple lore,
Or to itself a mind that strayed and doted.
But the wild notes nor nurse nor mind unstrung
Was like to know; and these the words she sung.

Will the sun never set?
    Will the twilight never fade?
·My heart is sick, my eyes are wet,
    With the night and his step delayed.
Go, loitering light, from the west!
    Sink, floating light, in the stream!
Fold, breeze, thy pinions, and rest!
    Rest: sleep; and dream!

The twilight lingers still
I hate the hues on the hill;
    I hate the sundown streak!
    Oh! if I could but wreak
    On crimson crag, on saffron peak,
My baffled will!

Come to me, silent as stars!
    Come to me, soft as the dew!
Come as the light through my bars
    When moons are new.
But come! come! come!
    My own, my sweet, my true!

        Oh! come!
I have flung the lattice wide,
    That the tendrils of the vine
May guide your arms as they climb and glide
    Nearer up to mine!
        Come! come! come!
        I cannot be mute, be dumb,
For I pine, I pine, I pine!

Hush! It is he! I heard
    A footstep in the laurelled walk!
Alas! 'Twas but a dreaming bird
    Chased by a phantom hawk!

I cannot await him longer.
    Love, ruffled against delay,
A moment fiercer, stronger,
    Beats,—flutters,—faints away!

LXXXVII

Thus like a bird that ceaseth its sad flute
Because none answereth, so on the dumb night
Died the warm strain, and Olive too was mute.
Glistened the grass like tesselated light,
The dewdrops hung upon the bough like fruit;
And at the window, motionless and white,
All but her golden hair, she nursed her dole,
And let the silence sink into her soul.

LXXXVIII

O purity of women who are pure!
They know, and yet they know not. In their breast
A fearsome, restless secret they immure,
Which to themselves is never quite confessed,
But oft withal, as though they can endure
No longer Nature's promptings being repressed
Escapes in flood of tears, or tell-tale praise
Of amorous song and poet's burning lays.

D

LXXXIX

They are like children playing on the beach
Of a mysterious ocean.   Fascinated
By the strange terror it inspires, let preach
As mother instinct may, their steps elated
Will trespass where the faint foam-fringes reach.
Cometh, asudden, wave precipitated
By the dread sea they toy with : how they fly,
From earnest peril, with a feeble cry !

XC

Olive had fled too late, and now her heart,
O'ertaken in its flight, was drenched with doubt.
Yes ! yes ! he loved her !   What ! he played a part,
When, as they watched the timid stars come out,
And the pale moon on her long journey start,
His voice had faltered?   He but meant to flout
At love's confiding promptness, when he pressed
His lips to hers, her breast unto his breast ?

XCI

Yet, if he did not love her !   Did love weigh
Impulse and prudence in a dangling scale ?
Did love, o'erawed by numbers, shirk the fray,
Or, when winds blew untoward, furl its sail ?
Was love a sage ?   What did those letters say ?
They breathed no strain of hope, no note of wail,
But in each pondered line there spake alone
Will's stately voice and wisdom's sovran tone.

XCII

Some six weeks later, Godfrid, who in vain
Had striven to lay the ghost of that dead time
Whose pleasure now had curdled into pain,
And whose reviewed delight seemed almost crime,
Striving to think that she would still retain,
For all their blight, the freshness of her prime,
Dogged by lame doubt, by self-reproach distressed,
Received a note by Olive's pen addressed.

XCIII

He tore it open with a trembling hand,
And with a greedy eye its message read,
Written, it seemed, in haste, and quickly scanned.
" I write to tell you my last news, instead
Of leaving it to gossip's busy band.
I am engaged, and shortly shall be wed.
Congratulate me, won't you?   All here send
Their best regards.   I fear that I must end."

XCIV

" Deign to accept," he answered, " from afar,
My fondest wishes for your future life.
May you be happy, as you gentle are,
And what you were as daughter, be as wife !
I pray in Heaven there move some vigilant star,
To ward from off you sorrow, loss, or strife,
And circle round you smoothly to the end.
Farewell ! with homage from your grateful friend."

XCV

O thou eternal secret, woman's heart !
Now, as when Eve was fooled, profoundly hid.
Man into life hath forced dead tongues to start,
Wrested dumb truths from stony pyramid,
Spanned the high hills, made of blank seas a chart,
And through the stars triumphant pathway thrid ;
But woman's heart, the riddle still unread,
Confounds the living, and confutes the dead.

XCVI

In that sad season of the bygone year,
When rise the mists and downward flows the sap,
And beggared Autumn, with a silent tear,
Empties her gold leaves into Winter's lap,
Another guest, lord in the hills severe
Whose harvest is the heather, and where flap
Crag-cradled kittiwakes round splintered foam,
Had crossed the porch of Olive's gentler home.

XCVII

Him had her sire through prickly stubble led,
Marked for him coign of vantage on the track
Where towered the slow-flushed pheasant overhead,
And shown him, eager, where the twinkling pack,
Mute as though muzzled, work the gorsey bed,
Till gleeful throat to gleeful throat peals back,
Then sweep o'er rolling down and dipping vale,
Straight as trim barks that head a following gale.

XCVIII

Men praised his steady nerve, true hand, quick eye,
Tall granite frame, clean limbs, and mien robust ;
Yet, softer critics, though they scarce knew why,
With colder voice his vaunted parts discussed.
" No, not the man to wake a woman's sigh :
Goodly, no doubt, brave, generous, helpful, just ;
But lacking in the mien, the tones, that draw
The charmed heart onward by some subtle law."

XCIX

But every lip averred that Olive's grace
Bounded the horizon of Sir Gilbert's eye,
That, noon and eve, her side seemed still his place,
And he was vacant when she was not nigh.
Yet could they read no tremor in her face,
No flush of pride, no cautious dread descry,
No sudden glow of fondness chilled by fear,
To show she felt that Love was walking near.

C

At first she started at his name, as starts
A free-born colt when cunning bait is brought,
And broke away.   But when with winsome arts
Her parents followed still, and still besought,
She, like the colt, when its wise dread departs,
Came to their beck, and nibbled, and was caught.
Then, still like it, which yields when o'er its head
The halter slips, she let herself be led.

CI

So unto them at least it seemed, whose past
Had only skimmed the inland lakes of life,
Whose sails had still swung lightly round the mast,
Nor once been swelled and strained by winds of strife.
They little guessed what made her yield at last,
Or, when she promised to be Gilbert's wife,
She would have wed the wintry wind, or laid
Her head on pillow smoothed by sexton's spade.

CII

He was a man of not uncommon worth
In this determined isle whose tongue we speak,
The only one he had been taught from birth,
Except a little Latin and less Greek.
England he deemed the navel of the earth,
And night and morning blessed the silver streak,
Holding the faith there lived beyond its waves
But papists, revolutionists, and slaves.

CIII

He knew the trick of every bird that flies,
Of every fish that swims, and could have told
When those would lie quite close, when these would rise,
How to entice the shy, outtire the bold.
He laughed to scorn the boast of sunny skies,
Of marble cities, orchards hung with gold,
Vowing one day's rough tramp through gloomy heather
Worth a whole year of stagnant Southern weather.

CIV

He felt no tremor when the evening star
In the moist west the vanished sun succeeds,
And in the heart the sense of things afar
Grows a religion deeper than all creeds.
How, in such moments, flesh and spirit jar,
And deepest joy still deeper anguish breeds,
He never owned, nor yearned for that vague goal
To which some god still goads the panting soul.

CV

The contemplation, and the pangs profound,
That fain would plumb unfathomable seas
Of light, and colour, darkness, silence, sound,
Life's straining aches,—he nothing recked of these.
Brute-like, he walked with eyes upon the ground ;
He heard no promise in Spring's dimpling breeze,
No buried hope in Autumn's curdling dirge,
Nor shared the secret of the wailful surge.

CVI

Yet do not scorn him, you whose finer strings
Move to the murmur of the faintest wind ;
For oftentimes the soul in hidden springs
And subterranean currents dwells confined.
And haply should the loss of cherished things
Force for it sudden passage to the mind,
Its pent-up waters will outflow, and borrow
A tardy channel through the clefts of sorrow.

CVII

And even now he vaunted all that lends
An outward glamour to domestic state,
Birth, lands, position, multitude of friends
Among the splendid, privileged, and great.
And if these merits hardly make amends
For gaps confessed, add a most noble gait
And blameless life, he was, 't must be allowed,
A man of whom might any girl be proud.

CVIII

And Olive was not slow to note and feel
His dumb desert and modesty sincere ;
And if at times another voice would steal
Betwixt him and her only half-lent ear,
As on an adder straight one plants one's heel,
She trod its whispers down with foot of fear
Which breeds a cruel courage, even to dare
Trample the hapless thing it fain would spare.

CIX

At times her voice would falter, and her eye
Fill with the moisture of a causeless tear,
Or her frame tremble, as 'neath sunniest sky
Creeps a strange shiver over windless mere.
And ever and anon with sudden sigh
Checked she quick mirth, as flying cavalier
Reins in his steed an instant, and looks back,
And listens, is one following on his track.

CX

So passed the weeks ; summer no longer reigned,
And nearer moved the looked-for marriage morn ;
Autumn came slowly through the yellow-grained,
Soft-whispering slopes, and took away the corn.
The harvest moon unto a sickle waned,
Hung o'er the golden harvest it had shorn,
High up in heaven, still brightly curved but idle.
The next would shine at full on Olive's bridal.

CXI

Musing on no such theme, but from the seat
Of hospitable laird in shaggy Perth
But just returned, to where deserted street,
Famed haunts of Splendour tenantless, and dearth
Of all that fills the void for urban feet,
Made London seem the loneliest place on earth,
Resolved at once to quit it for another,
Godfrid encountered Olive and her mother.

CXII

The shop whence they that moment had emerged,
Plainly bespoke their errand up to Town.
The colour to the maiden's temple surged ;
To Godfrid's rose—but quick repressed,—a frown.
The kindly parent farewell visit urged.
" It was no distance. Would he not run down ?
'Twould quiet be, but quieter anon ;
For, three weeks more, and Olive would be gone."

CXIII

A heartier invitation ne'er was given.
Old fears were laid.　Had Olive once to fight
Against her heart, she not in vain had striven,
And had not Godfrid long been lost to sight?
He, by he knew not what emotion driven,
But grown incautious in his own despite,
Gave to the honest pressure swift consent:
Yes, he would go; on Friday.　And he went.

CXIV

In the slant sunlight of the young October,
Dew-dashed lay meadow, upland, wood, and pool;
Mid-time delicious, when all hues are sober,
All sounds an undertone, all airs are cool:
When Nature seems awhile to pause and probe her,
Asking her heart if her eventful rule
Hath blest the earth she loveth, and to brace her
Against the wintry darksome days that face her. ·

CXV

Then, side by side, and unaccompanied,
But now for all their nearness more divided
Than if between them swayed an ocean's tide,
Forth through the wonted ways they slowly glided.
It seemed as if the summer life had died
In their hearts too, where once it had resided,
And Autumn had infused her solemn mood
In them, as in the sky, the mere, the wood.

CXVI

And as nor pipe of bird, nor foliage fluttering,
On the air's quiet pensiveness intruded,
But only ever and anon the muttering
Of loosened leaf from branches scarce denuded,
So from their lips, once so profuse in uttering
All love-swayed sounds, at intervals exuded
Unwilling word,—a syllable,—a sigh,—
Stirred by no inspiration, dropped to die.

CXVII

At length they halted where a lake, hemmed in
By wheeling bank, its liberty asserted,
Rushed for a gorge beyond with forceful din,
O'er boulder leaped, through moss-lipped crevice spirted,
Scattering its strength, but resolute to win.
Here Olive sate, with countenance averted,
Gazing adown the fall, while he surveyed
The springing cataract, the crouching maid.

CXVIII

Their silence now seemed natural.   The lake
Was silent too, but from its bosom sent,
Not less for their than for its own sad sake,
This infant stream, whose vagrant babblement
Made speech for all ; as in oppressive ache
Of those who, suffering, fain would hush lament,
A child's gay talk, irrelevant and quaint,
Acquits the air of silence and restraint.

CXIX

Her head was turned away ; her further cheek
Rested upon her hand ; he could but see
The nearer tresses, rippling, soft, and sleek,
The outlines of her form's mild majesty,
Shoulders whose curve a Phidias well might seek
To leave in marble, had we such as he ;
And just one small unconscious foot to hint
Of symmetry without excess or stint.

CXX

He scarce had time to knit his will and brace
His heart against the rush of tender feeling,
With which the sight of loveliness and grace,
In youth electric, sets the pulses reeling,
Before she turned, but quick again her face
Averted,—all too late !   For he saw stealing
Down it those tears which silently betray
More than all tongues can speak, all words can say.

CXXI

Omnipotence of tears in woman's eyes !
She threatens, and we flout the weak pretender :
Cold, and we beat her at her own disguise ;
She trusts to scorn, with keener scorn we rend her.
She smiles on others, we disport a prize.
She still shall win.   She weeps, and we surrender.
Artist ! amend your craft.   With shields nor spears
Mould me your Venus Victrix, but—in tears !

CXXII

And Godfrid, who but now against delight
Had fought and won, succumbing to distress,
To Olive's side straight hastened at the sight,
And tried each tender tone, each near caress.
He called her by her name as brothers might,
Stroked her soft hand, smoothed every truant tress,
And, when the tear-shower gathered unto storm,
Curved his strong arm around her fragile form.

CXXIII

She leaned away, she hung athwart the ledge
Of the young torrent, and with quivering lips,
"Don't," she cried, "don't! My pledge! my sacred pledge!"
But he, like one whose foothold slowly slips,
Once it hath passed the precipice's edge,
And with each struggle only deeper dips,
Felt all his purpose leaving him, and held
Her form more close the more her words repelled.

CXXIV

And lips that once have met in days gone by,
Meet easily again in days that are ;
And kisses seem best answer to a sigh,
When silence were too cold and words would jar.
How, too, might she compassion's touch deny,
Now he was near who had so long been far,
Or more than feebly, fruitlessly withstand
Kindness which conquers surer than command ?

CXXV

And though the lips, since now no more forbidden,
At length from cheating sympathy desisted,
One hand, which hinted half the yearning hidden,
With daintier hand was feverishly twisted,
While one, at first withstood, at last unchidden,
Strayed o'er her cheek, and the warm curls that kissed it;
And thus, to love love's guile no more abhorrent,
Silent they sate, and watched the tumbling torrent.

CXXVI

And when the spell of silence was uncharmed,
" Let us go home," she said; "'tis better so."
But they who fight with love are soon disarmed,
And bare their breast in striking the first blow.
So, lulled by that same lure which late alarmed,
Over the stepping-stones, for weal or woe,
Hand-linked they went, their eyes upon the ground,
And finding even in silence too much sound.

CXXVII

There was an arbour woven all of leaves,
Woodbine, and briony, and clambering hop,
Wild clematis its roof, wild brier its eaves,
And living trunk of fluted elm its prop.
Its floor was such as thrifty autumn weaves
Of last year's moss and this year's faded crop
Of white wood-sorrel, and coy flowers that grow
In nooks where sun scarce comes and winds ne'er blow.

CXXVIII

And some one of the branches had contrived,
In its unseen recess, a rustic bench,
Whence you could watch the lake's life, snugly hived:
How flashed a trout, how plopped a greedy tench,
Now skimmed a waterfowl, now dabchick dived,
Where came the kine their lazy thirst to quench,
Or swans, with feathers white as fluttering spray,
Like floating islands on the water lay.

CXXIX

And save the lake, its denizens, and the woods
That girt it round, there nothing was in sight:
Fair face of changeless water, tacking broods
'Mong tall reeds motionless;—such spot as might
Selected be by sandalled sisterhoods,
Who from the world have taken timid flight,
Craving to find from lustful fumes release,
And in chaste Nature's lap a pious peace.

CXXX

And, trailing slow, still hand in hand, beside
The rushy brink, at length their footsteps came
Unto the arbour; which when Godfrid spied,
Halting and bending forward his tall frame,
To peer within, "What a sweet nook!" he cried.
"Who trained these branches was not much to blame.
Shall we not use their shade, and see, unseen,
The yellowing Autumn trench on Summer's green?"

CXXXI

Nothing there was he now could ask but she
Had yielded speechless and enslaved assent;
So like to one who bows to fate's decree,
Under the hospitable boughs she went,
Where, hands still joined and laid upon his knee,
They sate down in the leafy tenement,
Sighing to think, beyond this cloistered mere,
Lay a rude world of noise, and hate, and fear.

CXXXII

Nor when around her gently-curving frame,
Their palms disjoined, a gentle arm was curved,
More than soft-footed fawn that hath grown tame
Starts at a human voice, shrank she or swerved.
And when her face burst suddenly aflame,
His shoulder for a screening pillow served,
Whereon she leaned her sorrow-drooping head,
Passive as though it were her bier or bed:

CXXXIII

And there remained.　No word, no look, no sigh,
Her stillness stirred.　She felt the hour bestowed
Bliss she were well content to take and die,
Would they but off her lift life's weary load.
She did not wish, she did not think, to lie
Nearer than this, but felt that pity owed
At least one brief indulgence unto woe,
Ere dear to-day changed to dead long-ago.

CXXXIV

O purity of women who are pure !
Could men but fathom it !   Longwhile she leaned,
Quiet as sleeping babe and as secure,
Upon the rugged pillow, where she gleaned
Glimpses of things unseen, but not less sure :
Till, feeling that she had too long been weaned
From fount that fed her fondness, she upraised
Her face, and full into his features gazed.

CXXXV

But when she saw, responsive to the look,
A sultry glow slow gathering in his eyes,
Presaging passion's flash, she could not brook
The thought that she should make less good and wise
Her new, her only idol, so betook
Her head again to its late paradise,
And said, with plaintive voice and still-born smile,
"Talk to me, Godfrid ! talk, a little while."

CXXXVI

"Talk of what, Olive?   Of sweet days gone by,
Or bitter, girded will is bound to face?"
"No, of yourself," she said, "the theme that I
Could muse as time still ran his endless race.
Love, though an egotist, can deify
A vulgar fault, and drape the gross with grace.
You are myself, and I would hear of you :—
What you have done, and what you hope to do."

E

CXXXVII

"What have I done? What do I hope to do?
Just to sit patient, Olive, in the shade,
Till the old creeds re-form, or gospel new
Their thinned disintegrated ranks invade.
But hug the hideously false for true,
Because what, since deemed vital truth, was made
Our bosom's idol, in our arms lies dead!—
Better be Rachel, and not comforted.

CXXXVIII

"Dead, yes, stone-dead, though simulating life
In reflex action, lingering minds mistake.
But because now no more the dual strife,
Fought on this earth, holds a safe Heaven for stake;
Shall our sole weapons be the glutton's knife,
The banker's shovel, and the croupier's rake?
Because in doubt if soul the flesh survive,
Shall flesh be lord while soul is still alive?

CXXXIX

"Look round! 'Tis lord, 'tis king, sole suzerain,
Bedizened fetish of the carnal crowd;
The oracle of joy, the god of gain,
Hope of the humble, comfort of the proud.
'Give us,' they cry, 'fat peace, with piled-up wain,
Cover our daughters with a golden cloud,
Unto our sons dispense pomp, pleasure, ease!'—
—Better a couch under the forest trees!

CXL

"So I must wait, and mayhap wait in vain,
Till death the janitor shall give release;
For life may prove to me, poor feeble swain,
As sometimes to the strong, a bootless lease.
Meanwhile I will not hire my soul for gain,
Nor strut the scarlet popinjay of peace;
Cozen chawbacons, coax the civic crowd,
Proud to the humble, humble to the proud.

CXLI

"If in my brain there glowed the poet's fire,
I then might try to rouse the sluggish time
By clanging all the octaves of the lyre.
Alas! for me such strains are too sublime,
Who pipe but lowly.   I can but aspire
To bear in august Action's heat and grime
A private's part.   Would that the hour had come!
Meanwhile my arm must rust, my voice keep dumb."

CXLII

He ceased.   And then no sound was there to break
The Autumn's shimmering haze, which seemed to rest
Low on the woods, the woods upon the lake,
The lake, asleep, on brooding Nature's breast.
There was no wind nor wandering breath to shake
Even the long lithe water-reed's ripe crest:
The swans' white prows, glassed in the unstirred stream,
Kept turning on themselves in downy dream.

CXLIII

And as she gazed upon the placid mere,
The ripples of her woe too died away;
And from her lips came comfort, calm and clear,
Even as the lake which hushed before them lay.
For she descried a future, vineyards near,
That should redeem the desert of to-day:
A Promised Land, which, from its summit high,
Her love could show, not reach,—since it must die.

CXLIV

And then she pointed to a great Beyond,
Which he might conquer with a freër stride,
Because not fettered by too close a bond
With her dwarfed nature; withal, fortified
By knowing she would keep an outlook fond
Still on his steps, whatever might betide,
Even when some one worthier should have gained
The heart she feared she only had profaned.

CXLV

A melancholy wonder filled his face.
His eyes were turned from her, and wandered out,
Not in the quest of Nature's varied grace,
Such as sometimes the spirit seeks without,
When vexed within, but blankly upon space,
As in a vision trancëd and devout.
At length in words significant and slow,
"Let us go home," he said.   "'*Tis* better so."

CXLVI

So home their way they wended by the lake
Left among hushing woods, and past the fall
Whose swift untutored music shall forsake
Never their ears till death hath silenced all.
For time which heals, still leaves a cold numb ache,
Whose shootings ever and anon recall
The original sharp wound, and wring from pain
Fresh tribute to old joy's abandoned fane.

CXLVII

Long lay the shadows on the sleepy lawn
Afront the Hall, as from the covert ways
Issuing, their feet magnetically drawn
Sought the soft sward where they in summer days,
When their untroubled intercourse had dawn,
Exchanged inaugural looks of love and praise.
Now, all was ended.   Praise and love were said ;
And, cut off in his prime, young hope lay dead.

CXLVIII

There was a marble basin, mid-sward placed,
Where falling fountain-sprays subduedly tinkled,
And, as they kept afalling, still retraced
The broken fragile rain-dome which they sprinkled.
Here, on its brim they sate, their loiterings paced,
Watching the water by the drops scarce wrinkled,
And seeing in its calm but hazy deep
Each other's face, as one sees face in sleep.

CXLIX

Once when he turned to hide recurring frown,
And dipped his hand into the imprisoned wave,
Hers plunged and seized on it as though 'twould drown,
Low-moaning in the tone of them that rave,
"Oh! if we could but drag each other down!"
But he, with soothing voice and aspect grave,
Said "Upward, you mean, Olive! as, so far,
You have drawn *me ;*—no siren, but a star!"

CL

The muffled mist came trailing up the leas,
Hemmed in the landscape, front, and flank, and rear.
Huddled the leaves more closely, and the trees
Drew in their shadows stealthily, for fear.
Then, as the horizon faded by degrees,
More plainly plashed the fountain on their ear;
And in their hearts they louder seemed to hark
The drip of doom, more all around grew dark.

CLI

Dew-dashed again and silent, in the morn,
Lay the apparent woodlands; but not more
Silent and dew-dashed than the gaze forlorn
Of her who in her inmost being bore
A woe that humbled pride, that outbraved scorn.
The morning mounted, and the moments wore;
Moments no grief can hurry or delay,
Save when we scare them with our call to stay.

CLII

The tokens of departure met her eyes
And ears bewildered, and upon her rushed
As with the shock of uninformed surprise.
Her consciousness had been too wildly flushed
For her the sober truth to recognise
That he was really going; that lives crushed
Are nought to Fate, whose car indifferent drives
Betwixt exulting or o'er mangled lives.

CLIII

Farewell! Farewell! She drew him to a nook,
Still bright with lingering flowers her winning ways
Had coaxed from summer when it went, and took
From out her breast something that caught the rays
Of broken sunlight, and with voice that shook,
Said: "Take it and wear it in the after days!"
"Take it?" he answered. "Yes,—as I would take
A shell,—a kingdom,—for your gentle sake."

CLIV

Then to the porch returning, where awaited
Motionless equipage and champing bay,
Wonted adieux he made with voice that mated
Ill with the looks that always will betray.
Harshly the wheels upon the gravel grated,
Drew back a moment, and then rolled away,
Under the branches, through the farther gate,—
She gazing after, trothed and desolate.

CLV

"I send," wrote Godfrid, "but a worthless song,
Yet one whose notes my feeling so express,
I nurse the hope it may, devoid of wrong
To any other, speak your own no less.
If so, we might perhaps be made more strong,
Nor quite so lonely in our loneliness,
If, keeping lines in which our thoughts are blended,
You sent a transcript with your name appended."

CLVI

Awhile seemed utter silence sole retort.
But just as tardy prudence 'gan to turn
And gibe temerity, came message short.
"They kept your letter from me. How I burn
(I have been angry: Heaven forgive me for 't !)
With shame to tell you what I only learn
This very eve. Well, I have had my way,
And send the verses, copied." These were they.

Accept it, Olive? Surely, yes ;
    This ring of emeralds, diamonds too :
As I would take,—no need to press,—
    A leaf, a crown from you !
No rudest art, no brightest ore,
Could make its value less or more.

Gone is my strength. 'Twere useless quite
    To tell you that it is not hard

To have one's paradise in sight,
    Withal, to be debarred.
And yet the generous glimpse you gave
Was more than once I dared to crave.

Hard ! very hard, sweet ! but ordained.
    We know 'tis God's own world, at worst.
And we have only partly drained,
    And so still partly thirst ;
While others parched remain, or seize
Fiercely the cup and drain the lees.

So let us strive to deem it well,
    However now we stand aghast.
Earth, Heaven, not being parallel,
    Perforce must meet at last.
And, in that disembodied clime,
A clasp more close may not be crime.

You loved me too well to deny :
    I loved you far too well to ask.
Only a kiss, a gaze, a sigh,
    A tear,—and then a mask.
We spared the fruit of Good-and-Ill ;
We dwell within our Eden still.

O sunshine in profoundest gloom,
    To know that on the earth there dwells,
Somewhere, unseen, one woman whom
    No noblest thought excels ;

And that by valour to resign,
I make her more than ever mine.

Too late, too late, I learn how sweet
    'Twould be to reach a noble aim,
And then fling fondly at your feet
    The fulness of my fame.
Now—now,—I scarce know which is best,
To strive, or lay me down and rest.

O winter in the sunless land !
    O narrowed day ! O darker night !
O loss of all that let me stand
    A giant in the fight !
I dwindle : for I see, and sigh,
A mated bird is more than I.

God bless you, Olive !   Even so
    God bless your husband !   He, if true
To his sweet trust, to me will grow
    Only less dear than you.
But should he hurt his tender charge,
Why, hate is hot where love is large.

Yes—yes !—God bless your wedded lot !
    My beautiful !—no—no—not mine !
I scarce know what is, what is not,
    Only that I am thine ;—
Thine, thine, come aught, come all amiss.
No time, no fate, can alter *this !*

CLVII

Strange? Yes! the human heart is subtle strange,
And, even when most stoutly ruddered, drives,
Through winds that veer and over waves that change,
Unto some port, not that for which it strives.
Tides turn its track, storm-gusts extend its range,
The tempest strips it, and the lightning rives;
Till, poor black hull, it seems itself to aid
Each howling buffet, and each watery raid.

CLVIII

When unto Olive Godfrid bade farewell,
Carrying the faithful pledge of her distress,
Still from his side unable to dispel
The dogging memory of despair's caress,
And all of sweet sad sorrow that befell,
Down to the edge of parting's wretchedness,—
His steps he bent to where, 'mid lordly lands,
An empty, roofless monastery stands.

CLIX

A river journeyeth past its ancient walls,
Whereon hoar ivy thrives and night-owls build.
Its only chant is now a waterfall's,
Which swells, and falls, and swells, as it is filled
With music from the hills. The cuckoo calls
Throughout moist May. When August woods are stilled
In sleepy sultriness, the stock-dove broods
Low to itself. The rest is solitude's.

CLX

But many a mile before the river sweeps,
With gentle curve, around the Abbey gray,
Straight through dense woods, in whose umbrageous deeps
A mystic muteness lurks, it keeps its way.
Now through a throttling gorge it gurgling leaps,
Now flows, slow, smooth, silent as those that pray,
'Twixt sylvan sanctuaries, whose green aisles slope
Up to bare moor, with the bare sky for cope.

CLXI

And here it was, unwisely, Godfrid sought
Solace for joy which yesterday was wrecked,
But nothing found there, save the loss he brought.
For Nature is a mirror, to reflect
Man's many moods, faith, doubt, fear, fancy, aught
That may rejoice his spirit or deject,
And, as she back projects them, to infuse
Into their image her own lively hues.

CLXII

Thus Olive, who seemed earthly fair when viewed
In her own lineaments, now she was glassed
In wood, and stream, and abbeyed solitude,
All known, all pictured loveliness surpassed.
Then, prompt Imagination's airy brood
Their immaterial textures wove and cast
Around the ethereal image, till his eye
And heart abode with unreality.

CLXIII

But Godfrid, who scanned first this perfect flower
With gaze of tranquil homage, could not now
Bring back the freshness of the faded hour.
In vain the passionate verse, the rhymëd vow !
This was but fancy's mist, the mere heat-shower
Which from imagination's sultry brow
Falls in quick rhythmic drops, to slowly clear
And leave behind a serene atmosphere.

CLXIV

But Olive, though she too might boast to have been
Nurtured in Arcady, was woman first
And last of all things.   With an ear akin   .
To each sweet sound that ever was rehearsed,
By bird or bard, on lyre or mandolin,
Withal deep down within her heart she nursed
That passion for the actual and the real,
Which still remain the woman's true ideal.

CLXV

So every line by molten passion coined
In the chill mould of Godfrid's hollow song,
She to her life's most cherished tokens joined,
And secret wore, lest they should suffer wrong
From vulgar gaze, or haply be purloined
By envious hand, and not be hers for long.
Each wailing strophe, warbled by fancy's throat,
With her indelible heart's-blood she re-wrote.

CLXVI

And when her parents fain had brought the ring
Back to her hand, and sent the rhymes away,
She, like a gentle fearful-hearted thing
Whom motherhood makes fierce, stood dumb at bay,
Prompt to rebut, and ready even to spring,
Should any seek to make her prize their prey.
And in her eyes so wild a look she wore,
And in her mien such force, that they forbore.

CLXVII

And as the time drew nigh for her to quit
For ever the familiar porch of home
For the vague land where unknown spectres flit,
She waxed as pale and restless as the foam
Frayed by sunk rocks whereon doomed vessels split.
From chamber unto chamber would she roam,
Vouchsafing broken answers now, now none,
And waiting for the setting of the sun.

CLXVIII

But when the days of respite came to close,
And dawned through low dun clouds the bridal morn,
She smiled, but like to one who mocks at woes,
And laughed, but as they laugh who laugh for scorn.
They said she looked like a white shut-up rose
That haply burgeons in a time forlorn,
When she stood veiled, and that she walked the nave
As straight and cold as coffin goes to grave.

CLXIX

Then Autumn fired the woods, and crimson glowed
Fringed bole and feathered bough, and topmost spray,
Which, as fell in the shrivelled foliage, showed
Roofless and bare, that late shut out the day:
While hurrying Winter's drifting storm-showers flowed
From hissing heavens, and slowly died away
The colour from drenched Nature's face.   And then?
Black trunks, and dirgeful winds, and dripping fen.

END OF ACT I

ACT II

F

ACT II

PERSONAGES:

OLYMPIA—GODFRID—GILBERT—OLIVE.

PROTAGONISTS:

LOVE—RELIGION.

PLACE:

SPIAGGIASCURA—MILAN—FLORENCE.

TIME:

MARCH 1858—MAY 1859.

ACT II

I

THERE is a little city in the South,
A silent little city by the sea,
Where a swift Alpine torrent finds its mouth,
And billowy mountains subside smilingly.
It knows nor weeping skies nor dewless drouth,
No seasons, save when April's glancing glee
Slow steadies unto Summer's still-poised wing,
Or mimic Winter lifts the mask from Spring.

II

Once on a time it was a famous city,
Famous for love, and song, and stately strife,
When men were knightly still, and women witty,
And court and camp with revelry were rife.
Now is it hushed as long-forgotten ditty,
Secluded almshouse of a bankrupt life,
Refuge for him, who, after days of riot,
Seeketh the safe monotony of quiet.

III

No traveller's busy footstep cometh there,
No pallid form, more painlessly to die ;
No gainful barter thither doth repair ;
Even the boatman's oar and net pass by.
No clattering wheel and whip offend the air ;
Its streets but lead to mountain, sea, and sky,
And, when gaunt Winter stalks our shivering isle,
Bask, backed by hills, in ocean's rippling smile.

IV

Within it is a lovelier little chapel
Than ever wealth ordained or genius planned
For those famed shrines where art and splendour grapple,
· Vainly, to blend the beautiful and grand.
No gold adorns it, and no jewels dapple,
No boastful words attest the builder's hand ;
Sacred to prayer, but quite unknown to fame,
Maria Stella Maris is its name.

V

Breaks not a morning but its snow-white altar
With fragrant mountain flowers is newly dight ;
Comes not a noon but lowly murmured psalter
Again is said with unpretentious rite ;
Its one sole lamp is never known to falter
In faithful watch through the long hush of night ;
From dawn till gloaming, open to devotion
Its portal stands, and to the swell of ocean.

VI

Never did form more lissom thread the dance
Than hers that scours the hill to find it flowers ;
Never did sweeter lips or holier glance
Watch for the striking of the sacred hours ;
No hands so leal e'er decked the warrior's lance,
As those which tend its lamp as darkness lours ;
And never since dear Christ expired for man,
Had holy shrine so pure a sacristan.

VII

Beyond its threshold she nor hearth nor home,
As tender maidens wont, had e'er possessed :
Only a window just above the foam,
Less like a chamber than a sea-bird's nest.
No mother's voice forbade her steps to roam,
No father's joy enslaved her to his breast ;
And all but answered, asked you of her line,
" A daughter of the sunlight and the shrine."

VIII

This year when streams enfranchised by the Spring
Came bounding to the ocean from the wolds,
Just as the callow broods were 'tempting wing,
And bleating voices heard about the folds,
And almond blossoms trusty news did bring
Rude winds had scampered to their northern holds,
Within the chapel a strange face was seen,
Where for long days no stranger's face had been.

IX

When transubstantiated wine and bread
In mystic mass renewed the gainful loss
Of cruel Calvary, or tonsured head
From carven pulpit banned as worthless dross
All that the flesh can win, or doleful tread
Followed the tearful Stations of the Cross,
At Vespers' chant, at Benediction's prayer,
Or *Quarant' Ore*, was the stranger there.

X

Presence so constant she could scarcely fail,
Despite her own devotion, to perceive ;
Since there, as elsewhere, save the old and frail,
Or such as had some sudden cause to grieve,
Or when the Church's mandate must prevail,
Men came but seldom, and to quickly leave.
So she gave thanks one callous bosom less
Should mitigate the Sacred Heart's distress.

XI

Oft had he come, and knelt, and gone away,
Often returned and often knelt again,
Before her eyes, which, too absorbed to stray,
And not avoiding, rarely met the ken,—
As though as yet she scarcely knew that they
Had aught to do with, aught to fear from, men,—
Fell upon his, which, wont on her to gaze,
Forgot to curb their burning look of praise.

XII

Perhaps the woman's instinct failed in her.
Perhaps a maiden's bashfulness is more
A matron's lesson than our lips aver.
Shrank not her clear gray eyes his gaze before,
But dipping finger so as scarce to stir
The water in the stoup beside the door,
She held it out towards his without dismay,
Turned, knelt, and crossed herself, and went her way.

XIII

Half a moon later, while the morn, yet early,
Smiled to the sound of reawakening trills,
When, though the mist, discomfited and surly,
Slowly retreating, hugged the higher hills,
On slopes below, the wild-rose blossom pearly
Sparkled with scented dew its sleep distils,
And None's faint bells afar were heard to chime,
Their eyes and hands met for a second time.

XIV

The bright incarnate spirit of the Morn,
Upon a stone mid-stream he saw her stand,
Atiptoe, straining at a snow-white thorn,
Whose bloom provoked but still escaped her hand.
He, though of gracious courtesy inborn,
Yet by a sight so fairylike unmanned,
Sat like a statue that hath long while caught,
And keeps, immutable, some selfish thought.

XV

The ripple of the streamlet past her feet,
White thorn above her, whiter robe around,
The linnet-pipings nigh, the distant bleat,
Spiral lark-music in the blue sky drowned,
Blending of all, melodious and sweet,
To superficial sense and soul profound,
Steeped him in such oblivious trance, indeed
He in her beauty quite forgot her need.

XVI

Reaching a branch, she clutched it, but, alack !
It yielded as but yields a half-bent bow,
And with a sharp rebound sprang loosely back,
And all the bloom came showering down like snow,
Dappling the dark stream with a milk-white track ;
But where it fell on *her*, you could not know.
And then she gave a foiled despairing cry,
That sounded half a prayer and half a sigh.

XVII

Swift at the sound from selfish trance he woke,
And started up, and hastened to her aid ;
Sprang o'er the stepping stones, and deftly broke
A loftier bough in lovelier bloom arrayed,
And, as he tendered, reverently spoke :
" I pray you, sinless maiden."   And she said,
" Thanks, gentle sir ; my flowers are not for me,
But for our Lady's shrine afront the sea."

XVIII

"Then place these there," he said, "unless, indeed,
By my base touch their virtue be annulled;
And when your lips for other sinners plead,
Breathe one kind orison for him who culled.
In this cold world, where sunless lives we lead,
Faith oft grows petrified, contrition dulled;
But who would not feel blest to know that prayers
Mounted from lips like yours to ears like Hers?

XIX

"And if such favour may a stranger ask,"
He said in accents chivalrous and free,
That screened no foul presumption with fair mask,
"May I your pious steps accompany?
I still perchance can aid you in your task,
To crown with flowers our Lady of the Sea;
Or if that office but for you be meet,
May I not help to bear them to her feet?"

XX

Hers was a heart that knew not to deny.
Like the benign Madonna she adored,
She looked down ever with consenting eye
And smiling tenderness, whoe'er implored.
So, while the candid gaze made sure reply,
From parted lips a gracious welcome poured.
"Come then," she said, "but quickly; we are late.
We must not make our loving Lady wait."

XXI

So down the dewy hill they swift descended,
She treading first, he following fast behind ;
Anon by tracks that deviously wended,
Now by smooth paths as straight as blows the wind ;
Until the vineyards and the city blended,
And then those vanished, and their ears resigned
The mountain torrent's intermittent roar
For the tired waves that fainted on the shore.

XXII

The little temple's door stood open wide,
And all the place by sunshine was possessed,
From the groined roof which time had slowly dyed,
Down to the inlaid altar whitely dressed.
But the smooth walls that rose on either side,
Were marble ; marble was the floor you pressed ;
So that, withal, the spot seemed fresh and cool,
Even as shady grove or reedy pool.

XXIII

Full on the left an antique pulpit rose,
Of structure quaint, and it was marble too,
Where hands long numb had carven, as they chose,
Odd allegories, fair and foul to view.
Here virgins, calm as newly fallen snows,
Bearing curved palms, and singing hymns to you ;
There long lank demons gnawing damnèd souls,
And bastard animals, and nightmare scrolls.

XXIV

But from these fancies twain you turned full soon,
For on the right the mild Madonna stood,
Down from her flowing hair to sandal-shoon
The mystic type of maiden motherhood.
Below her feet there curved a crescent moon,
And all the golden planets were her hood ;
In comely folds her queenly garb was moulded,
And over her pure breast her hands were folded.

XXV

She looked the most immortal mortal being
That ever yet descended from the skies,
As one who seemed to see all, without seeing,
And without ears to hear man's smothered sighs ;
With all our discords the one note agreeing,
'Mid death and hate a love that never dies ;
A tranquil silence amid fretful din,
And still the sinless confidant of sin.

XXVI

And now the mountain maiden spread the store
Of wondrous whiteness from the hawthorn bower
Culled by the stranger, on the marble floor,
And from her lap discovered many a flower :
Proud cyclamens on long lithe stems that soar,
Retiring violets that meekly cower
Among green leaves, lilies that know not fear,
And the blue stars to parting lovers dear.

XXVII

All these her fingers fancifully wrought
Into festoons and wreaths and posies fair ;
Then from an inner sanctuary brought
Vases of delicate tint but simplest ware,
And round the statue, nimbly as her thought,
Ranged them, till not a single spot seemed bare.
Whereon she back retired a little space,
And eyed her handiwork with questioning face.

XXVIII

"There, it is done, tho' ill. Now let us kneel,
And beg our gracious Mother to accept
Our tribute poor, since paid with homage leal."
Therewith a pace or two she forward stepped,
And her fair knees the marble fair did feel.
He just a little way behind her crept,
And, forcing his proud limbs to bend, obeyed
Her sovran word, and watched her as she prayed.

XXIX

Her hands were clasped, her eyes cast meekly down,
Down her smooth cheek the tender tear-drop stole,
And under kerchief white and bodice brown
Heaved the pure tumult of her sinless soul.
Oh ! soon the Lady with the starry crown
Will sure, he thought, step from her flowery knoll,
And, subtly quickened by celestial charms,
Enfold this virgin form in virgin arms !

XXX

How long she thus remained, he noted not,
But, like to one whose count of time is stayed,
Still as she knelt, knelt rooted to the spot,
And when she rose, rose, following like a shade ;
And still, the place, the hour, the scene forgot,
Though sooth he should have bidden adieu, delayed ;
Until she timorously broke the spell
With the faint words : " I thank you, sir ; farewell ! "

XXXI

" Farewell ! " he said,—her shadow even in speech ;
But the sad sound dissolved his sunny dream :
" Farewell, farewell ! but may we, I beseech,
Not meet once more beside the rippling stream,
Or on the grassy slope, or pebbly beach,
Or even here, which meeter still would seem ?
And, to befriend me, tell me, ere I go,
The name in Heaven by which you are known below ! "

XXXII

" Still come, at your good will," she frankly said,
" Where the hills rise, or where the long waves fall,
Or where the stream runs babbling o'er its bed,
Or in this chapel, dearest spot of all,
And you by me will still be welcoméd,
If you, like me, will be my Lady's thrall.
My name, sir, is Olympia."   " Godfrid, mine."
And so they parted, with no further sign.

XXXIII

And she within the little chapel kept;
But he went downward to the shining shore.
The sun yet higher along the heavens had stept,
Withal to him it glowed not as before.
The morning's magic from the hills had crept,
The little city a dimmed lustre wore;
The waves had lost their music, and his breast
Heaved, beneath load of vacancy opprest.

XXXIV

Not of the climes where song and sunshine steep
The blood in honeyed idleness was he,
Where waking hours are but a conscious sleep,
And noons, like nights, delicious vacancy;
But of that restless race who work and weep,
Whose hearths are warded by the surly sea,
A swordlike stock, half vigour and half gloom,
Which, when it smites not, must itself consume.

XXXV

But he had fallen upon mournful times
When all great deeds were stagnant.   Tales of fame
His isle still haunted, and in sounding rhymes
Were sometimes sung, barren of future aim.
The leaders of the land were supple mimes,
Greedy of passing plaudits, sold to shame;
By whose base drugs, into deep slumber cast,
A once great Realm lay pillowed on its past.

XXXVI

The sacred Sceptre's virtue was confessed
Therein no more ; no man no man obeyed.
They had disarmed Authority ; the best
Were worst of all, few, feeble, and afraid.
Religion, long inviolable guest,
A menial first, an alien now was made ;
There was no end, no means, to prompt or please,
Save poor brute toil, or rich imbruted ease.

XXXVII

But he was of the strain of those who still
Are noble or are nothing ; who in days,
Empty of worthy purpose, curb their will,
And, though instinct with action, stand and gaze.
Secluded vale and solitary hill
Are more to them than ignominious praise ;
And o'er the world when night and dark are drawn,
Silent they wait till God brings back the dawn.

XXXVIII

So home he left, and o'er the vain-ploughed sea,
Through groaning cities, and long, silent fields,
Past poplars tall, and many a crocused lea,
To where the vine its clustering fruitage yields,
Onward he journeyed, until herb and tree
Still scantier grew, and their protecting shields
The Alps threw out, and on his cheek he felt
Airs that but blow from snows that never melt.

XXXIX

Yet not longwhile within the cold embrace
Of the unruffled mountains did he stay,
Nor by hushed lakes that still reflect their face,
Darkly by night, translucently by day,
But by snow-suckled torrents sought to trace
His devious, lone, and uninstructed way,
Until they led him to that tideless sea
That laps the shore of what *was* Italy.

XL

Thence to Spiaggiascura passed he on,
That silent little city by the shore,
Whence stir of busy life longwhile hath gone,
And where the laugh of youth is heard no more.
He fain earth's fardels ne'er again would don,
But henceforth only simple right implore
To sit i' the sun, and wise ensample win
From pale Lent lilies that nor toil nor spin.

XLI

The tenderness which drenches the lone mind,
Insensibly as dew distilled at night,
Made him, of late, cast many a look behind
Of fondness towards a Creed abandoned quite.
He felt his hands clasped by a parent kind
In infant prayer; he saw each dear old rite;
He heard the hymns of childhood, and he breathed
The scent of flowers with sacred incense wreathed.

XLII

For not in scorn, but he, bowed-down and blenched,
Had passed out from the Temple.   Ere he went,
With secret tears the altar-steps he drenched,
Aware he sped to utter banishment.
From home, hearth, Heaven, reluctant heart he wrenched,
The stern exiler of his past content;
Bidding adieu to Faiths which, well he knew,
Cease not to comfort, ceasing to be true.

XLIII

Thus with mute wisdom seated in his mind,
And tenderness chief tenant of his heart,
He left the wasteful, turbid strifes behind,
In which the understanding ne'er take part;
And, by his very loneliness inclined
To welcome a new anodyne for smart
Not yet quite old, he found his footsteps halt
Where Spiaggiascura fronts the waters salt.

XLIV

There found he all the disenchanted crave:
Beauty, and solitude, and simple ways;
The quiet-shining hills, the long lithe wave,
Now white-fringed fretting into rough-curved bays,
Now swirling smoothly where the flat sand gave
A couch whereon to end its stormy days;
Plain folk and primitive, made courteous by
Traditions old; and a cerulean sky.

G

XLV

In this new home, the fretful or the proud
Had trivial deemed, he with a windless will
Let his soul rest, as rests a summer cloud
On the soft summit of a rounded hill.
He joined the little city's mimic crowd
On early market morns, when down each rill
That marks a mountain track, with faces brown
Tall peasant folk came winding to the town.

XLVI

But long before the sun was hot and high,
They up the hill again were mounting slow,
And soon their forms were lost in cleft and sky.
Then Godfrid through the quiet streets would go,
Greeting and greeted by chance passer-by,
Or sometimes halting where, with locks of snow,
A bent old dame sate spinning at her door,
Then saunter downward to the vacant shore.

XLVII

But now the spot endeared to him before
By fair simplicity and lonely grace,
Had to his heart grown dearer more and more,
Since he had gazed upon Olympia's face,
Had seen her with up-raisëd eyes adore
The sinless Mother in the sacred place,
And carried in his arms her garlands sweet,
Swift down the hill following her fawnlike feet.

XLVIII

He thought how good, how restful it would be,
How cool of shade when fierce suns glare and scorch,
What placid haven from a plunging sea,
If he within the little temple's porch
Might dwell in reverent quietude, while she,
Purer of heart, still fed the altar's torch,
And live, despite his doubt, to her almost
As near as she to Heaven's angelic host.

XLIX

He saw her with the broadening sunlight come
Over the hills, over the mountains gray;
He heard her in the rising dawn-wind's hum,
He felt her in the warmth of growing day.
She sang to him when all the groves were dumb,
Peopled the pine-slope's solitary way,
Walked the long sands, leaving no print the while,
And in the rippling wave infused her smile.

L

Thus while his heart grew rooted to the spot,
The sea lay dimpling with perpetual smiles,
Calm as a babe that sleeps within its cot,
And hushed as lake, dotted with fairy isles.
The winds were all shut up in Æolus' grot,
Heaven free from cloud that darkens or defiles,
And not the frailest blossom fluttered down
From drooping branch within the tiny town.

LI

But when a sunny sevennight had passed,
Up from the south there came a trailing cloud,
And in its train an ever-rising blast,
That soon was singing high in sail and shroud ;
And, as it waxed, the sky grew overcast,
Lurid and low ;—whereat the breakers proud
Curved their strong crests, flung up their forelocks hoar,
And, madly rearing, plunged against the shore.

LII

And still as waned the day the wrathful ocean
Higher and higher rose, and to and fro
The slippery billows slid in shapeless motion,
Now dense and dark, now shivered into snow ;
Then once again as thick as hell-hag's potion,
Clotted with briny litter from below :
Like leaden coffins yawning first to sight,
Then swiftly hidden with fringed shrouds of white.

LIII

And where the sun would have been seen to set,
If sun had been, the sky was darkened most,
And drooped the welkin lower and lower yet,
As Night stole on without her starry host.
Anon, with flapping wings and stormy threat,
Foul seagulls came, and screamed along the coast ;
Then utter dark closed in, before, behind,
And over all loud growled the wolfish wind.

LIV

'Twas midnight, and the waves were rolling in ;
But in the little town were none who slept,
Save dotage deaf or childhood free from sin.
Pale in their beds, the rest scared vigil kept,
Crossing themselves, and listening to the din ;
And, as it swelled, the women wailed and wept,
And wrung their hands, thinking of those at sea,
Then hushed their babes, waked by the threnody.

LV

But one there was who neither wept nor prayed,
Nor sought a wakeful mockery of repose,
Was by the restless waves unrestful made,
And whose wild pulse still with the billows rose.
He, through the darkness, lone and unafraid,
Courted the storm and braved the tempest's blows,
Heard the rough surf's reverberating beat,
And felt the firm shore shake beneath his feet.

LVI

When all at once he marked a steady star
Spangle the gloom,—small, but surpassing bright,
Which seemed to shine nor near nor yet afar,
But glow suspended on the breast of night.
'Twas luminous as clear-faced planets are,
And then he saw it was the succouring light,
The Stella Maris, that Madonna's flower
Tended within the lonely chapel tower.

LVII

It led him on; he left the deafening tide,
And to the silent portal nearer drew,
Until no more the star could be descried,
The low porch hiding the tall tower from view.
But still across the bounding waters wide
Its steadfast ray a rippling pathway threw:
A glittering wedge of light that clave in twain
The obdurate dense night and murky main.

LVIII

But now the chapel door was closed and barred;
So on the smooth cold step he sat him down,
And pitying thought of the stout hearts that warred
With the fell surge, or dropped their hold to drown.
Ah me! but life is dear, and death is hard,
Though, when life smiles, we only fret and frown;
From its full breast, sick nurslings, turn and cry,
To clutch it wildly as the stream runs dry.

LIX

So for awhile he mused.   But soon his brain,
Careless to solve, let go the tangled theme;
And then strange thoughts, a desultory train,
Unbidden came and went, as in a dream.
Now he was tossing on the seething main,
Now at a shrine, lit by one pale lamp's gleam,
Kneeling with worshippers composed in prayer;—
And then, anon, whirled thro' the empty air.

LX

How long he thus sat dream-bound, could be known
To darkness only.   But at length he heard
A sound that neither was the billow's moan,
Nor howl of storm, nor scream of wheeling bird.
The porch behind him shook, and the numb stone
Whereon he sat, it seemed to him, was stirred ;
And in the doorway, wimpled with a hood
Of flowing folds, the mild Madonna stood.

LXI

So, for an instant, to his sight it seemed ;
But, by the fantasy not long beguiled,
He saw it was Olympia's self that beamed
Upon the darkness and the waters wild.
Yet was she heavenly as the thing he dreamed,
As pure, as potent, pitiful, and mild ;
And at her beck he looked to see dismissed
The unruly winds, and the loud billows whist.

LXII

But still the storm raged on.   "Olympia ! see,
See, I am here !" he said, still cowering down ;
And when she heard him not, about her knee
His arms he curved, and kissed her sacred gown.
"Godfrid !" she cried, "Godfrid ! oh, come with me,
Come quick within, and pray for those that drown !
In vain I watch and sue with many a tear ;
But if we both should pray, She still will hear."

LXIII

"She hear!" he pleaded; "hearken rather thou!"
Holding her robe, and suppliant at her feet;
"For never storm broke over failing prow
As on my breast life's whelming billows beat.
A long-tossed mariner I, behold me now
Straining to shore, craving for haven meet.
Oh, lift me, feeble, from these fearful waves,
And fold me, shipwrecked, to the heart that saves!"

LXIV

"O Godfrid, talk not wildly thus!" she said;
"I will be tender, so you will be calm;
There is no woe can not be comforted,
And for worst wound Heaven holds some blessëd balm.
I ne'er wore heavy heart or aching head,
But that I found, in psalter or in psalm,
Or silent mental prayer, or simple beads,
A swift and certain medicine for my needs."

LXV

"Yes, but," he answered, "mine a deeper woe,
Than bead, or prayer, or psalm can hope to probe.
I at my mother's knee was taught to throw
Myself on Heaven, and cling to Mary's robe;
But, like yon waves that wander to and fro,
Homeless and aimless through the whirling globe,
I flow now where Fate bids me, nor demand
Why there I ebb, and here I hug the strand.

LXVI

" Still to the Sovereign Will I humbly bow,
If I no longer grace or gifts implore ;
And, Heaven's own handmaid, listen to my vow,
Or Hope will die, where Faith had died before.
And see, Olympia !—is't not so ?—I now
But seek one intermediary more.
You through Madonna all your wants prefer ;
Well, I will pray to you, then you to Her."

LXVII

Then rising, with his face he sought her face ;
But on what altered sight his sight now fell !
Though buried in her hands, withal apace
From her loved eyes he saw the tear-drops well.
And as he strove, with reverent embrace
And words of pious tenderness to quell
Her surging grief, " Not pray ! Not pray !" she cried ;
Then bared her gaze, and wailed out at his side :

LXVIII

" Alas ! that ever by the rippling stream,
Under the blossoming thorn, our steps did meet !
Alas, alas, that I to you should seem
Winsome, and you to me undreamt-of sweet !
I thought you loved Madonna ; was it a dream
I saw you carry garlands to her feet ?
I told you—did I not ?—I was her child,
Hers only, wholly, till you came and smiled.

LXIX

"And I *am* Hers—not yours, not yours indeed.
Nay, urge not, speak not, Godfrid! for your tongue
Is but a dagger from whose strokes I bleed.
Hither return when the first lark hath sung,
And I meanwhile will watch, and weep, and plead
You yet may pray, even as you prayed when young.
Now go and rest!   And in her hallowed keeping
Madonna hold you, while your cares are sleeping."

LXX

She ceased, and with the cadence seemed to raise
Her hands to bless, whereat he bowed his head.
But when again he craved her lenient gaze,
The door was closed, the angelic vision fled.
Alone and outcast in the moaning ways
He stood, with winds and billows for his bed:
It seemed as if Heaven's self had thrust him out
To utter darkness, for the fiends to flout.

LXXI

Radiant with smiles, with limbs of rosy hue,
Up from Tithonus' couch Aurora came,
Her golden chariot scattering sparks of dew,
Her glowing coursers breathing genial flame;
And, as of old, the glorious retinue
Of youth and beauty trumpeted her fame.
Fleet from her presence fled the winds; the waves
Crouched at her feet, owning themselves her slaves.

LXXII

You cannot kill the Gods.   Their shadows still
The cherished rites of Pagan eld renew,
Haunt the cool grot, or scour the thymy hill,
And in the wood their wanton sports pursue.
This very morn I heard Pan's pastoral quill,
And tracked Diana's sandals o'er the dew,
Caught dimpled Venus veiled in feathery foam,
And Faunus scampering to his sylvan home.

LXXIII

And if Jove prove not the last god dethroned,
But Heaven at length Olympus' fate should feel,
Deem not, withal, its choirs shall be disowned,
Or dumb oblivion o'er its seraphs steal.
Still shall calm Stephen smile on martyrs stoned,
Fair sinners still to Magdalen appeal ;
Cecilia's touch still wake the sacred lyre,
And lamblike Agnes spotless loves inspire.

LXXIV

Such were the thoughts that stirred in Godfrid's brain,
When morning rose above the horizon's rim,
And once again he slowly sought to gain
Olympia's side, as she had bidden him.
There was a silence on the shimmering main,
And the white city did in sunshine swim ;
You would have thought the griefs that make men gray,
Had, like the storm, been spirited away.

LXXV

The chapel door stood open wide; the air,
Within, was sweet and fragrant as the clove.
Gold-dappled bees were humming everywhere,
Fancying Madonna's shrine a honeyed grove;
And, overhead, fluttered by coming care,
A little bird flew to and fro, and strove
To find some niche secure from ravage rude,
Where it might build its nest, and rear its brood.

LXXVI

Over the marble pavement pure as snow,
Faint yellow butterflies flickered, gaily dight,
Whose shifting shadows you might scarcely know
From golden flaws within the spotless white.
But for the rest, around, above, below,
There was no breath, no stir, no sound, no sight;
It was as quiet as could quiet be,
And all the place seemed lapped in vacancy.

LXXVII

The glamour that in silent beauty dwells
Chased for awhile the pain love's doubtful daring
Woke in his heart; but soon, despite its spells,
He felt the moments somewhat sadly wearing;
Till from the sacristy, with snow-white bells,
Olympia came, a lily lilies bearing,
And, having laid them at Madonna's feet,
Gazed on him salutation sad but sweet.

LXXVIII

On her young cheek no more that rose did blow
Such as from hedgerow in lush June you pull,
But, in its stead, her face was washed with woe,
Though of the sort which maketh beautiful;
Her large orbs, swart and satin as the sloe,
Whose lustrous light no sorrow could annul,
Yet wore a strangely grave and settled look,
Like a dark pool, and not the laughing brook.

LXXIX

"Tell me my fate!" he cried, seizing her hand.
"Your fate!" she answered, "tell me rather mine!
Bend pride's stiff knee; no longer grace withstand,
And ours shall be the bliss for which you pine.
If not, then Heaven hath this dear bounty banned,
And my poor heart must your rich heart resign.
I am Madonna's child, come life what may,
Come death! O Godfrid! kneel with me and pray!"

LXXX

There was a moment's hush, brief but intense,
Long as perhaps a billow hangs to break.
Then, with a heaving of the bosom, whence,
More than the lips, the answer came, he spake,
And said "I cannot!" frightening thus suspense,
Which fled, and left a more enduring ache.
But tight he clutched her hand, as, in the wave,
Men bent on death still strive themselves to save.

LXXXI

And as he held her thus, her sight grew dim,
Her other hand on Mary did she lay,
And turned from him to her, from her to him,
As soul and sense alternately did sway;
Like one of those primeval seraphim,
Pure spirit, but love-chained to a child of clay,
Immortal born, with just that mortal leaven,
Seduced to earth, but quick recalled to Heaven.

LXXXII

When suddenly across her infirm gaze,
Bewildered lips, and vacillating gait,
There rushed a quick resolve, such as betrays
The heart when hope at bay grows desperate.
Lifting her hand from off the statue's base,
She clutched his arm as though she clutched at Fate,
And, gasping, said, "Will you with me repair
Where Milan's spires go up to heaven like prayer?

LXXXIII

"For in its busy ways and sinful crowd,
There is, as I have heard, a marble pile,
Whose topmost pinnacles are lost in cloud,
And, ere the mountains, catch day's dawning smile.
The gorgeous palaces that house the proud,
Yield to its spacious nave and thick-trunked aisle,
And wealth and pomp of courts are sordid things,
· To its rich worship of the King of kings.

LXXXIV

"And learnëd men its famous Chapter fill,
Learnëd and breathed on by the Holy Ghost,
Chief among whom, in days they talk of still,
This little town could for its pastor boast.
He in my budding soul was first to instil
Sweet precepts, tidings from the heavenly host,
Love of my dear Madonna, and a life
That never thought to find in fondness, strife.

LXXXV

"Come, let us go, and, if you will, afoot,
And to that far-off goal make pilgrimage;
And our joint journey in your heart may put
Wise counsel, and your cruel doubts assuage.
If not, then he—for I will set him to't,—
With heavenly argument and reason sage
Shall melt the ear which to my prayer is cold,
And win you back, lost sheep, to Christ's dear fold."

LXXXVI

Now woke the morn, fresh as a maiden wakes,
And, while the world still slept, forth hand in hand
Went Godfrid and Olympia.   Lagging flakes
Of silvery mist, by light gales curled and fanned,
Fled up the hill; from feathery-foliaged brakes
There rang melodious matins; on the sand,
And on the sea, glistened a pearly dew;
And, over both, bright bent the heavens blue.

LXXXVII

He had a leathern satchel at his back,
And in her breast a missal small she bore ;
And, their sole burden these, they took the track
That lies between the mountains and the shore.
On the smooth main was many a white-sailed smack,
Upon the hillside many a ruin hoar ;
With many a fluttering wing the air was sown,
But on the mountain road themselves alone.

LXXXVIII

Soon as they reached the last and loftiest crest
Whence could Spiaggiascura be descried,
Halting, they took their first brief snatch of rest,
By a bright well that bubbled at their side.
There, as she said a prayer within her breast,
He prayerless gazed upon the prospect wide ;
And then the twain, hands linking as before,
Strode on, nor saw the little city more.

LXXXIX

Through smiling tracts, defended from the snows,
All the year basking in the sun's warm ray,
And fanned by every genial gale that blows,
Tracts that are Eden still, their journey lay.
Leftward the far-receding mountains rose,
Upon the right ranged headland, creek, and bay,
And jutting promontories, round which the bright
Blue ocean ended in a fringe of white.

XC

High up the hill were smooth steep pastures green,
Whence tinkling herd-bells fitful reached the ear;
And in the rough and bosky clefts between,
Browsed shaggy goats, clambering where all was sheer:
While, but half heard, and only faintly seen,
There a thin silvery thread, a white speck here,
Dashed the precipitous torrent, soon to flow
Glibly adown the gradual slope below:

XCI

The smiling slope with olive groves bedecked,
Now darkly green, now, as the breeze did stir,
Spectral and white, as though the air were flecked
With elfin branches tipped with gossamer;
And then so faint, Godfrid could scarce detect
Which the gray hillside, which the foliage fair;
Until once more it dense and sombre grew,
Again to shift, just as the zephyr blew.

XCII

Nigher their ken were mulberry, fig, and vine,
This linked to those in many a long festoon,
'Neath which the wise, when days are long, recline,
Reaping the hours in a deep golden swoon.
The tendrils yet had but begun to twine
Round the pale stems that would be hidden soon;
But, in the cradling furrows lodged between,
Peeped sprouting maize, and grasses newly green.

H

XCIII

And here and there with glistering lemon bowers
The lower landward terraces were crowned,
Or shapely orange groves, whose fragrant flowers
Make of the land a bride the whole year round.
Pink petals from the almond fell in showers,
Making a vernal carpet for the ground;
Over the walls peered tufts of yellow broom,
And oleanders reddening into bloom.

XCIV

And ever and anon some quiet town
Came into view, and thro' it straight they passed,
Though once mayhap its name had won renown
In this strange world, where nothing great doth last.
With braided hair, bronzed limbs, and girded gown,
Ranged round a fountain flowing clear and fast,
Their eyes as bright as day, yet dark as night,
Bent stalwart women, washing linen white.

XCV

And round the open thresholds children fair,
Happy and lithe as lizards, romped and ran,
Their grandams sitting by in sunny chair;
But, in the ways, never a sign of man.
He was away, driving the ox-drawn share,
Trimming the vine-clasped elm to shapely span,
Or through his maize in many a trivial course
Scattering the rampart torrent's forward force.

XCVI

In each broad market-place a church there was,
With campanile soaring straight in air,
And open door for whosoe'er should pass.
And once or twice, to say a hasty prayer,
Olympia stole within, though he, alas !
Without remained, mute in the noontide glare.
But ne'er a shrine they saw which, to their mind,
Was half so fair as that one left behind.

XCVII

When, for awhile, the sea got lost to view,
Since landward now the hilly pathway wound,
By aromatic pine-slopes stern of hue,
Which shut the sunlight out, their gaze was bound.
Beyond their ken the shaggy summits grew ;
Grimly, below them, yawned ravine profound,
Wherethro' swift torrent a rough pathway tore,
Filling the sombre silence with its roar.

XCVIII

But soon again the black pass broadened out,
On them once more the welcome sunshine streamed,
And budding larches, dotted sparse about
Among dark firs, like fairy foliage gleamed.
In valleys green they heard the shepherds shout
To flocks that browsed and herds that dozed and dreamed ;
Torrent no more, the stream beneath them flowed,
Devious, yet smooth, e'en as their mountain road ;

XCIX

Seeking a softly undulating plain
With straggling red-roofed villages bestrewed,
Whence, as the light of day began to wane,
Ave Maria rang from belfries rude.
The air, the hills, the reappearing main,
Felt the soft touch of twilight's tender mood;
And every bosom in that region fair,
All, saving one alone, o'erflowed with prayer.

C

For at the foot of a tall roadside cross,
Whereon the martyred Godhead patient hung,
And round whose base soft-greenly grew the moss,
By hill-dews fed, herself Olympia flung,
And, like to one who mourns some bitter loss,
Yet hides the grief wherewith the heart is wrung,
There silently to Heaven her vows preferred,
Yet because mute, oh, not less surely heard !

CI

But when once more she rose up to her feet,
Still at his side to bravely trudge along,
Her heart, he saw, with quicker pulses beat,
And lo ! she broke, unbidden, into song.
It was a melody unearthly sweet,
Which the fond ear for ever would prolong;
And with her voice, as ceased the belfries' clang,
The craggy hollows of the mountain rang.

1

Oh, Mary Mother, full of grace,
Above all other women blest,
Through whose pure womb our erring race
Beholds its sin-born doom redressed,
                    Pray for us!
Thou by the Holy Ghost that wert
With every heavenly gift begirt,
Thou that canst shield us from all hurt,
            Pray for us!   Pray for us!

2

Tower of David, Ivory Tower,
Vessel of Honour, House of Gold,
Mystical Rose, unfading Flower,
Sure refuge of the unconsoled,
                    Pray for us!
Mirror of Justice, Wisdom's Seat,
Celestial shade for earthly heat,
The sinner's last and best retreat,
            Pray for us!   Pray for us!

3

O thou of Heaven that art the gate,
That to the feeble strength dost bear,

To whom no outcast turns too late,
Even when thy Son is deaf to prayer,
                    Pray for us !
O Morning Star, to chase the dark,
Cause of our joy through care and cark,
Thou of the Covenant the Ark,
                    Pray for us !   Pray for us !

4

Bright Queen of the angelic choir,
Of patriarchs, prophets, worshipped Queen !
Queen of the martyrs proved by fire,
And Queen of confessors serene ;
Queen of the apostolic train,
Queen that o'er all the saints doth reign,
O Queen conceived without a stain !
                    Pray for us !   Pray for us !,

CII

So ceased the strain, and with it ceased the day.
The mountains slowly wrapped themselves in night ;
Far off, the silent sea gloomed cold and gray,
Sky-sundered by one long low line of white.
Over the vale, far down, a flat mist lay,
Which for a phantom lake bewrayed the sight ;
And louder now they heard the watchdogs bark,
And cataracts dashing downward through the dark.

CIII

Therefore with eager eye and quickened pace
Descried they twinkling lights not far ahead;
But many a zigzag yet had they to trace,
Descending ever, ere their hopes were fed.
At length they heard the voices of the place,
Sought out the inn, and craved for board and bed;
Two little sleeping chambers side by side,
And what rude fare the mountains could provide.

CIV

Yet as that day full many a league their feet
Had traversed, and would dawn bring many more,
Olympia early rose from fireside seat.
Reverent, he saw her to her chamber door,
Bent o'er her hand, and wished her slumber meet;
Then, to the warm hearth fed by pine logs hoar
Returning, sat him down, and by their light
Mused, mute and mournful, far into the night.

CV

But she, when in her little room shut in,
First, on her knees, her prayers to Heaven addressed;
These said, her simple gown she did unpin,
And of their robes her modest limbs divest.
Some mountain jonquils, that had gathered been
By Godfrid, fondly to her heart she pressed;
Then on the pillow laid her weary head,
And guardian angels gathered round the bed.

CVI

So for three days they journeyed, till they came
Where once-proud Genoa sits beside the sea,
Striving her antique temper yet to tame
To the stern bidding of the days that be :
Ghost of gay Eld, the same yet not the same,
As when she shone, beautiful, brave, and free,
Her airy pennon flouting every strand,
And Neptune's trident glittering in her hand.

CVII

But, with the breaking of another morn,
They rose betimes and travelled with the crowd,
Roaring through tunneled hill, and loudly borne
On wings of wind past leagues of land and cloud,
Where the Ligurian hoed his patch of corn,
Or through his vines the Lombard peasant ploughed ;
Till, with mid-afternoon, they could descry
The pinnacles of Milan prick the sky.

CVIII

And soon, once more afoot, their steps were bent
Through intersecting streets whose broad slant eaves,
Stretching athwart the footway, made a tent
For the hot sun, almost as cool as leaves.
It seemed that the whole city with them went ;
And when they reached the piazza that receives
Many a convergent way, a mighty crowd
Streamed up the steps of the cathedral proud.

CIX

So, never halting in the glowing square
A moment even, though the fretted fane,
Flamboyant oriel, pinnacles poised in air,
One after one the eye would count in vain,
Bold-flying buttress, tall shaft tapering fair,
And dazzling front, might well their gaze detain,
For the main door they made with all the folk,
Till on their ear the pealing organ broke.

CX

A moment more, and lo ! they stood within !
A cry of wonder from Olympia burst ;
But on the instant seeing that He, whom sin
Doomed to dire death upon the rood accurst,
Shone on the altar, veiled by mystery thin,
Straight knelt she down, and, soon in prayer immersed,
Forgot the crowd, long aisles, and columns tall,
While Godfrid gazed and marvelled at it all.

CXI

Each valid foot of transept, nave, and aisle,
Was dense with living things absorbed in prayer ;
Young men and maidens, children without guile,
Gray sires with flowing beard and bosom bare ;
Smooth sinless faces here, that seemed to smile,
Even as they prayed, with eyes soft-closed ; and there,
Hard furrowed visages down which the tears
Flowed from the brackish fount of desert years.

CXII

With comely kerchief crossed o'er bosom brown,
The humble peasant fingered her worn beads,
Made at her side her youngsters nestle down,
And told Madonna of her simple needs.
Next her, a dainty dame of Milan town,
Voluptuous as but southern rapture breeds,
Bewailing in the dust her too frail breast,
Begged Christ to be her lover and sole guest.

CXIII

And many a tonsured head was there, that bore
The ascetic cowl, surmounting garments strict;
Here the brown serge the loving Francis wore,
There the black robes of active Benedict;
And Dominic's stern habit, splashed with gore,
Beneath which silently the hairshirt pricked;
And, dotted in the carnal crowd anon,
Were pale-faced nuns, meek, circumspect, and wan.

CXIV

Then from afar a long procession came
Of white-robed acolytes silver censers swinging,
And wreathèd flowers, and torches all aflame,
And golden bells melodiously ringing,
And fair young boys, with faces free from blame,
Tuning their callow throats to such sweet singing,
It seemed to eye and ear of faith and fear
That Christ and all His cherubim were near.

CXV

And as they sang, the stately pomp swept on,
Crozier and Cross, inlaid with many a gem,
Taller than those that bore them ; lights that shone
In golden candlestick with jewelled stem,
And many a bright embroidered gonfalon
Vaunting aloft the new Jerusalem ;
And scintillating reliquary rare,
And awful Monstrance, whereon none may stare.

CXVI

Last in the solemn train, in cope of gold
And snow-white alb, came venerable eld,
Mitre on head of more than earthly mould,
Led by grave priests, gorgeously chasubled.
And, as they passed, round arch and column old
Incense and organ music rolled and swelled,
Till the long line within the chancel poured,
And then with one acclaim they praised the Lord.

CXVII

" All ye works of the Lord," they loudly sang,
" Bless ye the Lord, Praise Him for evermore !
Praise Him, ye waves, with your sonorous clang,
Praise Him, ye winds, Praise Him, O sea and shore !
Mountains, and little hills, and clouds that hang
Over the deep, dews, snows, and pinnacles hoar,
Darkness and Light, storms that are silent never,
Bless ye the Lord, Praise Him for ever and ever !

CXVIII

"Bless ye the Lord, fountains and rivers that run,
Huge whales and monsters of the deep profound;
Praise Him, ye lightnings, moon, and stars, and sun,
˅ Birds of the air, and beasts that graze the ground!
Praise Him for all the wondrous things He hath done;
Praise Him on harps, Praise Him on cymbals of sound!
With sounding trumpet, timbrel, and organ, and chord,
Praise Him!　Let every spirit praise the Lord!"

CXIX

Then on the dense mass sudden silence fell,
˅ Each knee was bent, each reverent skullcap doffed,
Held was each breath, and, touched by unseen spell,
The organ fluted silvery and soft.
Then came the tinkle of a little bell,
And, all heads low, the Host was held aloft;
While glinted through warm panes day's dying gleam,
And the rapt soul touched Heaven in a dream.

CXX

Then once again the organ thundered loud,
Usurping the high edifice with sound,
Whereat with dumb accord the prostrate crowd
Rose, crossed themselves, and to the doorway wound;
And soon where, late, myriads of knees were bowed
In phalanxed prayer, reigned solitude profound.
The solemn notes waxed faint, then swooned away,
And died along the aisles the light of day.

CXXI

And now throughout the vague cathedral gloom,
That here and there with lone faint lamps was flecked,
Two forms alone were blackly seen to loom,
A kneeling maiden, and a man erect.
They looked like statues carven at a tomb,
Apeing the quick, with flowing drapery decked,
And praying with fixed lips and stony head
Till the last trump shall sound and rouse the dead.

CXXII

But, shortly rising, with a beckoning nod
She drew him forward through the weirdlike space,
And on the hard smooth marble as they trod,
Their feet made fearsome echoes in the place.
Anon she checked him : "Stay you here with God,"
Whispering she said, " I will be back apace."
Among stone stems he saw her disappear,
Though still her hurrying footfall reached his ear.

CXXIII

At length even that deserted him ; and then,
He was alone in the tremendous gloom :
Alone with God, far from the help of men.
Like empty vault of monumental tomb,
More felt than seen, the dark roof smote his ken ;
The long aisles stretched like avenues of doom,
And, in the distant chancel dimly lit,
Bodiless forms seemed noiselessly to flit.

CXXIV

Left with his dark and solitary ache,
" If there be spirits of solace and light," he cried,
"Swoop from your spheres, your unseen Heaven forsake,
And now no more my lonely doubts deride.
Sound-sleeping martyrs, from the tomb awake !
Palm-bearing virgins, through the silence glide !
Can you be false who are indeed so fair ?
And if I needs must pray, then hear my prayer !

CXXV

"And thou, Olympia's trust, once mine no less,
Of all the Gods gentlest Divinity !
Mother, and Lady of the mild caress,
Lend me thy face ! oh ! give me eyes to see !
If thou canst hear, why dost thou scorn distress,
Thou before whom demons of darkness flee ?
Let me behold thee once,—once, I entreat !—
E'en as Judea's mountains felt thy feet !"

CXXVI

Not such the prayers to which high Heaven replies ;
The lips of faith another language speak ;
Celestial visions visit downcast eyes,
And those who find, not arrogantly seek.
No answer came to his presumptuous cries,
Such as, 'tis said, descends on suppliants meek,
But only deeper darkness, and a sense
Of unslaked thirst and yearning impotence.

CXXVII

At length, again, a solitary tread
Upon the silence gained, though far and faint ;
Yet well he guessed 'twas hers, than whom the dead
And never dying vaunt no purer saint.
Nearer, and ever nearer, now it sped,
Until his fancy her fair form could paint
On the dark space, and then the dark space yawned,
And she herself, no fancy, on him dawned.

CXXVIII

"Come with me, now," she said, in accents low,
And straightway led him with such swift command
Among dense-columned aisles, it seemed as though
Athwart a lonesome wood where huge trunks stand,
Baulking straight steps, together they did go,
He strange, and she familiar in the land,
Where, overhead, thick-matted branches made
Day night, and night a more cimmerian shade.

CXXIX

But shortly shone a little light ahead,
Just level with their gaze ; a feeble flame,
Held by a priest in cassock habited
And in mid-doorway seen as in a frame.
He stood as still as stand the pictured dead,
When some deft hand makes death and life the same,
And bids one, doubtful, nearer draw, and seek
If that which gazes so, perchance will speak.

CXXX

But ere the living presence could be proved,
Olympia's aid had vanished from his side;
The tall dark figure in the doorway moved,
And with fine gesture welcome fair implied.
He, by the stately courtesy behoved
To pass within, with slow obedient stride
Entered, the other slowly following him;
Then the door closed, and all again was dim.

CXXXI

And where now was Olympia?   Ask you where?
She to the gloaming chancel back had crept,
And, hope and fear absorbed in silent prayer,
Lay prone, aye prostrate, even as though she slept.
The flowing tresses of her warm, soft hair,
Dark as the gloom, the cold white marble swept;
She moved not, spoke not, sighed not; even her breath
Came faint, like one that feebly copes with death.

CXXXII

But, slowly rising thence, her body first
She lifted, then her hands, and last her eyes;
And floods of passionate supplication burst,
Through lips long sealed, from breast o'ercharged with sighs.
She called on Christ, on Her who bore and nursed,
On every Saint and Seraph in the skies,
And vowed herself to pain, if Heaven would save
From death the dear imperilled soul it gave.

CXXXIII

"Oh, by Thine agony and bloody sweat,
Deliver him, O Lord!" aloud she cried;
"By Thy keen Cross and Passion, save him yet
Save by Thy crown of thorns and bleeding side!
Why did Gethsemane Thy tear-drops wet?
Why wert Thou scourged, why scorned, why crucified?
Why didst Thou die, why gloriously ascend,
Why send the Comforter, be this the end?"

CXXXIV

Then in a tempest of hot tears her cries
Were drenched and drowned, her weak words washed away;
Her tears were choked with sobs, sobs swooned to sighs,
Then sighs to silence, and there mute she lay.
Oh, if there be a Heaven beyond the skies,
A Heaven to hear, why was it deaf that day?
For since time's dawn, unto the realms of air
No holier heart e'er breathed a purer prayer.

CXXXV

"Rise, my dear child," a mild voice gravely said,
"Rise and accept your doom:" whereat she rose.
"In vain is Reason's dew when Faith is dead,
And Grace sleeps silent under Doubt's deep snows.
I can no more. The Paraclete hath fled;
Through his parched bosom prayer no longer flows.
By Heaven may yet the miracle be wrought;
But human ways are weak, and words are nought."

I

CXXXVI

Then, lamp in hand, through choir and transept dim
He led them, till they reached a little door,
And, having fatherly blessed her and him,
Closed it, and they beheld his face no more.
The sky was bright with starry cherubim,
Silent, and round them was the city's roar;
And, in their hearts, an anguish of despair,
Too deep for utterance, and too dark for prayer.

CXXXVII

There motionless they stood, bereft of speech,
As vessels stranded wait for some fresh wave
That yet perhaps will lift them from the beach,
And bear them buoyant o'er the breakers brave.
None came; yet still they lingered, each for each,
Two lonely mourners at an open grave,
Which holds the dead and must be filled with clay,
And neither hath the heart to turn away.

CXXXVIII

At length when too oppressive grew the strain,
"Will you not sleep in Milan, dear?" he said;
Thus seeking with life's need to fly from pain,
And have his instant sentence respited.
But she, who knew delay was worse than vain,
Raised deprecating hand, and shook her head;
"No, Godfrid!   Here, our task is ended quite:
Let us retrace our pilgrimage to-night!"

CXXXIX

So once again they fled without delay,
On wings of wind through leagues of dim-seen land,
Night and the stars accompanying their way,
And roar and blackness close on either hand;
Until the dark drew off, and with the day
They saw the sparkling bay and joyous strand,
White sails, brown oars, huge coils of briny ropes,
And fair proud city throned on regal slopes.

CXL

And soon the road they came by, which had run
Close by the sea, now smooth as woodland pond,
Saw them once more, love-woven dream unspun,
Facing farewell.   A little way beyond,
A sleek brown mule stood blinking in the sun,
For a long march rudely caparisoned;
And at its side a gentle mountaineer,
Who to their grief lent neither eye nor ear.

CXLI

"Hear me once more, Olympia!   Must we part?
Is Heaven so stern, and can your gentle breast
Inflict and sooth endure so keen a smart,
When charity could lull our pain to rest?
Is there no common Eden of the heart,
Where each fond bosom is a welcome guest?
No comprehensive Paradise, to hold
All loving souls in one celestial fold?

CXLII

"Here, 'twixt the mountains and the sea, I swear
That I your Faith will reverence as my soul,
And as when first I succoured your despair
By the dark streamlet and the blossoming bole,
I every dewy dawn fresh flowers will bear
Unto Madonna's shrine, that happy goal
Where our first journey ended, and I fain
Would have this end,—not snapped, as now, in pain!"

CXLIII

The foam-fringe at their feet was not more white
Than her pale cheek as, downcast, she replied:
"No, Godfrid! no! Farewell, farewell! You might
Have been my star; a Star once fell by pride:
But since you furl your wings, and veil your light,
I cling to Mary and Christ crucified.
Leave me, nay leave me, ere it be too late!
Better part here than part at Heaven's gate!"

CXLIV

Thereat he kissed her forehead, she his hand,
And on the mule he mounted her, and then,
Along the road that skirts the devious strand,
Watched her, until she vanished from his ken.
Tears vainly dropped as water upon sand
Or words of grace on hearts of hardened men,
Coursed down her cheek, while, half her grief divined,
The mountain guide walked sad and mute behind.

CXLV

But never more as in the simple days
When prayer was all her thought, her heart shall be ;
For she is burdened with the grief that stays,
And by a shadow vexed that will not flee.
Pure, but not spared, she passes from our gaze,
Victim, not vanquisher of Love.   And he ?
Once more an exile over land and main :—
Ah ! Life is sad, and scarcely worth the pain !

CXLVI

The sun was sinking where the sky-line bounded
The blue and scarcely furrowed plain of ocean ;
A moment more, was gone, and left confounded
Retreat of day and night's advancing motion.
Then came the moon, rayless, and red, and rounded,
As when sole mistress of our heart's devotion,
And slowly took her melancholy march
Up the ascent of Heaven's stupendous arch.

CXLVII

Dark were the thoughts that passed through Godfrid's mind,
As sleepless on the deck sleep made his own,
He skirted bay, and cape, and hills behind,
And in their hollows villages bestrewn,
Which, dimly seen, were beautiful divined,
And, since no sooner just descried than flown,
Held on his heart a fond romantic claim
For ever thence.   If life could do the same !

CXLVIII

But soon there crept a tremor overhead;
The billows shook their white manes, and uprose;
The sheathëd east more large and crimson spread,
Like an imperious rosebud when it blows.
Up came the sun, impetuous and red:
The moon turned deadly pale, fronting her foes;
Refused, spite overwhelming odds and ills,
To share her sway, and died behind the hills.

CXLIX

Then, from remotest summit to the shore,
And thickly dotted everywhere between,
As sped the vessel, frequent more and more,
On treeless slope, in stream-refreshed ravine,
Glistened the marble hamlets; some that bore
Upon the beach, others in distance seen,
Like maidens dipping white feet in the spray,
Or dipped, and going up the hills away.

CL

Smoothly he sailed past headland, bay, and frith,
Smoothly and softly, till the vessel drew
Its track to Leghorn's living port, wherewith
Even now the prophecy seemed coming true
Of Italy's birth; past Pisa, by its kith
Beggared of all save beauty; onward, through
Val d'Arno garlanded with Spring, he sped,
For Florence called, "Come and be comforted!"

CLI

And comfort came to Godfrid, as, caressed
In that fair city's whilom curving walls,
He owned the spell by none save it possessed,
Which stirs yet rests the soul, and never palls ;
Strange power, oft felt by many a pilgrim guest,
Of river and garden, convents, hills, and halls,
Palace, and shrine, and gallery, to slake
The spirit's thirst and lull the bosom's ache.

CLII

But when robbed Autumn wept herself away,
And the South's bright unweeping winter came
Down from the mountain tops where glittering lay
Her fallen tears congealed, the smouldering flame
Of love that, unextinguished night or day,
Burned in his vestal heart, began to claim
Fresh fuel, and he longed to see once more
Madonna's shrine and Spiaggiascura's shore.

CLIII

Love his sole escort, yearning his sole guide,
And but one stage his journey, he at last—
For long now seemed the pilgrimage,—descried
The shimmering Eden of his exiled Past.
There, the dell zigzagged up the soft hillside,
There, tripped the streamlet, frolicsome and fast,
There, stood the little chapel, and lo ! there,
Olympia's casement, open to the air.

CLIV

But as unto the spot he drew more nigh,
And hastened onward with remembering feet,
He saw with sinking heart and saddening eye
Madonna's chapel closed, that used to greet,
With open door, sunshine, and sea, and sky.
So on its silent step he took his seat,
As on that woful night, and gazing dumb   .
On the blue breakers, wondered would she come.

CLV

And ever and anon he cast a glance
Up at her casement, where was wont to stand
A pot of flowers.   Now,—was it only chance ?—
No flowers were there.   At length, from off the sand
He saw a bent and withered dame advance
Slow toward the shrine, her spindle in her hand,
Singing, to mind her of the days gone by,
A sweet love-ditty, low and plaintively.

CLVI

As leisurely she came, he leisured rose,
And, gazing at her well-remembered face,
Said, " Can you tell me why these doors now close,
And where is she, the guardian of this place ? "
"She ? she is gone ; and whither, no one knows.
Spiaggiascura sees no more her face,
Her feet no more !   And I have heard them say,
'Twas one like you that drove our dear away.

CLVII

"Sister of Charity they call her now.
She wears black serge about her fair young limbs,
And a white fillet, smooth across her brow,
Hides her once raven hair.   Elsewhere her hymns
She chants, and Christ hath got her virgin vow.
But many an eye in Spiaggiascura swims,
Vainly, to have her back.   Ah ! well-a-day !
That love and grief should drive our dear away!"

CLVIII

Then on she passed, with feet infirm and slow,
Plying her spindle still along the shore,
Unto her own pleased ears continuing low
The love-song of her youth that was no more.
But he from her reproach made haste to go,
Lest others came and echoed it, and bore
Straight thence to Milan, making for the pile
Which, ere the mountains, takes the orient's smile.

CLIX

Empty its vast space now, where once he stood
With myriads packed in prayer ; empty its nave,
Empty the aisles, trunked like a virgin wood,
Save of a verger wielding idle stave.
"Pray, tell me where to find a Father good,
Who once the simple folk their sins forgave
That live at Spiaggiascura," Godfrid said.
"Alas, sir ! he hath been this three months dead !"

CLX

Then seeing that life and death alike conspired
Against him, with unhoping heart he went
From Milan, and to Florence back retired,
Once more relapsing to that dumb content,
Which, when is nothing more to be desired
This side the grave, sits with its longings bent
Upon the other, and in patience waits
The tardy opening of death's grim-shut gates.

CLXI

Then oftenest his presence might you see,
Ever alone, in corridor and hall,
And mostly there where Venus of the Sea,
Lithe on her white pentelic pedestal,
And pure withal in utter nudity,
Stands, challenging the story of the Fall.
Wait, souls impatient! Art will manumit
The bondsman, Nature, when the times shall fit.

CLXII

Withal, with lively concourse and the gay
Prismatic multitude that daily troops
From broad piazza or from narrower way
Along the quay where mountain Arno stoops
To suit the lowly bridges, would he stray,
Glad with the gladness of the shifting groups,
And, when the afternoons grew bright and long,
Mix with the green Cascine's babbling throng.

CLXIII

But he was seen there rarely, for he most
Loved in the pale light of the afternoon,
When vespers had been chanted, and the host
Of monks had slipped away with slattern shoon
To cell or sacristy, to stalk like ghost
Through dim-lit aisles where none did importùne,
Or in the cloister garden hard beside
San Marco's shrine or Buonarotti's bride.

CLXIV

With him were fountain, walk, and flower-bed,
And frescoed wall, a little space beyond,
Of open corridor, whereon the dead,
With art ingenuous, reverent, and fond,
Have limned, through gratitude to him who led
Them, his disciples, never to despond,
In colours not like those of modern trick,
But glowing still, the life of Dominic.

CLXV

Then through the *Spezieria's* courteous gate
Emerging on the outer world, his eye
And heart felt overburdened with the weight
Of the fair streets, vast hills, and vaster sky,
Where all except himself seemed calm and great.
Then would he lean o'er *Ponte Nuovo* nigh,
Till did the arbitrary tears annul
A scene for his soft heart too beautiful.

CLXVI

But, with the springtide of another year,
There ran a light-heeled rumour through the land,
That Future palpitated-for was here,
And End to be accomplished, long time planned.
In every city pealed the joy-bells clear,
For War to wave anew her smouldering brand.
Men leaped from lethargy, and, as they passed,
Glared in each others' eyes, and looked, "At last!"

CLXVII

And women brought their children in the streets,
And held their nestlings to the martial mirth,
Ashamed no more to offer mother's teats
To those who, once it seemed, would curse their birth.
And maidens sent their other souls, their sweets,
Unwed, but proudly tearful in their dearth,
Thinking, "Rest childless in your patriot graves,
Or freight our wombs with sons no longer slaves!"

CLXVIII

For He, the self-crowned democrat, whose claim
Had herds, condoning violence, confessed,
Unequal heir of a too warlike fame,
Who 'neath the buckler wore a doubting breast,
Had let long-smothered purpose break aflame
Through clouding words, whose meaning still was guessed,
Thinking to vindicate the tinsel yoke,
He durst not lighten, by one noble stroke;

CLXIX

And thundered for his war-horse. On they came,
He at their head, the galliard plumes of France :
And when the record of her too much shame
Sadly ye read, forget not oft to glance
At one bright page ; for never since the name
Of Brother grew a password, had the lance
Been laid in rest, or war-spur stuck in steed,
For goal sublimer or for sorer need.

CLXX

Meanwhile, though press and platform might harangue,
Busy with self and turbulent with fears,
He rode him forth, alone, with martial clang,
All the waked centuries singing in his ears,
To drive the bandogs back whose greedy fang
Was fastening deeper with their victim's tears ;
Spontaneous rushed where Italy made moan,
To give her grandeur, or to lose his own.

CLXXI

Scared by the mighty name which whilom hunted
Their long gaunt backs, they half relaxed their grip.
She, scrambling to her feet, what spear unblunted
Was left her, seized, and stanched her bleeding lip ;
Donned armour seeming large for limbs unwonted,
And strode with France to battle, hip to hip ;
While Europe coldly prophesied disaster :
" See the fair slave making a change of master ! "

CLXXII

And Florence, gentle Florence, good to rule,
Rose from her sunny insolicitude,
Feeling that crafty mildness would befool
Her easy heart to tolerate a brood
Of hireling brows who deem the world a school,
Themselves the ushers.   At her altered mood
He fled, their Lord.   Without or hiss or groan,
They laughed the discrowned craven from his throne.

CLXXIII

Then all the Tuscan youth, like Helen's charmer,
Less for Bellona's than for Beauty's joust
In seeming fitted, donned withal their armour,
And followed in the wake the war-dogs loosed.
And Godfrid felt the passive blood wax warmer
Within his veins, and knew himself traduced
By servile lethargy and despot sorrow,
And sware to join the banners on the morrow.

CLXXIV

He had no mother, sister, maid, to leave,
But friendly faces had been bent on him,
And friendly hands stretched out to make him grieve
Less for a past which never could be dim.
His farewells he had ta'en, and, as the eve
On Florence drooped, was hurrying past the brim
Of snow-flushed Arno, in his soldier guise,
When on his arm a hand, and—Christ! those eyes!

CLXXV

The eyes of Olive, still as fair and fond,
The touch of Olive clinging to his side
In mute remembrance of the ancient bond.
Quickly she spoke: "Say, whither do you glide,
With blind gaze fastened on some goal beyond?"
"I go to fight for Italy!" he cried.
"O Olive! come not with that pallid face
To check me, now but started in the race!"

CLXXVI

"Hush! If it ever held you, prove it now!
I want your aid. Can Italy not wait?
But choose!" she said. "For death upon *his* brow
Beleaguering sits, and I am desolate.
Strange faces vex him, and, I know not how—
But, come or go! Why stand I here to prate?
You once were—— Well, I did believe that time
Might quench my love, not leave you less sublime."

CLXXVII

Swiftly together through the streets they sped,
Swift to the chamber mounted where he lay,
With all except the blankness of the dead.
"An English face, dear!" did she softly say,
"Whose name you know." Sir Gilbert from his bed
Turned a slow glance, and murmured, as a ray
Crept o'er his face of momentary bliss:
"An English face and voice? Thanks, thanks, for this!"

CLXXVIII

He was so feeble, so usurped by pain,
He could not say, articulately, more;
But pressure of the hand, and look, made plain
That this new presence made his smart less sore.
Then she explained to Godfrid how the twain
Had come through Umbrian hills from Capuan shore,
Arrived yestreen in Florence' swarming town,
And he by fever straight been stricken down.

CLXXIX

"The strangeness of the place will aggravate
His mental ache, and multiply his fears;
The sounds within, without, the hostel-gate,
Are unfamiliar to his homesick ears.
Can he be saved? Oh! think you 'tis too late?
Yes! he will die!" And rose the woman's tears,
And clung the woman's hands. These Godfrid pressed,
And whispered low: "Be calm, and hope the best!"

CLXXX

And then he set himself, as best he might,
With hand not quite so gentle as his heart,
Unskilled indeed, and all inapposite
For this new task, to play the nurse's part;
Urging meanwhile the unpaid debt of night
And travel's weariness, with specious art,
To her, he said, who must from slumber snatch
Strength to relieve him in to-morrow's watch.

CLXXXI

At last, reluctant, on a couch hard-by,
Still robed, she lay, and soon was deafly sleeping :
While darker waned the light in Gilbert's eye,
And o'er his temples came the death-dews creeping.
The fitful night-gusts from a murky sky
And hills of melancholy mist came sweeping ;
Till Godfrid's ears, excited, thought to find
The crash of battle flying on the wind.

CLXXXII

And then as darkness deepened, and the storm
Howled for the moon that came not, and the night
Scowled that she tarried, o'er the fevered form
Came writhing pangs and agonies to fright,
Which give to dying limbs a strength enorm ;
The which with gentle words, as best he might,
Strove Godfrid to assuage, beset with fear
Lest yon sound sleeper should awake and hear.

CLXXXIII

"Thanks, more than brother !   But I die, to-night !"
He breathed, and on the pillow weakly sank.
Colder the feet, the lips more pinched and white,
Clammier the hands, more moist the hair and lank.
Stole through the casement omens of the light
Of lagging dawn, but cloud-distressed and dank.
Then woke the fair flushed sleeper from repose,
Blaming her eyes that they could ever close.

K

CLXXXIV

He still was there, and through the doubtful morn,
Through struggling noon, once more defended eve,
Into another night was bravely borne
By hard-pressed dogged life that would not leave
The centre of its citadel, though shorn
Of hope that outward succour would relieve ;
Until it seemed that death, of late so eager,
Fell back from lines 'twas useless to beleaguer.

CLXXXV

A week, a puzzling, shapeless week, had gone,
When sunshine seemed to venture in the room,
Not through the window only, but upon
The learnëd brows so long enwrapt in gloom ;
And, the eighth morning, when they came to con
That pale sunk face, the very leech from whom
Comfort came rarest, whispered low at length,
"He yet may live ; 'tis an affair of strength !"

CLXXXVI

His whims waxed fewer, and his gaze less wild.
At last came sleep ; true, but a timid sleep,
Like wounded friend but lately reconciled,
Whom thoughts of past estrangement somewhat keep
Embarrassed still, withal a slumber mild,
Well-wishing, kindly, if nor long nor deep ;
Under whose covering influence might faint life
Repair the losses of its recent strife.

CLXXXVII

As the sick-chamber felt returning dawn
Of hope deemed set for ever, and tender heed
Might from the bedside partly be withdrawn,
Olive's fond gaze, which lately did but feed
On its vicissitudes, seemed now to fawn
More upon him Fate sent her in her need,
With look of thankful wonder in her eyes, .
Blent with affection, deeper for disguise.

CLXXXVIII

As dawn on night, as night on evening crept,
Strength summoned stealthy courage to invade
The slowly cooling channels lately swept
By subtle fever's enervating raid.
And when, the eleventh morn, the doctors stepped
Across the wonted threshold, and surveyed
The form that had so obstinately braved
The onset of close death, they murmured, "Saved!"

CLXXXIX

Then sleep, so generous still, if sensitive,
And anxious now to make a full amend
For absence long, approaches coy and stiff,
Seeming as though it never could expend
The kept-back love it long had yearned to give,
Nor prove itself enough the true old friend
Of former nights, found even night too brief
Wherein to bring the sufferer relief.

CXC

One morn, the fourth from that on which the words
Of promised life had life still more promoted,
From soundest sleep he woke.   Without, the birds,
Many, and musical, and swollen-throated,
Lustily carolled.   Voices of the herds,
From slopes unseen, into the city floated ;
With sunshine-shadow blended, and the sense
Of life come back, and Spring's young influence.

CXCI

Yes ! Spring had, jocund, danced adown the hills,
Filling the valleys with her footsteps fair,
And calling to the leaping mountain rills
Her swifter flight to follow, if they dare.
The dainty crocus and bluff daffodils
Pushed through the sod to drink the honeyed air.
The light lark into soaring treble burst,
To tell to Heaven what Earth had learned the first.

CXCII

" Godfrid !" he murmured.   But no answer came.
" Poor fellow ! he is wearied, and at last
Seeks the repose he has such right to claim,
Now that my peril, thanks to him, is passed."
He felt within so steady glow the flame
Of life late flickering, and so longed to cast
One look without, he slowly, stiffly, stepped
From his lone couch, and to the window crept.

CXCIII

He opened.   Just below, the city lay,
The marble shining city ; but, between,
Waved feathery trees in fresh-assumed array
Of many-shaded but harmonious green.
Seemed air, and sky, and mountain fâr away,
To swim and sparkle in a perfumed sheen,
And, nearer coming, to salute his brow,
And bid him own he ne'er had lived till now.

CXCIV

Roses, o'erburthened with their weight of flowers,
And drooping 'neath their own too luscious scent,
Hung over garden walls, and to young bowers
Transformed hoar gate and ruined battlement.
The nightingales through all the noonday hours
Sang, not for sorrow, but for heart's content ;
Nor round the circuit of the city fair,
But over penthoused street and broad bright square.

CXCV

It seemed as though the universe and he
Together had revived, and now his heart,
Hereto in sooth not over quick to see
The year's distinct emotions, had a part
In her new vernal geniality.
But unto him was solitude a smart :
He could not look, alone ; 'twas not his fate
To find in Nature friend and intimate.

CXCVI

So thence he tottered, weak, across the floor,
To an adjoining chamber.   Nought could be
More sweetly sunny or deserted more.
From world without came hummings of the bee,
And liquid linnet trills.   By open door,
Into another room he passed, to see
Godfrid on couch, asleep, with weary limb,
And Olive, nigh, intently watching him.

CXCVII

Down her fixed face, as alabaster pale,
The tears were trickling steadily and slow,
As tears will stream which neither flood nor fail,
Because from deep enduring source they flow.
He stood transfixed, reading the pictured tale,
And then completing it by his own woe:
Incarnate revelation, come at last,
Explaining each fresh puzzle of the past.

CXCVIII

All—all,—in that mute tell-tale group he saw:
The fettered heart he once had fondly deemed
Must love like his into love's orbit draw;
The cold consents which more like sufferance seemed
Than blood's response; obedience chilled by awe,
Not warmed by tenderness; the tears that gleamed
Oftener in eye than smile round lip or brow;—
In these,—in more,—he stood instructed now.

CXCIX

For in that concentrated gaze he read
Not love alone, but love's stern hopelessness,
Whose first, whose last indulgence was to shed
Thus openly the tears 'twould else repress,
Before that blameless, tranquil-sleeping head,
Unconscious cause of her, of his, distress.
He could not salve his woe with sense of wrong,
Nor anguish learn from vengeance to be strong.

CC

He turned away to go, as men will turn
From grief they cannot grapple with, and sought
Soft to retire, that so she might not learn
The ruin in his heart her heart had wrought,
And, unaccused, for other's heart might yearn.
But gently though he moved, the sound she caught,
And, keen as guilt for every step that stirs,
Read in his face the thought he read in hers.

CCI

No word by him or her was uttered then,
Or ever, of the truth, now both well knew,
And while she silently eschewed his ken,
He mute into his hollow woe withdrew.
But from that hour she sickened straight ; and when
Godfrid awoke refreshed with slumber's dew,
And came with hearty mien to greet them both,
He found her sunk in strange mysterious sloth.

CCII

At first he thought 'twas nature's self, that, wise,
Was but unstringing chords long overstrained,
And, when he marked no dread in Gilbert's eyes,
Deemed every torpid moment moment gained.
But when she sleepless lay in sleepy guise,
And hour by hour the pale-pink life-tint waned
From cheek but late with rosy youth aglow,
Fear gathered in his heart, foreboding woe.

CCIII

And when the leeches, come to take farewell
Of Gilbert, scanned her face and touched her hand,
She said she needed not the medicined spell,
Nor had she any ache they understand.
Nor could they, sooth, her lethargy dispel,
Or say what foe, of all the dismal band,
Was lurking in her blood, but sought to learn,
By questioning words, what skill could not discern.

CCIV

And when they questioned Godfrid if some woe,
Of old or recent canker, vexed her heart,
With stare for stare he answered, "Who shall know?"
Whereat they moved away and talked apart,
Then gravely said, "Believe us, that is so.
Hers is a malady beyond our art.
We know not whether she will die or live,
For we have neither death nor life to give:"

CCV

And so departed. Then she, like a light
That burns dim, dimmer, toward the break of day
Within an alabaster vase at night,
As Gilbert waxed in strength, so waned away,
Then, without warning flicker, went out quite,
And, all her sorrows silenced, smiling lay.
She looked so bland, so griefless, on her bier,
You would have thought she had been happy here.

CCVI

There is no name for that of which she died,
Unless we call it weariness of heart,
Which still can slay, however men deride
Its power and against it vaunt their art.
But she hath now the peace for which she sighed,
And never again will know or want or smart.
She never more will draw uneasy breath,
For she hath wed the faithful bridegroom, Death.

CCVII

There is a peaceful cemetery stands
Where the Fair City's walls once cast their shade,
Filled with the dead beloved of other lands;
And One sleeps there whose memory will not fade.
Their dreamless bed is made by stranger hands,
And in strange earth their limbs forlorn are laid.
No English flowers bloom there, but tapereth high
The solemn cypress, pointing to the sky.

CCVIII

There, with the restful, Olive hath her rest,
Borne thither from the restless, both by him
She loved, and him she should have loved, the best.
No pompous dirge was sung, no funeral hymn
Vexed the deep silence of her shut-up breast :
Only a few grave words, and tears that swim
In manly eyes when the cold covering earth
Takes all we had, and leaves us to our dearth.

CCIX

But when the sycophants of death had flown,
Among the white memorials of life's fate,
Gilbert and Godfrid, lingering, grieved alone.
Hard-by, they heard through Pinti's buzzing gate
The rolling wheels of war, and trumpets blown
By those who, not less eager because late,
Made for the front of Freedom's thickening lines
Through the choked passes of the Apennines.

CCX

And Godfrid's soul, like war-horse when it hears
The longed-for bugles blow, pricked at the sound.
" Now must I go !   This is no time for tears.
Farewell ! I speed me to yet holier ground.
I hear the summons of the harked-for years ;
At last, at last, a godlike Cause is found.
Who tends the dead, when betwixt Alp and wave
A buried Nation bursteth from its grave ? "

CCXI

And as he spoke, the fire that filled his eye
Was flashed from Gilbert's with reflected ray,
Who, as at grief enraged, thus made reply :
"Let me go, too.   Now wherefore should I stay?
Life still keeps something, so it be to die
In the hot hour of liberating fray.
How can I reck for what I fight, or whom,
So you but find me sword, and foe, and tomb!"

CCXII

So where the graves are quietest she lieth,
She who was so unfortunate, though fair.
While to the rest full many a footstep hieth,
To her hushed mound none ever doth repair.
But fleecy cloud, and sunny breeze that flieth,
Seem to have made it their peculiar care.
As for the twain, they vanished in the rattle
Of jolting tumbrils and the joy of battle.

END OF ACT II

ACT III

ACT III

PERSONAGES:

GODFRID—GILBERT—MIRIAM—OLYMPIA.

PROTAGONISTS:

LOVE—RELIGION—PATRIOTISM.

PLACE:

CAPRI—MENTANA.

TIME:

OCTOBER—NOVEMBER 1867.

ACT III

I

THE laggard Child of Liberty and Light,
Long travailed by the centuries, now was born :
She had put off the obloquy of night,
And like a Goddess stood, facing the morn.
Minerva's self had not more full-grown might
At her swift birth ;—a thing no more to scorn.
A turret-crown crested her forehead clear ;
Calm was her front, and in her hand a spear.

II

The Long-expected of the Nations stood
Resplendent on the mountains ; Morning sang
For heart of joy, and o'er the crisp blue flood
That laves soft shores, a jubilant pæan rang.
There was a stir sent through the old world's blood,
And long-hushed lyres lent dithyrambic clang.
Hope was rethroned upon her ancient seat,
And pining peoples came and kissed her feet.

III

No more by stagnant water, oozing walls,
Listening to silence, Venice crouched and wept;
A glow was on her palaces; her halls
Echoed once more to sounds that long had slept.
Last of the dull Barbarian's dainty thralls
To feel her limbs, up to her feet she leapt,
Clasping her Lombard brother by the hand,
While throbs of welcome trembled through the land.

IV

For, ere her woe had moved the heart of ruth,
Day on her lone divided kindred broke.
The bright Parthenope renewed her youth,
And lithe Etruria slipped the tyrant's yoke.
Umbria shook off the gnawing church-wolf's tooth,
And, happy once again, Campania woke;
And round rent Savoy's Cross as hot they pressed,
Italia clasped her children to her breast.

V

All—all,—save one! Rome still in bondage lay,
Writhing beneath the Hierarch's heavy heel;
The eldest-born of that renowned array,
From franchised kith cut off by warding steel.
For fitful Gaul, whose horns were first to bray
Salvation o'er the hilltop, feebly leal
To its own dream, from such high quest had ceased,
Playing scorned gaoler to a trembling priest.

VI

So every eye and heart were turned to Rome,
And hands were sworn to vengeance.   Maidens thrust
Their lovers from them, spurning peaceful home
While blade still crouched in scabbard, lolled in rust.
As with the share they ploughed the rippling loam,
Or round their limbs there plashed the purple must,
All sang of Rome : "Rome, Rome shall yet be ours !
Sleep, Tyrants, sleep ! we count the ripening hours."

VII

The sickle's arm caressed the lissom corn,
To strains that throbbed of Rome ; the blade that pruned
The shading elm or lopped the straggling thorn,
At each brave stroke to songs of Rome was tuned.
The shepherd boy upon the hills forlorn,
When his tired flock to sweet siesta swooned,
On his rude reed piped plaintively of Rome,
And, tiny patriot, heaved a sigh for home.

VIII

The wind that shrilled through each adventurous shroud
That skimmed the Tyrrhene sea, rang loud of Rome ;
To songs of Rome were timed the arms that bowed
O'er Hadria's oar or clave Liguria's foam.
The quarry's hollow bosom echoed loud
The self-same note ; and where the chamois clomb
In fancied fastness, 'twas that ditty sweet,—
Sweet if yet sad,—that scared its flying feet.

L

IX

Round the warm hearth or under chilly stars
Men gathered, 'mong themselves discoursing low ;
And as the stalwart grimly stroked their scars,
Bold striplings murmured, "We, too, sure shall go ?"
Now every brawny babe was gat of Mars,
And suckled by a she-wolf; bred to grow
To kingly valour, by its blood impelled
To rear a Rome diviner than of eld.

X

But they who ruled the land since death had dragged
Down to its greedy cave the daring mind
That staked, to swell, its fortunes, sate as gagged,
And in the swathes of policy confined.
With halting gait the would-be leaders lagged
Behind the led, and feebly watched the wind,
Nursing a craven hope that Fortune's wheel
Would drop the prize they feared to snatch by steel.

XI

So to the rocky home of him who still
Bore Aspromonte's bullet in his flesh,
Men's hope was turned, that soon his chafing will
Would whet the blade and lift the flag afresh ;
That he, their Cincinnatus, tied to till
Idly the niggard soil, would rend the mesh
The alien round him wove, and, long-implored,
Beat out at last his ploughshare to a sword.

XII

There is an isle, kissed by a smiling sea,
Where all sweet confluents meet : a thing of heaven,
A spent aërolite, that well may be
The missing sister of the starry Seven.
Celestial beauty nestles at its knee,
And in its lap is nought of earthly leaven.
Girdled and crowned with loveliness, its year
Is circling summer ; winter comes not near.

XIII

'Tis small, as things of beauty ofttimes are,
And in a morning round it you may row,
Nor need a tedious haste your bark debar
From gliding inward where the ripples flow
Into strange grots whose roof is azure spar,
Whose pavement liquid silver.   Mild winds blow
Around your prow, and at your keel the foam,
Leaping and laughing, freshly wafts you home.

XIV

They call the island Capri ;—with a name
Dulling an airy dream, just as the soul
Is clogged with body palpable ;—and Fame
Hath longwhile winged the word from pole to pole.
Its human story is a tale of shame,
Of all unnatural lusts a gory scroll,
Record of what, when pomp and power agree,
Man once hath been, and man again may be.

XV

Terrace and slope from shore to summit show
Of each rich clime the glad-surrendered spoil.
Here the bright olive's phantom branches glow,
There the plump fig sucks sweetness from the soil.
Nigh fragrant blossoms that through the Zodiac blow,
Returning tenfold to man's leisured toil,
Hesperia's fruit hangs golden.   High in air,
The vine runs riot, spurning human care.

XVI

And flowers of every hue and breath abound,
Charming the sense; the burning cactus glows,
Like daisies elsewhere dappling all the ground,
And in each cleft the berried myrtle blows.
The playful lizard glides and darts around,
The elfin fireflies flicker o'er the rows
Of ripened grain.   Alien to pain and wrong,
Men fill the days with dance, the nights with song.

XVII

Upon a beetling cliff, eyeing the flood,
Stood one in prime of years; but there was that
In his grave gaze which told of storms withstood,
And on his brow a lofty patience sate.
His was the tranquil mien of one who would
Wrestle with fate and lay obstruction flat,
But lets the meaner ills of life go by,
Bears small shafts dumb, nor gives lewd tongues the lie.

XVIII

With Italy's flowing fortunes Godfrid's sword,
On victory's wave upborne, had followed still:
Fleshed on that day when first the Austrian horde
Was swept from Lombard plain, nor sheathed until
The unclean Bourbon monster lay and roared,
Like old Typhœus under Ischia's hill,
And from Romagna's gangrened flesh and worn
Amortised limbs, were priest-clinched shackles torn.

XIX

Then came that chilling pause, when though from peak
Of Apennine and Alp to dimpling wave
The glow of Freedom mantled o'er the cheek
Of the fair land, in shadow of the grave
Rome grovelled mute, and Venice, pale and weak,
Sobbed 'neath her Teuton ravisher,—lovely slave,
Who, reared at Liberty's maternal knee,
Yearned for the pure embraces of the free.

XX

Even to her, deliverance came at last,
Yet not in the sweet guise brave men had dreamed.
Though Italy aside the scabbard cast,
Upon her blade no ray of victory gleamed.
But 'mong the realms by force and fraud amassed
While rival robbers each from other schemed
To filch a province for his own domain,
Then Venice seized the hour, and slipped her chain.

XXI

Not on Custozza's baleful field, but where
Trent cleaves Tyrolean Alp, had Godfrid fought,
And, when the sword was sheathed, within this fair
Famed isle at once a home and watch-tower sought,
Waiting for day to dawn on Rome's despair ;
And hither oft would come, and, steeped in thought,
Silently watch from Capri's sunny brow
The soft sea lave its feet, even as now.

XXII

Here, too, when drooped awhile the wind of war,
Which, blowing up from Freedom's freshening wave,
Scattered the clouds that dimmed Italia's star,
Returning to its sheath reluctant glaive,
Had Gilbert safe retired, and from afar
Watched for the day to dawn on priest and slave,
And fill the lungs which now drew sleepy breath
With the awakening watchword, "Rome or Death!"

XXIII

When first the noise of battle smote his ears,
He was as one who, reckless of dismay,
Seeks but to reach the bristling hedge of spears,
And on their point to fling his life away.
But wayward death, which follows him that fears,
Fears him that follows, still refused to slay
One who pursued its steps from field to field,
And found in scorn of life life's surest shield.

XXIV

But as in vain he fought for his own doom,
Winning but glory where he sought for rest,
The Cause espoused in hope to find a tomb
Began for its own sake to wed his breast.
There, once ensconced, it drove out idle gloom,
Bade sluttish sorrow do male will's behest,
Aired the close chamber of his grief-locked brain,
And through his life made ordered purpose reign.

XXV

The wealth he had inherited, not won,
Which most who win or herit, swinish spend
Luxuriously lolling in the sun,
Till their plethoric wallowing comes to end,
Seen with his opened eyes, belonged to none,
Not even to him, except as Freedom's friend,
A passing trust which Heaven would judge at last,
Bequeathed to endless future by the past.

XXVI

Something of this from Godfrid had he learned,
Who, earlier versed in wisdom's generous lore,
When once he found his counsels were not spurned,
Urged them on Gilbert ever more and more.
But many the bark that never hath returned
Unto the hand that pushed it from the shore;
And, Gilbert once inspired by Godfrid's mind,
The pupil soon the mentor left behind.

XXVII

The frantic watchword which, when blown aloud,
Hath ofttimes fooled the good, but ne'er the wise,
Of "Rulers, pass your sceptre to the crowd!"
Godfrid could but distrust, indeed despise.
Nor because he himself had disallowed
The altar's claim to bind or bow his eyes,
Joined he with those who, reckless of the end,
Treat as his direst foe man's kindest friend.

XXVIII

But few there be who in a world unfair,
Unbalanced, still keep equitable mind.
And Gilbert, giddy with the bracing air
Of freedom, looked before him nor behind.
Of its swift treacherous tempests unaware,
Nor his sails reefing with the rising wind,
The mad gusts circling in his un-taut shrouds,
Unpoised he drifted with the drifting clouds.

XXIX

Thus each crude enterprise and yeasty vow
That borrowed freedom's flag had Gilbert shared,
Though Godfrid stood apart with blaming brow,
Nor moved till clear the Royal trumpet blared.
∨ And as it had been hitherto, so now.
The self-made track which tortuous rashness dared,
Still pushing on towards Rome, while one essayed,
One by the king's highway the journey made.

XXX

But never near the twain came grudge or wrath
To flaw the friendship sanctioned by the grave ;
And Godfrid, leaning on the mossy cloth
Which draped the wall that overlooks the wave,
Far down soft-fretting into pearly froth,
Or lithely crinkling into gravelly cave,
Was joined by Gilbert, who had left his skiff
Tethered below, and climbed the staircased cliff.

XXXI

Awhile they both were silent ; side by side,
Gazing across the scarcely-rippling bay
To the low shore where, curving deep and wide,
Then up the hill half climbing, Naples lay.
Or, did one speak, the other scarce replied ;
For only triflers spoil the summer-day
With purposeless quick babble, vexing ears
That fain would list to sound which silence hears.

XXXII

But when this silence seemed to reach its noon,
Gilbert began, with slowly earnest tone,
To speak of freshly burgeoned hope, which soon
Would into full luxuriance be grown,
That foully-ravished Rome no more should croon
Upon her desolate hearth, but, vengeful grown,
And driving tonsured Tarquins from her door,
Renew the conquering Commonwealth of yore.

XXXIII

Godfrid had listened to the ardent tale,
Unmoved, nor wondering.   But when it was done,
Fixing his gaze on a white-bosomed sail,
Far off, which, lightly heaving in the sun,
Seemed its own guide, own counsel, and own gale,
And in the track of its own hope to run,
With unpremeditated words which take
Shape from past meditation, thuswise spake :

XXXIV

" You trust me still, and you do well to trust :
For I who yet must blame, shall not betray.
Brighten your blade then.   Mine, alas ! must rust.
Sage peace is sadder than insanest fray.
Yet once more hear me, Gilbert ! and be just.
Is Aspromonte's lesson thrown away ?
Is the throne false ?   The nation's hunger dulled ?
Or Turin's senate's solemn vote annulled ?

XXXV

" By all the lineal titles of the past,
By this to-day's inheritance, by ties,
Already future-sanctioned, that shall last,
Rome will be gathered to Italian skies.
Wait ! they but stumble who would step too fast.
Foresight and fate, the foolish and the wise,
Alike push on the hour that snaps the yoke.
Watch we the moving hands, and bide the stroke.

XXXVI

"Enough to purge this land of alien lords,
And weld its many sceptres into one;
And thanks to smiling Heaven and smiting swords,
The patient piecemeal task is wellnigh done.
I see the straining of the worn-out cords,
By potent hands in other ages spun,
Potent no more, and know that Rome will be
The crown, that was the crib, of Italy.

XXXVII

" But though from the Tiara we must strike
One storey of the too proud edifice,
Need we assail the crook to wrench the pike?
Ah! Gilbert! Gilbert! We should do amiss.
'Ware how you weaken force and faith alike.
Reason and reverence first must learn to kiss.
The centuried growth it is which props the walls.
Tear down the ivy, and the ruin falls."

XXXVIII

Gilbert replied not; for the closing words,
Like melancholy music, made him mute.
Mute too was all, save where the slow sea-birds
Plained, or behind them dropped some o'er-ripe fruit,
Or, in far cleft, bleated the bearded herds.
At length, with scant farewell and hasty foot,
He turned him from the spot, and, to the shore
Descending,—Godfrid stood alone once more.

XXXIX

Absorbed in luscious idleness he seemed,
Watching the languid ripples crawl to land,
As one whose bliss was deepest when he dreamed,
And who earth's beauty rather felt than scanned.
Yet oftentimes the soul all sailless deemed
By trivial gaze, with inward fire is fanned,
And, neither baulked by wave nor helped by wind,
Cleaves life's rough surf, when gay barks lag behind.

XL

But brief his re-found solitude ; for soon,
Among the vines which clustered thick behind,
There came a maid, singing a mountain tune.
And, as she moved, vagrant as summer wind,
The bright green leaves into a long festoon
She wove, and round her crimson kirtle twined.
Crimson her bodice, white her brimming vest,
And white the kerchief folded o'er her breast.

XLI

Her skin was lustrous as the ripening grape,
And, like the grape's, the sanguine flesh beamed through ;
Her eye could match the olive's dainty shape,
And far outshone its darkly-burnished hue.
Twisted in coils above the massive nape,
Her classic hair grand memories might renew,
Back from her brow, free from fantastic wiles,
Rippling like ocean, when dark ocean smiles.

XLII

She was not learnëd in that bookish lore
Which men call knowledge; but her arms could ply
In the stiff surge withal a valorous oar,
And quick hands make the flashing shuttle fly.
It was her fingers wove the dress she wore,
What time the night held more than half the sky;
And when the days were long, from dawn to close
Still would she climb, nor ever crave repose.

XLIII

And yet she was a woman,—gently framed
For loving purposes.   The murderous snare
She never set, nor barrel deadly-aimed
At bird or beast consented she to bear.
Even in the fishers' net her hands disclaimed
All helpful service; but when none were there,
Oft she disported in the genial tide,
With surging breast keeling the foam aside.

XLIV

The womb that bore her, like a tree with fruit
Too rich and rare, had perished with her birth;
And, ere she lisped, her father's voice was mute
For aye, and she was left alone on earth.
No, not alone; for every native lute
Was tuned to move her little feet to mirth;
And now along the mainland, many a mile,
Men sang the lovely Orphan of the Isle.

XLV

In either hand a bunch of grapes she held :
The left were garnet, opal were the right ;
Clustering and tapering, full-veined, sunshine-swelled,
They would have filled Iacchus with delight ;
One of whose Charities of early eld
She seemed, with every genial grace bedight ;
That gentle Triad who the innocent earth
Girdled with music, modesty, and mirth.

XLVI

And as she came anear, the juicy bells
She merrily held and dangled in his face.
" Eat, eat of these ; for old tradition tells
They melancholy's darkest cloud can chase ; "
Then with that frank simplicity which dwells
Alone with unsophisticated grace,
Archly went on, " Accept the simple cheer ;
My tithe to him who preaches all the year."

XLVII

" Thanks for my tithe, dear Miriam," Godfrid said ;
" Perchance it is a trifle overdue ;
But lo ! you pay me interest instead :—
I cross old scores, and we commence anew.
'Tis fortunate you came ; for in my head
There runs another sermon.   Nay, 'tis true,
And I *will* preach it.   Come, be patient, dear.
See, there are only we, and waves, to hear."

XLVIII

"Suppose,"—and on the rocky ledge that lay
Between them and the leap to death below,
He spread the comely gift,—"suppose that they
Who coaxed the unreflecting vine to throw
Its tendrils out, and trustingly display
The swelling beads to heaven's seductive glow,
When they were ripe and bursting, even as now,
Should turn away, and leave them on the bough?—

XLIX

"Leave them to shrink and wizen in the wind,
For the hot sun that fostered root and stem
To scorch their moist pulp, burn their cooling rind,
And all the airs of heaven to rifle them,
Though caves meanwhile with empty vats were lined,
And throats as dry as some trite apophthegm?
Suppose that this should happen,—here,—to-day,—
Here, in our Capri,—what would Miriam say?"

L

"Why, that the folks were mad.   But there's no fear.
Your parable lacks truth.   Nay, look around!
The joyous vintage hours are circling near,
And wine-stirred feet ere long shall beat the ground.
They come, they come, the merry band! I hear
Our light-long toil in songs of plenty drowned;
We wreathe our brow with vine-leaves, and we sing,
While cape and creek with laughing echoes ring."

LI

" Right merrily answered, Miriam, and right true.
Yet hearken to me, dear !   There is a God,
To whom the God of Wine is a deity new,
A thing of yesterday, a faun, a clod,
A tipsy nothing !   Nay, I warrant you,
That long ere Bacchus breathed into the sod
The secret of the grape, the God of Love
Owned this fair world and shared the world above.

LII

"Yes, wine is good ; it thaws the ice-bound breast,
And fancy's fretful-pawing steed unchains,
Rouses the torpid soul from churlish rest,
With floods of summer flushing wintry veins.
'Tis wine that flutters the poet in his nest,
Plumes his light wing and warms his liquid strains,
Curtails long nights, and hath the charm to steep
Outwearied limbs in deep undreaming sleep.

LIII

"Yes, wine is good, but love is better still ;
For it assails the pulses of the heart
With swift yet soft suffusions.   Love can fill
Life's vacant hollows, worse than any smart,
With pleasant tumult, surging joys that thrill
The silent soul to music.   'Tis an art
Which maketh poets of us all ; we sing
Like Sappho's self, when love once tunes the string.

LIV

"Its children are delicious dreams, that haunt
The brain awake or sleeping ; its bright lures
Alone confer the ecstasy they vaunt,
The one divine delirium that endures.
On love's light step attend no shadows gaunt,
And all its own sweet wounds its sweet self cures.
It fans but feeds the warmly-glowing flesh,
And slakes the thirst it still creates afresh.

LV

"But love, like these fair tokens of the vine,
Hath, too, its times and seasons.   First, its spring ;
Days of sweet doubt and fear, when smiles like thine,
Daintier than tendrils, to the fancy cling.
Next, its enticing summer, when the bine
Of hope unfolds its tremulous covering,
And softly-swelling vows, love's crowning gift,
Fed by its life-blood, peep through each green rift.

LVI

"Then, last of all, love's luscious autumn time,
When all its dreams have ripened.   Fear hath fled.
No more the heart suspicion's chilling rime
Or blight of scorching jealousy need dread.
Love's hour is here ; love's vintage-bells may chime,
And love's festoons be wreathed round board and bed.
He reels with ripeness : press his sweetness out,
Whilst the hills echo with the valley's shout.

M

LVII

" But haply should we scorn mature desire,
Nor love's full-teeming wealth make haste to press,
Why, then it shrivels of its own spurned fire,
And straight its goodly promise perishes.
Then shall no love-cup cheat the toils that tire,
Nor care be chased by wedlock's staunch caress.
Yes, mad indeed, we have squandered all our store,
The harvest of our youth, which comes no more.

LVIII

" Nay, listen to me, Miriam ! for I speak
A parable that lacks nor truth nor aim.
Answer me truly : have I far to seek
To point the moral that I scarce need name ?
Do I not read in rosy-glowing cheek,
In palpitating vein, in eye aflame,
Love in your heart would build himself a nest,
If you will only house that gentle guest ?

LIX

" Why, why repel him, why indeed delay,
Since he hath come in so mature a guise ?
Look down ; 'tis Gilbert's bark that cleaves the spray
Far at our feet, his arm the oar that plies.
What if time's touch hath flecked his beard with gray,
It veils a breast more steadfast and more wise.
Ah ! Youth in man is fickle ! Not the fire
That warms the hearth is fed on green desire.

LX

" He is a noble gentleman and true,
Whom sorrow hath made firm.   He loves you, dear,
And still will love you when the dazzling dew
Of youth no more shall in your cheek appear.
I am no messenger ; no more than you,
Hath he confessed his secret to my ear.
But Love is a silent babbler, and I need
No words of his or yours, your hearts to read.

LXI

"Nor can you plead him alien in blood,
For he hath made your country's cause his own.
Have I not seen him in the sanguine flood
Through which she waded to her rightful throne,
And by the bayonet's threat and cannon's thud
Marked his tame port of peace heroic grown ?
And when he deemed the hour to do or die
For Rome had struck, did not his soul reply ? "

LXII

"O yes !" she answered, glowing as she spake,
His last words flushing her dark cheek with fire,
"I know that he would die for Italy's sake,
And that is why—I swear it by my sire,
My mother's sacred dust, my country's ache !—
I yet will give him all his soul's desire !
Thou art my more than brother ; he shall be
Second to none,—not, Godfrid, e'en to thee !

LXIII

" Yet listen to me in turn, albeit I sound
Beggar in fancies that enrich your tongue.
I said but now that none so mad were found,
Who, when these clusters full to falling hung
From stalk and stem, and o'er the happy ground
From tree to tree in drooping garlands swung,
Would scorn the sweet pulp bursting through the rind,
And leave the jocund juice to feed the wind.

LXIV

" But see!   Our vintage dawns.   Yet do you doubt,
That if to-morrow, though brave loins were girt,
Brisk sleeves knit up, our baskets spread about,
The scoured vats all agape for wine to spirt
Down their huge throats, we heard a sudden shout
Of 'Rome or Death!' and saw the brave red shirt
Flame like a beacon,—we should, one and all,
Leave vat, leave vine, responsive to the call?

LXV

" Should we not quit the harvest of the year,
To gather in the harvest of all time?
He,—you,—yes I!—leave grape and grain, nor fear
To reap 'mid thirst and want a store sublime?
Swords were our sickles then; the dewlapped steer
No more with purple load our slopes would climb;
Its peaceful flank in warlike wains would foam,
Splashed with their blood who barred the path to Rome!

LXVI

"Bear with me then, I pray, my brother kind,
And bid him bear awhile whose love I prize.
So long as the Priest-King my kith shall bind
In Peter's chains,—well, Rome hath all my sighs!
I have no heart for tenderness, no mind
For pillowed sweets, no ear for baby cries.
Oh! I should blush were conflict's thrilling noise
To reach me, cooing over selfish joys!"

LXVII

She ceased; and he was silent in his soul,
Drinking her noble rhetoric.   But while each
Watched mute the creamy ripples landward roll,
Up the rude path that zigzagged from the beach,
A bright-eyed urchin, with a fluttering scroll,
Skipping and tumbling came,—too blown for speech;
His damson-coloured cheeks with speed aglow,
And tangled curls, left in the breeze to blow.

LXVIII

Hearing the swift step, Godfrid turned his head,
And quick the little Mercury, pressed for breath,
Thrust in his hand the scroll, then, panting, said,
"Read—read! the game's afoot of 'Rome or Death!'
See! Garibaldi from his isle hath sped,
And the whole land to join him hasteneth.
All Naples is astir; and look! they write,
This time the King will cheer, not foil, the fight."

LXIX

And as he spoke, and Godfrid scanned the scroll,
And saw that he spoke true, again the shout
Of "Rome or Death!" burst on his startled soul.
And half-way down to wave, where jutted out
From skeleton crag a green and grassy mole,
Down-peering spied they Gilbert, waving about
A blood-red flag, and loud with lusty breath
Crying, "Come! Godfrid! Miriam! Rome or Death!"

LXX

As swift as light, Miriam round Godfrid's neck
Flung tight her arms, and nigh as quickly loosed;
Then, without more ado or ever a check,
Down the steep path they ran, like streams unsluiced:
So fast, that soon the summit was a speck
Where late they stood,—the sea-bird's stormy roost.
And audibly now they heard the billows bound,
Which there had seemed to die without a sound.

LXXI

And, ever as they sped, waxed loud and oft
The cry, "Rome, Rome or Death!"   Each feathery holt,
Each sinuous down, each peak that pricked aloft,
Flung back the words, echoing the grand revolt.
And swift from vineyard, terrace, garden, croft,
As, straight on lightning, swoops the thunderbolt,
Flashed all the folk, in gathering crowd and roar,
And with one pulse descending to the shore.

LXXII

Thither too, whooping loud, thronged untamed boys,
Bare-browed, bare-breasted, gemmed with eager eyes,
With rapid questions heightening all the noise,
Then breaking off, nor waiting for replies.
And glowing maids were there, full ripe for joys
Not found in battle : Goddesses in size,
With massive pitcher on their heads, at ease
Standing like stalwart Caryatides ;

LXXIII

Nor moving lip, but with full gaze intent
On lovers yesternight intent to woo,
Who now no more coined words of blandishment,
But arched their blades, and felt the edge was true.
Over their serried shoulders forward leant,
With craning necks and faces sharp to view,
Low-chattering crones, wailing the lonely lot
Of these thus left, who heard but heeded not.

LXXIV

And, last of all, grave matrons joined the throng,
Babe upon arm, that only lisped as yet
The name of Rome and mother ;—grave and strong,
With thoughtful brow and eye, but cheek unwet :
While through the crowd bent graybeards hobbled along,
Blessing the Lord that, ere their sun had set,
They had seen this day ; yet railing half at Fate,
That sent salvation, for their aid too late.

LXXV

Then high debate arose who first should go,
Who linger last, and who at home must stay.
Some, fledged with shafts of death from tip to toe,
Vowed none should snatch or turn them from the fray ;
Some could a rusty matchlock only show,
And some a rough-edged billhook but display ;
These from the hearth had snatched up smouldering brands,
And those had brawny thews but empty hands.

LXXVI

But, once upon the mainland, arms would swift
For all be found.　And, as they babbled, came
Women and girls with many a farewell gift :
Strings of fat quails for which the isle hath fame,
And figs distilling honey through each rift
In their moist pulp ; bread, worthy sure to name
Even as to give ; huge bunches from the vine
Now newly plucked ; and flasks of rosy wine.

LXXVII

Meanwhile from where, under the frowning cliff,
In days gone by long waves had worn a cave,
Godfrid and Gilbert dragged a light-oared skiff,
And straight the sharp keel through the shingle drave.
A moment at the sand-bar halting stiff,
It heeled, then lurched ; and, as it touched the wave,
The waters rose to take it, and it lay
Trembling with gladness on the circling spray.

LXXVIII

Her uncowled face lit by a steadfast smile,
Into the boat first Miriam lightly stepped ;
Two sinewy youths, the pick of all the isle,
Followed, and briskly to their places leapt ;
Then Gilbert, and last Godfrid. Poised awhile,
Down swooped the oars, and swift away they swept :
The lined shore crying after them, " Death or Rome !
Swift speed your bark ! we follow in its foam."

LXXIX

Soon on the left rough Massa rose to view,
Then soft Sorrento. Now they swept along
Past populous shores where vine-veiled ashes strew
Cities that echoed once to dance and song.
Far to the right dark Ischia flecked the blue,
Where Nature's penitent hand smooths ancient wrong ;
And soon the mighty cone began to loom,
That floods with streams of death its fiery womb.

LXXX

But close behind them now they caught the hum
Of many voices, and the rising roar
Of noisy Naples, mingled with the strum
And twang of sharp guitar along the shore.
A moment more, and with the cry " We come,"
Bare-legged and Phrygian-capped, upon them bore
A rush of boatmen, voluble of speech,
Who drew the light skiff swiftly up the beach.

LXXXI

Then out they sprang,—first Miriam, Gilbert next,
Last Godfrid,—and the eager host pressed round;
Rude fishermen, hoarse women half unsexed,
And nude sea-urchins frisking o'er the ground.
Each with chaotic shout their ears perplexed,
Question and answer in the hubbub drowned,
O'er which there surged alone, as springs the foam
Above loud waves, the cry of " Death or Rome !"

LXXXII

But as they thrust the frenzied crowd aside,
And pushed on to the city's beating heart,
At every step their hopes grew verified,
And warlike omens bade their doubts depart.
Men, new in arms, gathering from far and wide,
Made but a martial muster-ground the mart.
Churches were changed to barracks ; and the cars
Of Ceres' self were given up to Mars.

LXXXIII

The very streets volcanic seemed and roared
Like Somma's fiery self, and seething flowed
With streams of living lava, ever poured
Hot from the City's innermost abode.
And, over all, ever and anon there soared
Convulsive detonations, such as goad
To agony of madness feet that fly
Waveward, when roused Vesuvius shells the sky !

LXXXIV

And then night fell, and fairy lamps shone out
From balcony and lattice.   High in air,
Gay gonfalons were lightly blown about,
And at the windows crowded faces fair.
Shrill lads upon the pavement thronged to shout
The great news forth, and in the shining square,
Hard by the Palace, flushed with jets of light,
Men stood in groups and fought the coming fight.

LXXXV

Just ere the hour drew near for lamps to fade
And the dense crowd to melt away to rest,
Far up Toledo shrilling trumpet brayed.
Straight at the sound, thither all footsteps pressed,
And, as if ranged for battle's stern parade,
Formed in deep files and long lines drawn abreast,
And, close in phalanx packed, with ringing cheer,
"Evviva Italia ! Evviva !" rent the ear.

LXXXVI

Rang out once more the clarion's cleaving blare,
And rudely rumbled hollow-bowelled drum ;
Then strains of martial music stormed the air,
And away they strode, steps sounding but lips dumb.
But at the windows, still, cheered voices fair,
And waved white kerchiefs gallantly ; while some
Sweet flowers drew forth from bosoms yet more sweet,
And showered them down to kiss the tramping feet.

LXXXVII

Then midnight tolled, and all the city was still.
Inarime lay darkling on the sea ;
Faint spikes of flame tipped Somma's murky hill,
And on the shore the waves died silently.
The fabled fields the Mantuan's wizard quill
Steeps in undying glamour, seemed to be
Once more Elysian, and the night-winds lay
Cradled on Baiæ's ruin-pebbled bay.

LXXXVIII

Gay broke the morn, and now along the land,
On with the day the joyous tidings grew ;
Passed the fleet spray round Spartivento's strand,
And raced with Manfredonia's billows blue.
Swifter than falcon by Libeccio fanned,
Up the long straggling Apennine it flew,
And, lithe as mist by sunrise skyward drawn,
Scaled Alpine peak and, bright, proclaimed the dawn.

LXXXIX

It brought the lilies out in Florence fair,
Flooded with life Bologna's grim arcades,
Fluttered the doves in Venice' marble square,
Filled Milan's thrifty streets with generous blades.
Perugia's griffin laid his talons bare,
The lion leaped from Padua's learnèd shades ;
And Turin's generous beast, prompt at the sound,
Lowered his horned front, and, pawing, shook the ground.

XC

Far off upon the mountain's marble side,
In rough-hewn amphitheatres whose bold tiers,
Scaling the sky, white crowned with blue, defied
With unprotected front the pitiless years,—
Round huge blocks coiling nervous rope tight-tied,
Or urging sinewy bullock with goads and jeers,
Carrara's sun-scorched toilers at the sound
Unwonted paused, and wildly stared around.

XCI

Steadying with brawny thews through rich brown soil
The unwieldy antique plough that Rhea's son
Drave round his regal Palatine, lusty swains
The challenge heard, and, as at signal gun,
Left the unfinished furrow ; left their wains
Standing half-piled ; left their sleek oxen dun ;
Left helpful wife, smooth babe, and clambering boy,
Nor stopped to snatch one desultory joy.

XCII

They left the long unstrung festoons half-stripped,
The tall deep crates half-filled, the vats unpressed,
In the first trough their hands empurpled dipped,
Doffed work-day gear, and called for gay red vest ;
Then, with brief, brave farewell, away they slipped,
Eager as fledglings from forsaken nest,
And not one hand was raised to bid them stay,
One tear let fall to clog them on their way.

XCIII

And Godfrid, Gilbert, Miriam, like the rest,
Ever on foot, now journeying with the crowd,
Now solitary skirting Samnian crest,
Trackless, by many a dried-up torrent ploughed,
On toward the Roman frontier panting pressed,
Nor halted till they saw Alatri proud
Look down on Collepardo, and descried
Soft Liris winding round rough Sora's side.

XCIV

But to the sword's goal nearer as they drew,
Omens of slackening purpose met their feet.
Men 'gan to ask each other what they knew.
Had not the Royal drum been heard to beat?
And were not those the Royal trumpets, blew?
Yet could it be they did but sound retreat,
Without one blow to break the bonds that wed
Longwhile the living to the loathsome dead?

XCV

Where was the Chief?   Had he yet left his isle?
Yes ; foiling nimble lurchers of the law,
He treads the mainland.   Did a sceptic smile?
Swift was the answer : here is one who saw . . .
Ay ! but how now?   A dungeon's well-clamped pile
Coffins his rashness.   He will burst it . . . Faugh !
Back to Caprera, oath-bound, see him led,
To gnaw his heart out on its barren bed !

XCVI

Godfrid the loud sardonic babble heard,
Silent and gloomy.   'Neath a trellised vine,
As evening paled, chary of heed or word,
He sate with Miriam.   Flask of Volscian wine,
And fare by hospitable hands preferred,
Untasted stood.   And when, at Miriam's sign,
The host withdrew, neither the silence broke,
Till, Gilbert, suddenly entering, thuswise spoke :

XCVII

" 'Tis as we feared.   The King clanks back his blade
Into the scabbard, and we stand alone.
The royal troops, late marshalled to invade,
Now guard, the frontiers of the priestly throne.
Some they turn back by force, and some persuade ;
Some through their nets have broken, and are flown
On to Mentana, resolute for Rome,
Save the Chief fail them too, and call them home."

XCVIII

So saying, mute he stood, biding reply.
But Miriam, who, the while he spoke, had gazed
On him alone, now glanced with anxious eye
To where sate Godfrid with his face upraised
And propped upon his hand reflectingly ;
Over whose aspect suddenly there blazed
The light of hot resolve, and, starting up,
He seized the flask and drained a brimming cup.

XCIX

And as he laid it down, "Too late," he cried,
"To turn back now! See! I will go with you.
In vain we would discern; the Fates decide,
And fool us to the task they'd have us do.
So will I not be wanting at your side,
Though deep I pray we shall not live to rue
The madness of this hour. I cannot stem
The waves I loosed not. I must ride with them:

C

"Though be it to dismay. But, Gilbert, this,
This bear in mind, if I should fall, you stay:
Though destiny now shapes my steps amiss,
And I am by its current swept away,
I drew the sword, only to bridge the abyss
Which severs Rome from Italy; and say,
If chance some voice of my last deed inquires,
He ne'er assailed the altar of his sires.

CI

"Enough,—alas! too much,—of my poor name;
But there be those whom I, in death, would spare.
Now, go with Miriam where the tongue of fame
Reports our camp: I will towards Rome repair,
And learn if chains have made her courage tame,
Or if, not too disheartened still to dare,
She finds her feet, and through her prison walls
Answers the voice of Liberty that calls.

CII

"Now farewell, Miriam! Gilbert be your guide
Till I unto you both my steps retrace."
Whereat she rose, and going to his side,
Soft laid against his beard her tender face,
And murmured: "For your journey Heaven provide!"
Then he to her gave brotherly embrace,
And, grasping Gilbert's hand, as brave men do,
Went, and down vine-slopes vanished from their view.

CIII

But when the morrow's dawn broke wild and red,
Afoot once more, Gilbert and Miriam clomb
Many a hillside, crossed many a torrent's bed,
Tracking through shaggy wood, past tumbling foam,
That faithful band who, by one instinct led,
Swarmed at the Sabine heights that look towards Rome;
There where Nomentum still keeps, half consoled,
Its Latin name and Bacchic fame of old.

CIV

And these, if few, yet steadfast, o'er the rim
Which severed still the freedman from the slave,
Had crept or burst, and in embattled trim,
Five thousand breasts, wooed glory or the grave.
Purged of the waifs that on the surface swim
Of noisy venture's swift but shallow wave,
Shrunk was their volume now, calm, gathered, deep,
Even as the cataract's, ere adown it leap.

N

CV

But on the mountainous ledge that dips towards Rome,
They still hung pausing; for the Chief yet lagged.
Cursed be the knaves that to his far-off home
Had yet again his limbs reluctant dragged!
Fools! would they coop the wind or curb the foam?
Soon flashed the news upon their spirits fagged,
That he unhelped had slipped the net once more,
And wind and wave were wafting him to shore.

CVI

Yes! steering tiny shallop, all alone,
From rock to rock 'mid perilous shoals, then tost
On tumbling billows by the mistral blown,
Till space 'twixt sea and sky seemed wellnigh lost,
Long ere the snarer guessed their bird was flown,
He gripped Sardinia's coast, its mountains crossed,
And thence by leal hands led and fair gales fanned,
Near Leghorn's beach leaped once again to land.

CVII

Then swift to arms and flashing ranks they flew,
Shoulder to shoulder, heart by brave heart, ranged,
Quick with whose every beat He nearer drew.
Yes! 'twas the Chief, from venture unestranged,
As when his grasp the Bourbon hydra slew
At tough Marsala, and a kingdom changed.
Upon his brow were threatening thunders piled,
But round his mouth love's playful lightnings smiled.

CVIII

"My children!" when their jubilant welcome waned,
With resonant clear voice he said, "I am here.
The French Jove's minions thought to hold me chained,
Lest I spread fire through this cimmerian sphere.
Oh! how his eagle rent me, as I strained
To rid me of my rock's engyving gear!
But herculean destiny, which foils
Olympian counsels, came and cut my toils.

CIX

"And lo! I stand among you yet once more,
Sons of my heart and scions of my soul!
I see ye are still, all that ye were of yore,
The valorous stuff Alcmene's self might foal.
Behind, lies shame in ambush,—peril before.
Which do ye choose? Speak! whither is our goal?"
He paused; and like a thunderclap, the breath
Of their charged breasts roared loud, "To Rome or Death!"

CX

"'Tis well. Look there!" And as he spake they turned,
Following his finger with immediate eyes.
"There, there is the vent for which your lives have burned,
Your goal or grave, your sepulchre or prize.
Gods! where the suckling she-wolf's bosom spurned
The cruel priest's decision, darkly wise,
The foul hyæna's bastard litter tugs
At Italy's breast, poisoning our Mother's dugs!

CXI

" Will ye not, stalwart war-hounds, help me scare
The unclean foster-whelps from such a shrine ?—
This brood of Hell, that Heaven's fair front would wear,
From hearths which, even in ruin, keep divine ;
Ruins, your own inheritance ?   Now swear
By all the godhood in Rome's royal line,
By the Republic's virtue, by the brow
Of Empire calm, ye will reclaim them now !

CXII

" Lend me your youth, I give to you my years,
The steadfast wisdom of the life that hangs
Upon death's gaze and calmly waits the shears,
Nor cares o'ermuch when the dark portal clangs.
So that I see the glimmer of your spears
Frighting the foemen's eyes, and mark your fangs
Fast in the hirelings fleeing from the list
Of final war, then let me be dismissed.

CXIII

" My task will then be finished.   But I waste
In sterile words the sunlight.   Now, to arms !
Yon citadel, within whose walls disgraced
A host of motley mercenaries swarms,
The savour of your valour first shall taste.
Now blow the sanguine bugle's shrill alarms !
Cleansed of its levy of Batavian boors,
Monte Rotondo must, ere dark, be yours ! "

CXIV

Though light their panoply, their valour great.
No Vulcan's limping thunderbolts delayed
With cumbrous help their impetus elate;
Theirs the straight barrel and the swooping blade,
The fleet advance—the pause—the crouching gait—
The forward rush—the well-seized ambuscade;
Till, in thin trusty lines spread out, they feel
The circled city with a grasp of steel.

CXV

Then straight its pulse responded.   Loudly bayed
The deep-mouthed cannon from the walls, and woke
The slumbering citadel, which swiftly made
Its mouth a teeming womb whence martial folk,
Born ready-armed, swarmed to the rampart's aid,
Crested the walls, and glimmered through the smoke
Of sulphurous din, whose war-clouds thundered black
'Gainst the long sinuous hills, that bellowed back.

CXVI

"Fire me the gate!" the Chief exclaimed, "and smoke
These skulking vermin from their darksome holes!
Why waste your breath in many an idle stroke
Against the intangible air?   Unearth the moles!
Look! you must break the shell to seize the yolk!
Then fire the gate, ye young and valorous souls!
Swiftly let torch and faggot be their guests,
And burn yourselves an entrance to their breasts!"

CXVII

Then, under cover of the deepening dusk,
As now the foe, in fancied fastness, drowned
With draughts of cheering wine the homely rusk,
Weening the day with conquering laurels crowned,—
With fascines girt and many a well-dried husk
Of last year's corn, soft to the gate they wound,
Whose solid jaws, deemed doubly safe till dawn,
Stood grimly clenched, with all the guards withdrawn.

CXVIII

Others too brought, but with like stealthy stride,
Bales of coarse tow in liquid resin steeped,
With kegs of shining pitch, and,—high and wide,
Faggot on straw, straw upon faggot heaped,—
Thrust them between, and then their torches plied.
Swift at the touch the prompt light crackling leaped,
And, darting tongues of fire from quivering frame,
Spread through the loose sere heap its own fierce flame.

CXIX

Nor till the goodly pile was all ablaze,
Was the alarum raised within ; when straight
The slack carousers, smitten with amaze,
Snatching their arms, rushed wildly to the gate.
But those into the darkness, far from gaze,
Softly drew off, instructed well to wait
And pour, with obvious aim that could not fail,
Through its reopening jaws a deadly hail.

CXX

And soon, the monstrous bars and bolts drawn back,
The huge gates groaned, then slowly opened wide,
And straight in front uprose the blazing stack,
Though through the gap no foe could be descried.
So 'gan they all, emboldened, to attack
The burning barricade, and thrust aside
This fell approach of fire that strove to spread
To their defences its contagion dread.

CXXI

Thus as they rushed with ardour to undo
The invisible assailants' crafty task,
And with unguarded breasts swarmed full in view
Of those who wore the distance for a mask,
Came sudden such a crashing volley through
The screen of sputtering twig and boiling cask,
That, staggering, back they fell, and, ambushed mesh
Dreading at hand, rolled back the gate afresh.

CXXII

But ere its ponderous lips could meet and clang,
The fiery mass fell in and choked its jaws.
Then once again a rattling volley rang
Straight through the chasm, and, all unseen the cause,
With deadly aim dealt many a mortal pang.
Then silence came,—a momentary pause,—
Then blinding smoke ; and then, all barriers snapped,
The gate, without, within, in flame was wrapped.

CXXIII

The wolfish watch-dogs from uneasy sleep,
As though the moon were up, uprose and bayed,
While the rude herd, slow-roused from slumber deep,
Crept from his hutch and the weird sight surveyed.
Leaning with hands that neither sow nor reap
On his long crook, there statue-like he stayed,
As one who wondered not, and in whose veins
The instinct flowed of fire and ravaged plains.

CXXIV

Unsheltered kine in unhelped labour lowed,
Coupling their throes with yet more deep dismay;
While stolid oxen, freed from yoke and goad,
Rolled their large eyes, and wondered was it day.
Troops of wild colts, no lord as yet bestrode,
Gathered in clouds, stopped, sniffed, then tore away;
And low-browed buffaloes, into terror lashed,
Through jungled swamp, snorting and bellowing, splashed.

CXXV

It seemed as though the centuries had rolled
Their sepulchres back, and all the disarmed dead
Were coming forth anon, and, as of old,
Round Rome's seductive realm of ruin spread,
Would in their coils its feeble walls enfold,
And on its wreck a fresh destruction shed;
That Goth, Gaul, Vandal, Hun, did all conspire
To wrap what yet remained, in final fire!

CXXVI

And still the greedy flames kept crawling round
Monte Rotondo's ivy-buttressed wall,
Whence gloomy owls, as if from under ground,
Flapped out, and with their melancholy call
Would ever and anon the deepening swound
Of dying ears with fantasies appal,
Vexing their souls with terror as they sank
Through yielding life into the deep dread blank.

CXXVII

Nor till the dappled curtain of the East
Rose on the chorused dawn,—by surfeit choked,
Had the fierce fire from random foray ceased.
But long ere then, their sleepless limbs yet smoked
With grime of battle, and their rage increased
By yestreen's blood that still their garments soaked,
With bayonet couched and fury-flashing sword,
Through the charred portal had the Red-shirts poured.

CXXVIII

And still as they advanced, from thresholds freed
Came forth the exultant populace, and blessed
The arms that brought salvation to its need.
Their blackened hands the trembling grandsire pressed ;
The tearful matron brought the welcome meed
Of mother's kiss ; the soft-eyed maid caressed ;
Whose brothers swelled their ranks, to lead them where
The routed hirelings clung to central lair.

CXXIX

In a grim palace whose huge entrance seemed
Portcullis more than hospitable gate,
And through whose grim-barred embrasures there streamed
No ray of cheering sunshine soon or late,
Whose hoary walls were but too truly deemed
To boast the dungeon's thickness,—desperate,
And like to wolves whom baying throats surround,
The cowering foe had final covert found.

CXXX

But when once more the threat of fire was hurled,
And torch and bavin to their hold were brought,
And round the basement tall the black smoke curled,
Quick from within a parley was besought,
And high o'erhead a small white flag unfurled.
Curt the conditions.   These : All who had fought,
Would in the courtyard pile both gun and blade,
And straight across the frontier be conveyed.

CXXXI

So on the morn of that auspicious day,
By valour won, Monte Rotondo fell,
Making fagged limbs with freshening triumph gay,
And sinking hearts with surging hope re-swell
That henceforth neither foe nor fate could stay
Their supreme star and front invincible.
Lo !   Yonder column rose, and tower, and dome,
In the blue air !   Why not at once to Rome ?

CXXXII

But quick the Chief with tranquillising smile
Checked their untimely ardour. "Not to-day.
Blown with the race of victory, breathe awhile,
Nor tempt too much your yet but mortal clay.
Another morn, and yon cross-crownëd pile,
That glistens in the sun, shall point your way;
Nor shall its dome above the twilight soar,
A second time, ere Rome be God's once more!"

CXXXIII

So wounds were blithely drest, and blood-stains dried,
And, as day broadened, short siestas snatched;
Some, stretched supine on the bare mountain-side,
Some, slumber-shaded under a pine detached.
And some lay gashed and shattered, open-eyed,
On pallet rough in hovel rudely-thatched;
And some, alack! in their last bed were laid,
Nor heard o'erhead the beating of the spade.

CXXXIV

But, with the waning of the sultry glare,
About the camp a fitful movement grew.
Here, these prepared the evening meal, and there,
From bellied vats those beaded beakers drew.
Others with busy brows and muscles bare
Rubbed their accoutrements to flashing hue.
Some sang; and oft, a solitary neigh
Shivered the air, then eddying died away.

CXXXV

Scarce a good bowshot from the bustling throng,
A farmstead stood, irregularly built,
Its walls of unhewn stone, yet square and strong,
Held in old days by arquebuse and hilt.
Alone of all the tenements along
Those sparse-clad heights by sunset softly gilt,
Nor strident voice nor desecrating hoof
Filled the apt shelter of its ample roof.

CXXXVI

But if a curious eye had cared to scan
Its hidden life, two forms might now be seen,
Busy within ; a godlike-statured man,
And grave-browed maiden, moulded like a queen :
A type to show what sovereign Nature can,
When stunting progress cometh not between
Her and her handiwork ; a shape unmarred
As, goddess-born, was sung by Scian bard.

CXXXVII

And like a queen of old, her fingers fair
Played busily with stuffs of various dyes,
Red, white, and green, of which, with loving care,
She made, when shaped to strips of equal size,
A banner, such as Freedom's champions bear ;
While Gilbert watched her with unmoving eyes,
Leaning against the threshold, while his hands
Smoothed a rough stake, mute slave of her commands.

CXXXVIII

" 'Tis done," she said, and as she said she rose.
"Now to the staff affix me Italy's flag!
As veers the vane unto the wind that blows,
So, once breeze-fluttered, never shall it lag
Behind the storm that breaks upon our foes,
Lead where it will, and though to death it drag!
Follow this symbol, Gilbert! you will find
Peril in front, but victory hard behind!"

CXXXIX

The colours from her fair brave hands he took,
But quick the fair brave hands themselves he pressed,
Drawing them upward, and with touch that shook,
Laid and soft held them on his ample chest.
And as some acorned oak bends low to look
On tender fern that girds its rugged breast,
So he, now bending her fresh form above,
Dropped in her lap the autumn of his love.

CXL

"Yes, Miriam! to its flagstaff will I bind
Your banner fast, and follow it as true
As watching vane obeys the wandering wind!
But when our blades have hewn a pathway through
To Rome or Death, then should I chance to find
The better doom, oh! unto me will you
Be as this steadfast pennon to its pole,
To bark its sail, unto the flesh its soul?

CXLI

"You, Miriam, you! my standard, symbol be,
And I could bear you through a cloud of foes!
The glorious colours you, upborne by me,
From battle's onset unto victory's close."
Then, holding flag and staff asunder, "See,
What soul or spell hath this apart from those?
But knit them close, and then, its flag unfurled,
Even this sere branch might rouse a slumbering world!

CXLII

"And yet a humbler, happier fate I crave,
Than to renew such task as brings us here.
Once let yon sky no longer roof a slave
In this fair land, and I our bark would steer
Back o'er that blue and siren-rippled wave,
To me through you, to you through kinship dear,
And, fondly tethered to its narrow isle,
Live in the sunshine of your wifely smile."

CXLIII

She started at the word, and from his grasp,
Hereto endured, had fain her form withdrawn,
But that he gripped her wrists with tightening clasp,
And to her, helpless as some poor meshed fawn,
Sued with yet bolder lips and quickening gasp:
"Stay near me still, even as to night the dawn!
Fair life, fair love, with no dread gloom o'ercast,
Wherein I drown the darkness of my past!

CXLIV

"Thy land, thy race, is mine, and thy young hopes
Are round my heart entwined, as a fair flower
Scales with its delicate bine and tendrilled ropes
The lonely gaps of some untenanted tower,
Where the bat burrows and the night-owl mopes.
O, be to me a beauty and a dower!
Fill me with light and colour, till men bless
Me, the poor wall, that props thy loveliness.

CXLV

"Dead in the grave she lies, dead in the grave,
Who should have loved me, but she loved me not.
Pierced through the heart by passion's glittering glaive,
Thus did she leave me, who were best forgot.
Snowdrops and lilies her lone sepulchre pave,
White as the sheets over some infant's cot,
Where innocence lies sleeping. She too sleeps;—
Happier than one that wakes, and wants, and weeps.

CXLVI

"I would not wake her, for she was not mine.
Sound be her sleep and sweet; sweet be her dreams!
She will not dream of *me*. She was divine,
And I am earthly; so at least it seems.
Yet did she pour out all my life like wine,
And leave the goblet empty. O for streams,
Streams of full love that to the heart are wed,
As some deep river to its deeper bed!

CXLVII

"That is not Love which is not loved : 'tis nought
But vacancy of pain, unfuelled fire,
A sigh by silence choked, a speechless thought,
Insanity of soul, diseased desire.
And love is won no more than sold or bought ;
'Tis a spontaneous giver, whom inspire
The Gods alone, whose promptings we forsook.
The fault was mine.   She gave me—what I took.

CXLVIII

"Streams roll not back, nor deem that I e'er could
To that dim past revert which was my bane.
I am as one who quits a darksome wood,
And sees before him sunlight-smiling plain,
Thankful to stand no more where late he stood.
Country and kin to me were symbols vain.
Thou art my kindred, and thy land shall be
Land of my love and true nativity.

CXLIX

"But "—and yet tighter, as he spoke, he clenched
His nervous grasp—"by the Enduring Powers,
By all the tears that ever drowned and drenched
The cheek of hopeless love through lonely hours,
Whose parching fire can by no tears be quenched,
By thy sire's ashes, by the sacred flowers
That roof thy mother's grave, I thee conjure,
Spare me not now !   Strike home ; I will endure.

CL

" Strike, but once only ! I can nurse that pain ;
Nurse it in solitude which doth repair
Even worse wounds than that.   But there's a chain
No mortal twice consentingly would bear,—
The chain which binds with its tormenting strain
Two pulsing lives that one life do not share.
Love me with love that knows nor ebb nor flow,
As I love thee ! or, Miriam, bid me go !"

CLI

Thereat he loosed her hands, and his own fell,
Mute, to his side ; and like some giant stone,
Poised on its base by old enchanter's spell,
So that it rocks e'en to a touch alone,
So now he stood, mightily movable,
And through the glamour that is all love's own,
Despite his manhood, ready to be stirred
By the soft touch of her responsive word.

CLII

A moment mute remained she, with her head
Bent on its stem, like some dark crimson rose
When winds have been too rough, which, since, have fled.
But soon, like bud that to the sunlight blows,
Her face she lifted to his gaze, and said,
" Did he not tell you ?   For indeed he knows.
He wrung my secret from me on the day
Our joyous war-bark bounded o'er the bay."

O

CLIII

"What!" he exclaimed, as future, present, past,
Confusedly before him 'gan to swim;
"What! Godfrid!   Comes he then once more to blast
My burgeoning hopes?   Oh! how love's sight is dim!"
"O, thou mistak'st me quite!" she cried, aghast;
"For thee he pleaded, and I answered him,
Straight from my soul, as now I answer thee :—
Love me, and I will listen,—when Rome is free!

CLIV

"Till then,—but hark!"   And ere one grateful word
Could from his bosom burst to ease his joy,
Out through the threshold, like a startled bird,
She flew, he following like an eager boy.
And lo! the camp with some strange news was stirred,
And, as a flock of wild-fowl to decoy,
Skimming the reedy pool, are blindly urged
On instant wing, toward one spot converged.

CLV

Thither, too, Miriam, Gilbert at her side,
Straight made with breathless eagerness her way,
The rush of supple striplings opening wide
To let them pass athwart the armed array.
"See the brave band returned from Rome," one cried.
"Then Godfrid's back!" and he could hear her say,
With murmuring lips, as low as breathing shell,
The rapid prayer, "Pray Heaven! alive and well!"

CLVI

Soon was all doubt dispelled; for toward the crest
Of the steep range whose face towards Rome is set,
A handful stood, by thirsty march distressed,
Hot, haggard, silent, dashed with gore and sweat;
And in their midst, towering o'er all the rest,
As, 'mong tall fir-trees, tall pine tops them yet,
Stood Godfrid, gloomy, dark with dust and smoke,
And to the gathering crowd thus curtly spoke:

CLVII

"Yes, we are back, or those at least you see,
A remnant, safe; the best are left behind:
Of freedom reft that others might be free,
Or dead, that worse than dead fresh life might find.
Cairoli fell o'erborne, one against three,
But not till two of three first fed the wind.
His Spartan dam may smile; one son remains;
Not here,—but wounded, captive, and in chains.

CLVIII

"What did I hear you ask? Doth Rome not rise?
Who rises with the heel upon his neck,
Or greets the dawn with joyfulness, whose eyes,
Long shorn of sight, the greedy vultures peck?
Alas! Of heaven-fed Freedom's lusty cries,
What can emasculated serflings reck?
Rome rise? Yes,—when you raise her. Not till then.
Shall she long wait you? Not if ye are men!"

CLIX

With which, the keen-eared group aside he ploughed,
And, greeting Miriam with fraternal speech,
Passed, linked with her and Gilbert, from the crowd
To that lone dwelling placed beyond the reach
Of the camp's tumult.   Then, like storm-charged cloud,
The black news circled, each one questioning each,
And vowing deep, as swift the story spread,
To rouse the living and avenge the dead.

CLX

But when with morn the heights and slopes began
To prick and burgeon into armëd life,
The dense red ranks spread out like gaudy fan,
To bass-toned drum and treble-fluted fife.
From mouth to mouth the gladsome rumour ran,
The hour was here to kiss the lips of strife,
With battle's breast to blend embrace and breath,
And rush, delirious, on to Rome or Death!

CLXI

And as they gazed, and every bosom rose,
High-leavened with the thought of combat nigh,
Far off they saw, as when a ground-mist grows,
Or distant copse shows feathery to the eye
When first the early-budding sallow blows,
About the walls a haze ambiguous lie,
Which, when it once had shape and substance ta'en,
Rolled itself out, and crept along the plain.

CLXII

Shortly the moving mist began to gleam
And glitter as when dawn's returning rays
Strike on the ripples of a shadeless stream,
Until it glowed one scintillating blaze,
Flickering and flashing in each morning beam.
And then they knew it was no vaporous haze,
But foe come forth,—bayonet, and blade, and gun,—
Shining and shimmering in the cloudless sun.

CLXIII

Swift through their lines a thrill electric ran,
And, as it died, girt by that faithful few
Whose spendthrift lives had still been in the van
Since first his banner of redemption flew,
'Mid men heroic looking more than man,
Serenely strong, the Chief came full in view;
While through the ranks, with sabre-sounding clang,
A shout of welcome and defiance rang.

CLXIV

" Hail, noble champions of a noble Cause ! "
Flashing them back their greeting, thus he spake.
"See, Fortune smiles.   The beast whose greedy claws
Ye have come to clip, doth from his covert break,
And, spurred by desperate terror, hither draws.
Now in your hands your shafts avenging take,
And bide his onset ! We will wait him here,
And let the rash fool rush upon the spear.

CLXV

" Then shall his lair be yours.　Gods ! what a lair !
The very cradle of your name and race ;
To Roman loins where Sabine women bare
A lusty birth from violent embrace :
Sons sternly strong, daughters divinely fair,
Celestial those in force as these in face,
Who, not unmindful of their getting, curled
Their sinewy arms around a ravished world !

CLXVI

" Look ! where your sires, disarmed by love's decree,
To their consenting brides at length were wed,
The Gallic harlot, fetched across the sea,
With venal limbs fouls your ancestral bed !
Your home, your hearth, your very nursery,
Where Roman babes on Roman tales were fed,
Hath grown a den defiled, a place of shame,
Barbarians mock, and patriots blush to name !

CLXVII

" Where trod the Jove-crowned conquerors of earth,
The stealthy shaveling slipshod creeps along ;
Where rang the echoes of triumphant mirth,
The trembling monk mumbles his drowsy song.
On the twin hill where Empire took its birth,
And the victorious eagles used to throng,
A spurious Cæsar drills his legions foul,
And flings his ægis o'er each crouching cowl !

CLXVIII

" And do ye live and breathe ?   Now live no more,
Save ye can purge the palace and the fane
Of prince and priest who barter grace for gore,
And God's and Cæsar's name alike profane.
Is Italy so fair, their native shore
Bounds their barbarian appetite in vain ?
Vainly the Alps arise, vain rolls the wave ?
Then sate their greed of soil.—Give them a grave ! "

CLXIX

Then with brief words, and indicating hand,
Along the heights and broken slopes he spread
The little cohorts of his clustered band.
Some in the shrunken streamlet's stony bed
He showed to crouch, and others bade to stand
Behind the waving ridge's sheltering head,
Watching, with eye alert and firelock low,
To deal prompt death on the presumptuous foe.

CLXX

And where the gray-trunked olive's purpling beads
Glistened among its shifting-coloured sprays,
He dotted children of the mountain-meads,
Who mark the chamois with unerring gaze
On track that only to the snow-line leads ;
While others in the down-cut corn and maize,
Cut but unstacked, he bade in ambush wait,
Patient as vengeance, pitiless as fate !

CLXXI

Hark ! the sharp challenge of a rifle rings
Shrill through the air ! then all again is still ;
Save where its eddying echo faintly clings
To the deep hollows of some distant hill.
But soon the breeze a fuller message brings,
Another,—and another yet,—until
A fitful musket-rattle spreads around,
And silence seems but waiting upon sound.

CLXXII

Awhile from hill and slope no answer came ;
Though many a sharp-fanged messenger of death
Tore through the leafy vine-stem's tender frame,
Scorched the gray trunks with its malignant breath,
And set the shocks of ripened maize aflame.
But as when long a storm-cloud lingereth,
And, since it loometh black, men wonder why
Its threatening javelins linger in the sky ;

CLXXIII

But when at length it bursteth overhead,
It bursteth all at once, and serried hail
Flashes and rattles on the torrent's bed,
And beats the corn as doth the thresher's flail ;
So now, at lagging signal swiftly spread,
The scowling muzzles pointing toward the vale
Hurled on the foe a hurricane of steel,
That made the foremost fall, the hindmost reel.

CLXXIV

"Now must be craven bolts, winged from afar,
Exchanged for bristling weapons, face to face,
And this too distant dalliance of war
Discarded for the grip of close embrace.
So, Latin lads ! show of what strain ye are,
And prove the unslacked mettle of your race
Against these mongrels of a lineage lewd,   .
The bastard sons of sires your sires subdued ! "

CLXXV

Thus through the hush of momentary truce
Rang the Chief's clarion voice.   But from his lips
Scarce had the words been fledged, than, as a sluice
Opens and quick its pent-up water slips,
Was all the volume of assault let loose,
And, wave on wave, the flashing bayonet-tips
Came streaming on, an ever-broadening ring,
Crested with banners of the Pontiff-King.

CLXXVI

Wave upon wave : As, when on some long shore
The tide comes rolling in, in ridgy sheets,
Surge after surge, with hollow-bosomed roar,
Plunges and breaks, then hurriedly retreats,
And the stunned strand stands solid as before,
But swift a fresh on-coming billow meets
The flying foam, and carries it along,
Back to the assault, with volume doubly strong ;

CLXXVII

So, endless, rolled the ridges of attack,
Line after line, valour at valour's heel;
Surged, roared, rushed, broke, then fell in fragments back,
Shattered and shivered on that shore of steel.
Yet waxed not then the tide of onset slack,
But as each ruined rank was seen to reel,
Another,—longer,—stronger,—onwards dashed,
And o'er the flying eddies curled and crashed.

CLXXVIII

Then forth from copse and vineyard, orchard, grove,
Farmstead and stony torrent's shielding bank,
And deep-set pool where the tall cane-stems wove
For ambushed feet a cover dense and dank,
Rushing and trampling came a mighty drove,
That swiftly formed in many a hornëd rank,
And, swarming on each open crest and crown,
Paused for the word to speed their valour down.

CLXXIX

Not fiercer, blacker, sweeps the Alpine storm,
When gorges howl and the fir-forests crash;
Not louder, ocean, when the dun waves form
Their monstrous heads, and rocks and breakers clash;
Not straighter doth the avalanche enorm
Its jaggëd path through crackling pine-masts gash,
Than swept the impulse of their gathered will,—
At once wind, wave, and lauwine,—down the hill.

CLXXX

Whereat the ranks that fenced the Triple Crown,
And, too unmindful of rebuke divine,
Drew Peter's sword afresh, soon as the frown
Of grim assault drew near in line on line
Of smoke and steel, flung blade and rifle down,
And, scattering wide o'er dip and steep incline,
Their faces set where safety led the way,
And fled in wildered flakes of loose dismay.

CLXXXI

Then all seemed won ; and victory's course that, first,
Steadied by curbing discipline had rolled,
Soon as it felt resistance' barriers burst,
Asunder swept and spread out uncontrolled ;
Dispersing as the fugitives dispersed,
By the wild rout made hazardously bold,
Till in the exultant lines,—left, centre, right,—
Pursuit had waxed disorderly as flight.

CLXXXII

When lo ! though nought as yet could they descry
Save friends behind and fleeing foes before,
Upon them weapons new began to ply,
New and unseen, that hushed the cannon's roar.
So thick came bullets now, they scanned the sky
To see if Heaven itself perchance did pour
The hellish missiles down, and foully mar
With unfair stroke the hard-got spoils of war.

CLXXXIII

As thus awhile they halted, and with eyes
Of wonder and of terror gazed around,
They saw the flying rout melt phantomwise,
And sudden, in its stead, as from the ground,
A new and unsuspected host arise,
Bearing the Tricolor with eagle crowned ;
Advancing not, but stemming their advance,
With the famed chassepots of Imperial France.

CLXXXIV

Then rage seized every breast ; and once again,
By warlike instinct ordered, swift they shrank,
Rallying each other both with voice and ken,
Into close file and steady marshalled rank ;
Though faster, thicker, rained upon them then
The lethal hail, and many a brave brow sank,
To rise no more, on which, a moment gone,
The upward light of dawning victory shone.

CLXXXV

In vain or force or feint, courage or skill,
Against a foe that seemed to multiply,
By some miraculous arm, its strength at will,
And, scattering death, never itself to die.
Maddened by pain, no more they cared to fill
The widening gaps, but with a desperate cry
Rushed in disordered valour, singly brave,
If not to make, at least to find, a grave.

CLXXXVI

Then many fled, and those who fled not fell ;
And, from that moment, Miriam 'mong the erect
Nor Gilbert saw nor Godfrid. In the swell
And surf of carnage lay their valour wrecked.
And ere she could descend and rush to well
Her love in dying ears,—unruled, unchecked,
The tide of flight came on, and as the spray
Lifts the light seaweed, swept her steps away.

CLXXXVII

The last she saw was a mute patient steer
Join its yoke-fellow in death's darkened stall,
Where it may slumber peaceful all the year,
Dreading no bondsman's stroke, no master's call.
The rest was like the tumult in the ear
Of waters o'er the drowning, or the pall
That falls on fainting eyes when pulses reel,
And even the living brain forgets to feel.

CLXXXVIII

Into sparse wattled sheep-pens many crept,
And by the rude but pitying herd were hid
Among his flock, that, all inhuman, slept.
But their bedfellows closed not weary lid,
And when pursuit's fierce waves had past them swept,
Up from the strange, warm, throbbing couch they slid,
And to their host, beneath the starlight pale,
With sobs of fury stammered out their tale.

CLXXXIX

They told him how the day dawned bright with hope,
How noon had seen the hirelings' onset foiled,
How they, triumphant, bounded down the slope,
And then,—with lips that faltered, blood that boiled,—
How their spent strength had with new foes to cope,
And Italy's dream, touching its goal, was spoiled.
Then, speech engulfed in surges of the breast,
Aghast they stood, and, silent, looked the rest.

CXC

Till one just mustered stertorous breath to tell
The shepherd son of Romulus who those were
That with their hellish sorcery broke the spell.
Whereat the hind shook his thick matted hair,
Unto their curses joined his curses fell ;
And bringing down his crook, high poised in air,
Sharp to the ground, as though it were a spear,   ,
Called on the avenging gods below to hear !

CXCI

Into Mentana's squalid ways,—for there
A little band, at daybreak left behind,
Still kept unbroken front,—the wounded bare
The dying, fain some pillow's prop to find
For these, oblivious of their own despair.
And soon the church with pallets rude was lined,
By which Franciscan priests soft-sandalled stole,
And sped with patriot prayers each parting soul.

CXCII

Just as the twilight faded into dark,
Voices were heard without ; and striplings four,
Who had escaped the foeman's deadly mark,
Into the nave a goodly body bore,
Stretched on a litter, seeming stiff and stark,
Whose torn red shirt was steeped in redder gore,
And to whose beard and hair of iron gray
The death-dews clung, like frost to wintry spray.

CXCIII

Behind them close walked Miriam, on whose brow
Black thunder-sorrow brooded, but who dropped
No tear of feeble anguish even now.
Slow at the sight each prostrate sufferer propped
His head upon his hand, and breathed a vow
Of dying love towards her.   She nor stopped,
Nor looked on either side, but followed pale
The mournful convoy to the altar rail.

CXCIV

There with arresting hand she bade them pause,
And on the altar step to lay him down,
And to a servant of dear Christ's sweet laws
Who wore the saintly Francis' habit brown,
Beckoned ; and as distressful beauty draws
Even the heart that wears the chaste cold crown,
He hastened towards her and said lovingly,   .
" My daughter dear, what can I do for thee ?"

CXCV

"Wed me," she said, "dear father, to this man;
Wed me this hour, ere he be man no more.
See! though his eyes be closed, his cheek be wan,
And though he soon will tread the heavenly floor,
He lives—he breathes! his sinking bosom can
Receive the vow I long therein to pour,
Ere he shall leave me but a deaf-eared clod,
And go to claim me at the Throne of God!"

CXCVI

The monk bent over the mute, hueless face,
And laid his ear against the blood-stained breast;
Then turned to her, and said: "Fair child of grace,
'Tis true that life hath not yet left its nest,
But even now for its true dwelling-place
Its wing it lifts, to fly away to rest.
'Twould be as though you wed a corpse, to wear
Eternal widowhood on your young hair."

CXCVII

"O yes, I know!" she only could repeat,
In hurrying words that burst through sorrow's dam,
"Father, I know!   But wed us, I entreat,
That I may plead, through him, before the Lamb,
For our wronged land!   It, corpse-like at my feet,
I ne'er can be more widowed than I am.
I,—I will live to plot, he die to pray,
That Heaven with Earth conspire to avenge this day!"

CXCVIII

The trembling friar took up the clammy hand,
Whose pulse beat faint, and laid it within hers,
While she repeated, at his grave command,
The solemn pledge which deathless bond avers.
And, on the instant,—o'er a silent land
As a faint breeze sometimes in summer stirs,
Then drops,—so Gilbert, for a moment's space,
Opened blue eyes, and smiled into her face.

CXCIX

Then grief had all its way, and wild she flung
Her body on his body, and loud wept ;—
Wept with the loosened nerves, late overstrung,
And with the passion that too long had slept.
A sympathetic horror stole among
The close-packed pallets : some from out them crept
Near her to kneel; and those who could not stir,
Died, weeping blood for Italy and her !

CC

Now far and wide the sterile-rolling plain
Lay in the shadow of the passing night,
Whose ebon wings, outstretched o'er land and main,
Move on,—slow,—silent,—none may mark their flight :
O'er stiff cold limbs for ever dead to pain,
O'er writhing forms whose cries still scared the kite,
Calling for aid from those that, happier, slept,
On, on, unhalting, pitiless, it swept.

P

CCI

There is a tall but crumbling tower that stands
Amid the lone Campagna's gloomiest waste,
Whose depths were dug by those Cyclopean hands
Which famed Cortona's massive circuit traced.
Above, its walls, like wrecks on littered strands,
Heaped more than built, rise up.   Each age has traced
Its record on the masonry.   Wouldst compare
Republic, Empire, ruin?—Scan them there!

CCII

Its corner-stones are waifs from submerged fanes,
Its mortar, marble gods.   Urn, statue, bust,
All that of porphyry temple yet remains,
Tumbled and trampled, shattered, ground to dust,
Chipped, splintered, fouled, besmeared with wintry stains,
Into its chinks and crannies have been thrust.
Religions, dynasties, to patch a rent
In its rude mail, their sepulchres have lent.

CCIII

The feudal bandit, flying from the proof
Of bloody deed,—a later, fiercer Goth,—
Oft to its shelter came with glowing hoof,
There fortress found, and braved a Pontiff's wrath.
Foxes and wolves have littered 'neath its roof.
But now alone, to sup his darnel broth,
And warm his agued limbs within its walls,
Thither at times the stricken shepherd crawls.

CCIV

To-night there shone a feeble light within,
And, in the one sole chamber time had spared,
Upon a pallet rough and mattress thin,
Was stretched a wounded man.   His throat was bared,·
But on his still-clad form was thrown a skin
Such as Rome's minstrels wear,—rude, shaggy-haired,—
That served for coverlet ; beneath his head,
A sheaf of straw for pillow had been spread.

CCV

Soundly he slept, though ever and anon,
As though he would awake, he groaned and gasped ;
But still a stout sword-hilt, from which was gone
One-half its blade, his right hand tightly grasped.
A little way aloof, with face that shone
With fervent prayer, and palms intently clasped
Before a crucifix, herself had laid
Against the wall, a wimpled Sister prayed.

CCVI

And, save these two, for many a league around,
No living mortal was : only the dead.
He, pierced and gashed, and plunged in sleep profound,
She, with her pure white veil around her head,
Between her God divided and each sound
That reached her from the slumbering sufferer's bed :
Her vigil's sole companion, one small lamp,
Such as you find in sepulchres old and damp.

CCVII

Sudden he woke, and with a battle-cry,
Raising his body upright in the bed,
Brandished the bright dismembered blade on high,
Struck at the foe, and rallied friends that fled.
He saw as yet with but half-waking eye,
And, bridging the abyss between the dread
Dark hour he fell and life's returning light,
Fancied himself erect in thick of fight.

CCVIII

But when the air resisted not, nor stroke
Of quick-retorting sword attested fray,
Slowly to complete consciousness he woke,
Stared wildly round, and wondered where he lay.
He saw the bare blank walls, the nun's dark cloak,
The little oil-fed lamp's ascetic ray;
Then on his broken blade and bloody vest
Looking,—half he recalled, and read the rest.

CCIX

The pale-faced Sister, startled by his cries
'Mid her mute prayer, rose promptly from her knees,
And, with celestial pity in her eyes,
Stole toward the pallet, soft as steals a breeze
Through open casement when the sunset dies.
" Brother," she said, " I come to bring you ease,
To nurse your wound and speed your parting soul.
Forget the fight: for Heaven is now your goal."

CCX

Her eyes were cast down meekly, and she seemed
As one who saw yet saw not.   On her brow
And round her mouth a tranquil radiance beamed.
Yet surely, surely not again, not now,
Not now,—as but a moment gone,—he dreamed
An empty dream?   That face, that voice, avow
Herself, her soul!   "Olympia!" loud he cried;
But on his lips all other language died.

CCXI

She started, and flung up her arms, like one
By bullet through the brain in battle shot,
Or fearful tidings suddenly undone.
"O Godfrid! Godfrid!   Tell me it is not,
Not thou, not Godfrid! whom at rise of sun,
At noon, at night, I never have forgot
In my poor prayers! not thou, the once adored,
I see with shattered, sacrilegious sword!

CCXII

" Yes, it is thou, sole vision of my heart,
Ere dearer Christ espoused me to His breast!
I must behold thee, even as thou art,—
His foe, His executioner confessed,
Stained with His blood.   When we were forced to part
On that smooth shore by smoother sea caressed,
How could I dream that we should meet as now,
A worse than brand of Cain upon your brow!

CCXIII

"Did all avail you nothing? Not the morn
When first we met, and you with gentle speech
Dissevered from the Maytime-blossoming thorn
The snow-white branch, I, feeble, could not reach?
Oh! did you ne'er recall, in hours forlorn,
The sunny shrine I tended on the beach,
Nor that all-trustful tenderness which made
Your alien presence welcome as I prayed?

CCXIV

"Did you forget my little chapel quite?
And did Madonna's statue, which your hand
Helped me to deck, as swiftly fade from sight
As morning's footstep from the evening's sand?
Did you bethink you never of that night
Of raging tempest on a blackened strand,
When you did seek my face, and I did weep
To hear your woe, then, blessing, bade you sleep?

CCXV

"You have forgotten it all. Our journey dear,
Our simple mid-day meal, our evening halt,
The tumbling cataracts, the sheep-bells clear,
The tall black pine-wood scaling Heaven's vault,—
Tell me how soon did these all disappear,
How soon was hateful memory sown with salt?
When, when did cold oblivion begin?
And when was all as though it ne'er had been?

CCXVI

"Well might my prayers, sin-weighted as they be,
Not reach the Throne of Grace.   But thou, O thou!
Thou mightst at least have not been deaf to me,
And, for my sake, have reverenced the brow,
Mangled with thorns, of Him who died for thee!
Though you believe not, was it hard to bow
To the remembrance of the words I spoke,
The tears I shed, the hoping heart you broke?

CCXVII

"No! all was vain.   Shore, mountain, sea, and stream,
Milan's cathedral, Spiaggiascura's shrine,
The silent grief that worse than speech did seem,
To me so sacred, since it half was thine,
Then when we parted,—these were but a dream!
Alas! *I* dream not.   Waking woe is mine,
Waking reproach.   Forgive, O loving Lord!
That I once kissed the hand that grasps that sword!"

CCXVIII

Thus as she spoke, he neither word nor sign
Let fall, nor muscle moved, nor eyelid dropped,
But, with lips parted, gaze slow-dimmed with brine,
Intently gazed and listened, till she stopped.
Then, one hand still to hilt he held divine
Clinging, his head upon the other propped,
Grave, he began: "With reverence have not you
Been heard, Olympia?   Reverent, hear me too.

CCXIX

"You are the bride of Heaven, and I, alas!
Earthy; but, even as you are heavenly, hear!
O, since that bitter parting came to pass,
Never an hour hath been, in year on year,
Whether the hills were hoar, or green the grass,
Or dimpling corn uplifted playful spear,
Or mellow bunches drooped from branch and wall,
I had not sped to you, had you deigned to call.

CCXX

"Forgot that morn! forgot that dewy spot,
Where Heaven, it seemed, dawned full upon my gaze!
Forgot the little chapel! and forgot
Madonna's statue, at whose flowery base
With you I knelt, my doubts remembered not!
Nay, if oblivion from my brain shall raze   ˙
Record of these, then back may Mercy roll   ˌ
Her opening gates, and clang them on my soul!

CCXXI

"Bear with me still, Olympia, to the end!
Full well I know 'tis not your love, your wrongs,
With which you now reproach me, or that rend
The heart which henceforth but to God belongs.
Vainly I now should call you more than friend;
Vainly, though every dear old feeling throngs
Back to my breast at sight of you once more:
Vainly,—though even I knelt and could adore!

CCXXII

"Too late! Too late! Denied to me awhile,
For ever are you ravished from me now!
Gone from your lips the sweetly mortal smile,
And Heaven's pure veil protects your sacred brow.
You are removed so far, you would beguile
My wildest vows, as did that virgin bough
Your straining hand, when in the mountain glade
I lent my help! . . . Alas! Me none will aid!

CCXXIII

"Yet though you did abjure me, and have given
Heaven all the love I once with Heaven did share,
The links which knitted me to you, are riven
Tighter by time, and have survived despair.
I may from many sins need to be shriven;
But one weight still I shall not have to bear
Before the judgment-seat. My love was pure,
Even as your own, and will till death endure!

CCXXIV

"When you had sought a haven in the sky,
I, from my haven driven, put forth to sea.
And lo! from every tower and turret high,
Rang out the glad peal, summoning to be free,
Free or for ever slave, the land that I
Loved not the less, because it fathered *thee!*
Land, crowned with snow and girdled by the foam,
Fair as her Florence, outraged as her Rome!

CCXXV

"Nay, bear with me, Olympia, bear alway,
If only for the sake of olden days.
Rome, still forgotten, still in fetters, lay.
I against you as soon my sword would raise
As 'gainst the altar where you kneel and pray ;
And though I lift no voice of prayer or praise,
In half-believing awe I bend me too,
Before the Faith that fosters such as you.

CCXXVI

"Not, not against the altar did I fling
My feeble body, counting life as dross :
No, but from Peter's hampered hand to wring
The carnal sword, and leave therein the Cross :
That Rome, unswathed, might from the sepulchre spring,
And Italy no more bewail the loss
Of her first-born, but grouped around her knee
Her dear ones hail,—not fair alone, but free !

CCXXVII

"Ah ! half in darkness on this earth we dwell,
Not in the light, but shadow, of the truth ;
Confounding good with evil, heaven with hell,
Misjudging rage and hate for love and ruth.
But, though our souls thus vainly gnaw their shell,
And manhood seem but disillusioned youth,
I still must hope, the lingering dawn despite,
That slow we move, through liberty, to light.

CCXXVIII

"And if there be, for close of all this ache,
This panting struggle, a celestial goal,
Come with me there, Olympia ! I will take
My blood-stained sword, and you your snow-white soul !
Perchance we there shall see that each doth make
Complete the other, and a godlike whole,
From human vision hid, will flash to life,
In that pure atmosphere where melteth strife.

CCXXIX

"But if I needs must go, leaving you here,
Pass solitary, silent, to my doom,
I will await you in whatever sphere
I may awake, of sunshine or of gloom.
For I will never, never yield you, dear !
While soul surviveth !   Meanwhile, tend my tomb ;
But still remember, that my latest breath
Blent, with your name, the cry of 'Rome or Death !'"

CCXXX

Faint came the final words, though tightly still
He grasped the bladeless hilt she would release,
To join his hands in prayer.   "Oh ! do His will,
And with the Heavenly Victor make your peace !
My heart shall keep a nook for you until
We meet in the Land where wrong and sorrow cease.
But oh ! bequeath me, ere you leave me lone,
Some hope that we *may* meet before the Throne !

CCXXXI

"Your words have meaning which you do not see.
All betwixt Rome must choose, God's Voice hath said,
And endless Death!" "Then, Death," he cried, "for me!"
And waved his broken brand above his head;
Then dropped the hilt, and fell back heavily.
Dragged down by woe, she knelt beside the bed,
And on the offending hand laid sobbing cheek :—
For love too strong, for martyrdom too weak !

CCXXXII

Now with light jocund step came young-eyed Morn,
Dancing and singing o'er the eastern hill.
The timorous twilight, blushing, fled forlorn,
And in each thicket awoke pipe and trill.
The world,—the old, worn world,—seemed freshly born,
Eden renewed, where man might drink his fill
Of brimming joy and beauty, nor e'er know
His naked self, that long bequest of woe !

CCXXXIII

The sluggish mountains, donning crowns of gold,
Uprose to greet the morning.   O'er the plain
Of blight and wreck a roseate wave was rolled.
Glowed in the sunlight aqueduct and fane,
No longer ruined.   Happy Gods of old
Would soon, it seemed, their ancient seat regain,
And rule once more, from oracle and shrine,
A scene for mortal empire too divine !

CCXXXIV

Rome, Rome itself, bathed in auroral sheen,
Its domes, towers, columns, fanned by buoyant gales,
Scanned from afar, one well indeed might ween
A sea of sunlight flecked with joyous sails.
Here, playful fountains leaped, and laughed between ;
There, bright-trunked stone-pines spread their sombre veils
'Twixt earth and sky ; the cracks in temples hoar
But dimples seemed, with which they smiled once more.

CCXXXV

From narrow humid street, in open square,
Sun-flooded, gathered an unwonted throng ;
And most where saint-crowned pillar clave the air,
Or spouting column soared like voice of song.
In every eye there lurked the angry glare,
In every nerve the self-suppression strong,
Of panther ere it leaps ;—a fearful pause,
Ere bounds the body, and out-curve the claws !

CCXXXVI

When, all at once, from lip to lip there flew
The rumour that the great Deliverer's tread
Nearer and nearer to the city drew,
Striding across the prostrate tyrant's head.
Some, shimmering in the distant sunlight blue,
Had seen his bayonet-tips and banners red
Stream o'er the crest of the Nomentan Way ;
And some, 'twas said, had heard his trumpets bray.

CCXXXVII

Then all the people started up and took
Hotly their way unto the Eastern gate.
The comfortable cripple left his nook,
And hobbled with the crowd.   With eager gait,
Dark matrons flower and lemon stall forsook ;
While timid maidens, fearing to be late,
Awaited not their mothers, but entwined
Their hands with baby boys, and ran like wind.

CCXXXVIII

Yes ! in the sunlight, pinnacles of steel
Flashed, and lithe pennons floated in the air ;
And from the ranks they crested rang the peal
Of thunderous drum and many a clarion's blare.
But, pitying Christ ! what do those notes reveal,
And what these ensigns, waved anear, declare ?
The Pontiff's pæan sounds 'neath banners black,
His hellish legions tramping in their track !

CCXXXIX

On,—on,—they came, with rhythmic-moving tread,
His hirelings first, their Gallic prop behind ;
And, last, with sullen step and unraised head,
A haggard, footsore file, whom Death unkind
Forgot to reap ; who neither fell nor fled,
But, caught in toils no valour could unwind
And reft of arms, now with the craven thong
Linking their limbs, toiled painfully along.

CCXL

Just ere the vanguard of the long array
The gateway reached, and bright warm bayonet-tips,
Dipping beneath its vault, from sheen of day
Passed, for a moment, into cold eclipse,
The crowd one last look gave, then slunk away :
The men with muttered curses on their lips,
Women with silent anguish in their eyes,
And hate, in hearts of both, that never dies !

CCXLI

Then, to the clang of cymbals and the sound
Of triumph-breathing instruments, swept on
The exultant host through solitude profound :
Past silent-nodding wrecks of Empire gone,
Sallust's choked garden, Cæsar's toppled mound.
What though bright fountain flashed, bright sunlight shone,
Loud pealed their trumpets, proudly waved their plumes,
Rome's dwellings seemed as empty as her tombs !

CCXLII

But as they, onward moving, roused the styes
Where modern squalor supersedes the reign
Of ancient ruin, swarms of black-robed spies,
Shavelings and sbirri, and their servile train,
Began through chink and crack with stealthy eyes
To peer and glance, as when from hole and drain
Foul-feeding vermin thrust suspicious snout,
Ere to their garbage-feast they sally out.

CCXLIII

But when they saw the Cross-Keys waving high,
And heard Gaul's pompous music fill the air,
Then out they came in shoals,—a various fry:
Some in brown serge, with feet and foreheads bare,
And hempen cord whence hung the rosary;
Some robed in white, long-bearded, comely, spare,
Whose lofty brows roofed Learning and the Law;
And some, black-frocked, with clenched ascetic jaw.

CCXLIV

Sudden, as though from underground they sprung,
File after file, came troops of tonsured boys,
To whose slim bodies gaudy cassocks clung,
And who from native Freedom's healthy joys
Had, babes, been weaned, and taught an alien tongue.
Their pretty voices swelled the monkish noise,
Their tender forms the sabre-sounding throng,
Their innocent hearts the festival of wrong!

CCXLV

They too, the coiners of the spurious smile,
That round the victor's chariot skip and bark,
Obsequious hounds, the vilest of the vile,
Came thick; and those, who know not light from dark,
Meek, timorous hearts, whom fear and faith beguile,
And who in storm cling fast to Peter's ark:
And, last, the sceptic souls, who from them thrust
Man's genial dreams, and in the fasces trust.

CCXLVI

So the armed host, by sycophant and slave,
Friar, and mendicant, and boyish band,
Followed and cheered, marched on with banners brave
To that famed spot on hoary Tiber's strand,
Where Papal statues arrogantly wave
Over the stream forgotten Pagans spanned,
And Papal gaolers, copying the gloom
Of death, have carved a dungeon from a tomb.

CCXLVII

Across the bridge they streamed, a hemmed-in crowd,
And up the narrow squalid Borgo passed,
Till lo ! the pile, whose head with sun and cloud
Converses, and whose feet are planted fast
In earth's foundation, rose before them proud,
Stupendous, soaring, dominant, and vast :
Type of that mighty Power which claims to quell
Man's soul, and rule the realms of Heaven and Hell.

CCXLVIII

Then, as a stream that finds a wider bed,
Over the broad piazza loose they poured,
Between the curving colonnades, and sped
Up the long marble steps, defaced and scored,
Though polished smooth, by many a pilgrim's tread ;
Until no more the glittering cupola soared
Up in the sky, and into shade they passed,
Like that the sun-confronting mountains cast.

CCXLIX

A moment more, beneath the atrium pealed
Fresh music, and an army new drew near :
The Church's spiritual ranks, that wield
'Gainst Satan's host the crosier as a spear,
And on their bosom wear the cross for shield :
Music that ravished the submissive ear,
And gorgeous companies whose pompous train
Dazzled the eye and dizzy left the brain.

CCL

Troops of fantastic friars, endless files
Of eremites and missionaries brought
From sun-scorched lands and ice-engirdled isles ;
Gold-mitred Abbots deep in prayer and thought,
And throne-defying Prelates wreathed in smiles,
Apparelled in rich copes with gems inwrought ;
Last, crimson-cassocked Cardinals, who curled
Proudly their lips, as though they swayed the world.

CCLI

Sudden shrilled silver trumpets, and out-flashed,
Quickly as sunlight flashes, mailëd men,
Across whose doublets,—black with yellow slashed,—
Glowed plates of burnished steel, that dazed the ken.
Next, brazen instruments and cymbals clashed,
Rending the lofty portico, and then,
So dread a sight approached, that they who saw
Dropped on their knees, and veiled their eyes for awe.

CCLII

For in mid-air, by men upborne, there came,
Enthroned, a venerable man, arrayed
In more than regal glory.   Eyes of flame,
Ravished from Juno's bird, his pathway made,
And, cushioned, shone his Triple Crown of fame.
Closed were his lids, but on his features played .
A more than mortal radiance ; and benign,
O'er the crouched crowd he made the Holy Sign.

CCLIII

When swept the long procession's final train
Into the august Temple's pillared nave,
Where statued pomp half baffles death's disdain,
And wrings its vauntful triumphs from the grave,
Army and concourse poured into the fane,
Distinguished now no more, but, like a wave,
Over the marble pavement rippling spread,
Till every slab was hid by human tread.

CCLIV

Then, with one voice, unto the Lord of Hosts,
Prince, priest, and people, Te Deum loudly sang :
Who hurls the waves against earth's granite coasts,
Swells with His voice the wingless tempest's clang,
And brings to nought the Mighty's impious boasts.
High up the spacious dome their anthem rang,
And in the air without, with rhythmic stroke,
The accompanying cannon's bounding pulses spoke.

CCLV

But with these proud Hosannas, and the boom
Of insolent artillery that cleaved
Rome's arching sky, ascended too the gloom
Of orphaned hearths, beds widowed, lives bereaved ;
Where He eternally abideth, Whom
Eye hath not seen, ear heard, nor heart conceived.
With sleepless eyes that scanned the nations wide,
Brooding He sate, His justice by His side !

END OF ACT III

ACT IV

ACT IV

PERSONAGES:

GILBERT—MIRIAM—OLYMPIA—GODFRID.

PROTAGONISTS:

LOVE—RELIGION—PATRIOTISM—HUMANITY.

PLACE:

ROME—PARIS.

TIME:

AUGUST 1870—CLOSE OF MAY 1871.

ACT IV

I

AND Miriam's prayer was heard.   The hosts of France
Low in the dust, low in dishonour, lay:
Broken her tumbrils, blunted was her lance,
And tinsel Empire vanished in a day.
The serried tramp of men, the war-steed's prance,
Pennon's proud smile and clarion's boastful bray,
Dominion's madness, glory's lustful dream,
Were swept like wrecks down Fate's unswerving stream.

II

For drunk by envy's ill-fermenting wine,
And each the other goading 'gainst a throne
Which late by force had proved its right divine,
And, vassal once, had now a rival grown,
Monarch and nation towards the peaceful Rhine,
Journeying through happy vineyards of its own,
Had urged the wheels of war, and, greedy horde,
Into the scales of justice flung the sword.

III

The sin of ancient years, unhallowed bed,
When, without love or honour, law or rite,
Bestial Ambition to the altar led
A ravished nation, giddy with affright,
And with vile lips the assenting victim wed,
Had borne its foul-got brood in all men's sight ;
A bastard offspring, wearing on their face
Brand nor success could hide nor pomp displace.

IV

And these had waxed to ripeness : sly distrust,
Which covers up its fear with mute assent ;
Curt sneers which sap, base gibes that fret like rust,
The irksome bond of spurious blandishment,
Disinclination deepening to disgust,
Overt reproaches, discord, discontent,
Divided purpose, longings ne'er the same,
And, lastly, naked scandal, dead to shame.

V

Thus from domestic petulancy grew
The itch of foreign venture.   Vexed at home
By weak disunion, throne and rabble threw
Distracting glance athwart the fencing foam.
Now into tropic seas their banner flew,
Now flapped forbidding over yearning Rome,
Now, lured and luring to dismay, unfurled
Its restless folds against the Western world.

VI

But bootless all.   The blight of failure fell
On each deft-trained design ere waxed it ripe,
Which straightway wizened just as it should swell,
And turned to ashes in the Schemer's gripe.
O'erbrooded purpose addled in the shell :
Kings donned their swords, hearing his peaceful pipe ;
And when he tricked them into strife, One rose
Colossal o'er a Continent of foes.

VII

Then, thus confronted, Prince and people wreaked
Their spite upon each other.   Baffled pride
Recalled that impious night when sobbed and shrieked
Through smothering hands the violated bride,
And morrow with her murdered kindred reeked.
While, thrusting condonation's pledge aside,
They who trooped willing slaves at Glory's heel,
Clamoured for freedom round its rusted steel.

VIII

Dazed by his dissipated dream, aghast
At ghosts he had deemed long laid, spurred by the cries
Of sullen crowds that gathered thick and fast,
Age in his limbs and death-rheum in his eyes,
With vacillating hand the rod he passed
To female counsels, perilous allies,
And pricked by priests and women blind with hate,
Passed to his doom through War's wide-opened gate.

IX

Then sleek corruption found its issue dire,
Teaching the obeisant multitude how vain
Is purple ostentation's eunuch choir,
When iron battle tramps the trembling plain,
Kneads the lithe golden grain to crimson mire,
And sings thanksgiving over sheaves of slain;
How forward splendour curlike slinks to heel,
When sabres clash and wrestling armies reel.

X

Servility, which brings the base to front,
Indiscipline, the mongrel jade that kicks
Against the whip and to the bit is blunt,
Yoked with confusion, twin in knavish tricks,
Loud braggart fear, that tempts then shirks the brunt,
And fireside luxury, which purrs and licks
Its velvet paws when wet winds wail without,
Swelled the loose train of predetermined rout.

XI

And these, by adulating courtiers led,
Lagged forth to meet where flattery smirks in vain,
A phalanxed people, mailed from heel to head,
And moved by law, as by the moon the main.
God, King, and Fatherland, the watchwords sped
From hearth to hearth, as from hill, vale, and plain,
They trooped to call, and drawn towards one sole aim
By one sole will, half-conquered ere they came.

XII

Then Meuse rolled red with blood and dark with shame,
And Sedan's bootless battlements concealed
Pale hosts of jostling fugitives that came
Clamouring for shelter from its fatal field.
Blind now to glory, deaf and dead to fame,
They sought in fear a friend, disgrace a shield,
And cowering mute in pools of comrades' gore,
Blessed the kind night that hushed the victors' roar.

XIII

But when the dark pall parted, and they saw
The day come forth and reascend the sky,
Full on them yawned the cannon's hungry jaw,
And on them glared its fixed, impassive eye.
Lo! round their terror moving myriads draw
The steel-knit network, surely, silently,
Nor strategy can foil nor valour tear,
Nor even death, though banded with despair.

XIV

Then foiled Aggression grovelled on the ground,
And France's Tricolor waxed deadly white.
Her legions to the Teuton's chariot bound,
Her Cæsar's sword surrendered, not in fight,
The spoil-clad victor through her vineyards wound,
Through ransomed towns, past camps too scared to smite,
On to the harlot City, which in dread
Whined to the world to save her from their tread.

XV

Whereat that other City, to the cup
Of her abominations sacrificed,
That she of lusts and glories false might sup,
City in turn of Cæsar and of Christ,
Though now of both long dispossessed, rose up,
And when Gaul's darkening flag no more sufficed
To cover her own bosom, freedom's sun
Felt on her face,—and Italy was One !

XVI

Then banned for ever was that bastard thing,
The regal diadem round priestly brows,
And a divine divorce decreed 'twixt King
Of carnal conquest and Christ's spotless spouse.
And though awhile her old affection cling
To the unnatural bond and impious vows,
She yet shall own, her alien banner furled,
That the soul's kingdom is not of this world.

XVII

Dragged from the clutches of tenacious death
By Miriam's love, who, when weak skill despaired,
Despaired not, feeding failing breath with breath,
And screening flickering life till life reflared,
Like flame that, hand-protected, brighteneth,
Gilbert, with her, that supreme moment shared,
When, through the gate Mentana's captives trod,
Burst Italy's flag and Savoy's kingly rod.

XVIII

And Godfrid, too, was there.   When first he woke
From that submerging swoon wherein he sank
With cry impenitent and raving stroke
That rent Olympia's heart, and saw life's bank
Once more in reach, round him were stranger folk.
He knew not whom to question, whom to thank.
There were no battle-stains his vest upon.
He looked : but lo ! his shattered sword was gone.

XIX

There was a little crucifix instead,
Of silver upon sandalwood, that lay
Close to his cheek, half slipping from the bed :
Which when he reverent would have drawn away,
He saw 'twas fastened by a hempen thread
Round his own neck, so could not go astray,
But, as he moved, moved still with him, and kept
A quiet watch upon him when he slept.

XX

He lay not now in squalid ruin built
Of mud and rifled empires.   Four white walls,
Blank, saving where there hung Who for man's guilt
Dies always, and in silent anguish calls
Sin to His feet, soft pillows, smoothened quilt,
A silence such as reigns in empty halls,
And by his bed a pot of fragrant flowers,—
These were his company through the muffled hours.

XXI

But he could hear, in corridor without,
The sound of swiftly, softly, passing feet,
That constant to some business moved about,
But did it without noise, or haste, or heat.
Sometimes this movement waned, and quite died out;
And, always then, he could catch voices sweet,
Just far enough away sick ear to please,
Chanting plain hymn or singing litanies.

XXII

And none e'er broke the silence of his door
Save white-cowled sisters, who, with modest speech,
Asked him if felt he happier than before,
Resmoothed his bed, placed food within his reach,
Then glided silently across the floor,
And left.   And each so like was unto each,
In office like, and all without a name,
He wondered were they others or the same.

XXIII

But one there was who never came, for whom
He ever looked with quickly-turning cheek
Whene'er a fresh foot comforted his room,
For whom he longed, of whom he dared not speak.
At length, one eve, as twilight's deepening gloom
Drove from his wall the sunlight's farewell streak,
He asked, "Where, sister, have I found a home?
Where am I now?"   She answered him, "In Rome.'

XXIV

Whereat, when she was gone, he wondering lay
Upon his bed. "Yes, Rome or Death!" he mused.
"The stern alternative of that lost fray,
Death, hath missed fire, and destiny refused
The other doom. But no! Did she not say
I am in Rome? Thus, thus the Gods amused
Fulfil the formulas for which we strive.
I am not dead. Is Italy alive?

XXV

"And where is Gilbert? Miriam, where? Where, she,
The maiden mistress of my soul, that knelt
With darkness, and the howling gusts, and me,
On that distressful midnight when I felt
My being like a bark that takes the sea,
And on known shore beholds dear figures melt
Into dim distance, and the waves and wind
Shut out the sense of all we leave behind.

XXVI

"Where is my dear Olympia? Dear, too dear!"
Then, down his cheek, like one last drop of dew
Hot noon hath spared, trickled a tender tear.
And when, at early morn, a nun-nurse drew
To his bedside, "Who was it brought me here?"
He asked. She answered: "One who prays for you,"
And changed his faded flowers for fresh, and went.
And he, being gentle, gathered what she meant;

XXVII

Nor questioned them again, though still his breast
Fluttered whenever fresh hand touched his door,
Fluttering for nought.   But when, self-kempt and drest,
He, all unhelped, could walk across the floor,
There came a sister older than the rest,
Who said, " You are our prisoner no more,
Who, elsewhere prisoned, would have found release
Hardly so soon.   Now, brother, go in peace."

XXVIII

And so he went, the little cross around
His neck, and silent sadness in his soul.
And by and by he wrote his thanks profound
To the good nuns who thus had made him whole,
And in whose cloister he had shelter found,
At their own risk, against the prying shoal
Of victor sbirri, pity their sole creed,—
And sent them humble gifts for humble need.

XXIX

Thence he returned to Capri, like a bird
That crawls back to its nest with broken wings ;
Lamenting, lonely, with a voice unheard,
The jar irreconcilable of things,
How at each other Past and Future gird,
How each one's music general discord brings,
And, with this grief which causeth the world's moan,
Blending a kindred sorrow of his own.

XXX

His sole joy seemed to gaze on the bland brow
Of meditating mountains, and the sight
Of that serene felicity which now
Made Gilbert's years seem few, his memories light,
Dead bond forgotten in a livelier vow ;
But who still lacked, vicissitudes despite,
The philosophic vision, which perceives
Some goodness even in that o'er which it grieves.

XXXI

So when the Gallic bayonets that suppressed
The yearning efforts of parental Rome
To fold her prosperous children to her breast,
Answering the cry of Paris, hurried home,
And Christ's miscrowned Vicegerent stood confessed
In his own strength, across the Tyrrhene foam
Gilbert and Miriam flew with eager breath,
To swell once more the cry of " Rome or Death ! "

XXXII

But Godfrid watched and waited, nor betook
His footsteps to the mainland till the Flag
Unto the breeze once more the colours shook
Which had freed Italy from cape to crag,
And, kingly still, to screen the Shepherd's crook
Now frankly waved.   Then no more did he lag,
But hastened with hot heart past strand and stream,
To clasp, no vision now, his life's one dream.

R

XXXIII

And thus he shared, with tears of trembling joy,
That consummating moment : moment rare
In this begrudging planet, where the boy,
Too oft, as man, sees high hopes melt in air,
Or descend earthward, mixed with base alloy ;
Moment admonishing no one to despair,
And that the nations which will watch and wait,
May even tire out time and rescind fate.

XXXIV

Upon the Palatine hill, presumptuous hands
Have swept and garnished, lending rival wrecks
Haphazard names, an enclosed space there stands
Of ruin unreclaimed.   No fribbles vex
The silent surface of time's drifted sands.
Untrained, unhindered, Nature hides and decks
Man's heaped-up failures.   Rarely human tread
Disturbs this green-grown dust-heap of the dead.

XXXV

And here, where desolation's final tide
Advanced and scattered, Godfrid musing lay,
Feeling like one who misses from his side
Something that ne'er before hath been away,
Now that the goal was reached whose course untried
Had filled the blank of many a lonely day,
And, to replace the past, that kindly friend,
Stretched an unfancied Future, void of end.

XXXVI

He ever and anon could catch the burst
Of pæans popular in far-off street,
Wherein he too had gladly joined at first ;
And as he mused that it were surely meet
This barren joy were not too oft rehearsed,
He heard the sound of slowly-winding feet,
He feared of strangers, but soon hailed, instead,
Gilbert's and Miriam's ever-welcome tread.

XXXVII

Straight, seeing them, he rose, that Miriam might
Choose some smooth seat, though choice in sooth was none.
But ere she reached the rude stair's topmost height,
Halting, she stood ; while Gilbert, like to one
Who, awkward, blurts unwelcome news outright,
" We must be gone before the set of sun,"
Abruptly said : " We are but here to tell
Our resolution, and to take farewell."

XXXVIII

" Gone before set of sun !   And farewell !   Why ?
What is this deed I with you may not share ? "
Godfrid exclaimed.   But neither made reply,
And with joint silence paid his wondering stare.
So he rejoined : " If it must be, good-bye !
For I shall miss you.   Yet one parting prayer
Grant me, at least.   Oh ! do not, insane, break
This moulded Italy you helped to make."

XXXIX

"Yes, Italy is made!" cried Gilbert, "though
Within its entrails priest and king still lurk;
And these must one day follow foreign foe.
This hour is not propitious for the work,
At least not here; and that is why we go.
At throat of throne-rid France is Teuton dirk;
But once by her Republic back are hurled
These bravo kings, she then will free the world!

XL

"The Chief has called us round him now once more,
Now for one final, universal stroke,
And Italy shall find on foreign shore
The means wherewith to snap her native yoke.
Thus, thus will we avenge Mentana's gore,
And coals of fire upon their hearths shall smoke,
Who, duped by despots, now themselves condemn,
Denied *us* freedom we will bring to *them!*"

XLI

He ceased.   But Godfrid made not haste to speak;
For well he knew that reason's clearest rays
Against the mists of passion are wan and weak.
So for awhile he did but stand and gaze,
Saying at length, "If find you what you seek,
You will be honoured in all coming days.
The world hath not yet journeyed to its end,
And he who helps it onward is its friend.

XLII

" But, oftener far, presumption's hasty hand
Mars the slow-shaping form it fain would mould.
Forgive me ! Your great Chief for this fair land
Hath done what long in story shall be told :
But that he quits her now for foreign strand,
Will leave me less regretful than consoled.
The rest she needs, it is not his to give ;
And he might kill whom once he helped to live.

XLIII

" But how of that ambiguous Cause he goes
To aid, will you the original sin repair ?
I look, but can see only kites and crows
Fighting for carrion in the empty air.
Sooth ! to be arbiter betwixt such foes !
Each, thanks to statecraft's need, hath borne a share
In Italy's redemption. She should stand
Aloof from both, her winnings in her hand.

XLIV

" Republic ! Empire ! Words that feed no want.
What are they but authenticated sound,
Fine names, not virtues, given at the font,
Affection's too fond labels ? Look around
At history's wide horizon ! Nay, fie on't !
Better, with millstone round one's neck, be drowned
In sludge of foul oblivion, than loose seas
Of blood 'gainst seas of blood for feuds like these !

XLV

"No! France must pay the ransom of the wrong
Done to herself at first, to others last;
Nor will just Time take dithyrambic song
In quittance of the madness of the past.
Eleutheromaniacs round her rudder throng,
And wild she drives.   Still, if the die be cast,
May you ne'er sigh, 'mid wreck of world-wide hopes,
For home's sure weal and Capri's narrow slopes!"

XLVI

Slowly the last words trembled to their close,
And, trembling still, who uttered them was dumb.
Dumb, too, were they, unwilling to oppose
To friendship's pleading voice the stifling hum
And heat of passion, better kept for foes.
So Gilbert said, "We knew you would not come.
But we must start forthwith.   Say, will you cheer
Our parting feet, or bid us farewell here?"

XLVII

"Nay, let us hence then," Godfrid said, and straight
Adown the ruins' twisting track they went;
Nor strove he more to turn them from their fate,
But only on last offices intent
Seemed anxious, more than they, they were not late.
And soon the remnant rapid hours were spent.
By Tullius' levelled walls they, silent grown,
Parted, and Godfrid was in Rome alone.

XLVIII

There he abode, his temperate sword laid by,
Content to scan, complete, the work it planned ;
With peaceful hand, soft heart, and searching eye
Tending the needs of his adopted land,
And paid by its soft tongue and smiling sky :
All through that long white winter, when the brand
Of war austere fired Gaul's luxurious roofs,
And her sons crouched 'neath havoc's scouring hoofs.

XLIX

For all in vain had scrambling tribunes snatched
From Cæsar's captive hand the sword and flag,
And against regal victors, fumbling, patched
The rents of Empire with the ready rag
Of a Republic, from the gutter scratched.
In vain the phrase-plumed rhetoricians' brag,
The strut of hucksters panoplied, the loud
War-prattle of an armed unmastered crowd.

L

Hemmed in by silent steel and the clinched jaws
Of them that bared its edge, that stronghold lewd,
Semiramis of cities, whose soft laws
Make licit the illicit, till, subdued,
Even genius panders to her self-applause,
Now with her own sleek self herself at feud,
Lacked, as she stood effeminate at bay,
The antlers male to hew herself a way :

LI

And loudly to her lovers called, to leap
To arms for her sore sake, that yestertide
In her delight delighted, and drank deep
Of her lascivious wine-cups, and but vied
To share the perfume of her wanton sleep:
But these had slipped away from her roused side,
And from far-off beheld the loveless spears
Couched at her breast and callous to her tears.

LII

Then wailed she to her kindred, who sate scared
In innocent plain homes, whose cleanness she
Had outraged with her harlotries and spared
Nor scoff nor stain in days when she was free,
Corrupting to her dainties those she snared,
And mocking those who wailed her infamy,
That they would beat the ploughshare to a sword,
And die for her who had but danced and whored.

LIII

But when, unhelped by gods or men, she saw
From off her sybaritic tables melt
The dainties dressed for her voluptuous maw
In days of fat concubinage, and felt
Mute hunger her fastidious entrails gnaw,
Then she, so long unused to kneeling, knelt,
And, kissing with her unkissed lips the dust,
Sued to the foe to do what deemed he just.

LIV

And he, because he *was* just, would have stripped
The tinsel from her forehead, and torn off
The mimic steel in which she was equipped,
Making of Mars a mock, of death a scoff.
But once more in the dust her brow she dipped,
And tearfully besought she need not doff
Her new-found gewgaws, but might peaceful wear
Spur on her heel and war-plume in her hair.

LV

And he, in part for scorn, in part that he
Knew she against herself would quickly turn
Her braggart weapons, once her limbs were free,
Bade her retain them, but with visage stern
Told her go find and fetch unto his knee
Ransom of gold she in the days could earn
When all men bought her pleasure, and until
She forfeit paid, his sword should guard her still.

LVI

This, from afar, foreseen with certain ken,
Had Godfrid watched, in Rome abiding still,
Through that lone winter, until Spring again,
That hastens nor delays for good or ill
Or aught that haps the fitful fate of men,
Came in her blushing beauty o'er the hill,
Kissing to softness air and earth and skies,
Youth's candid coyness laughing in her eyes.

LVII

Tidings the while had fitful reached him there
Of Gilbert and of Miriam : lines at first
Written in hope's free hand and symbols fair,
Then by a pen in dubious thoughts immersed,
And, finally, disfigured by despair,
That more betrayed than plain bespoke the worst ;
Blent with recrimination, rage, distrust,
Which railed at all, and paused not to be just.

LVIII

Now Earth, now Heaven, now kings, now crowds, were taxed
With burden of the failure.   France itself,
And its too prosperous sons, had craven waxed,
But caring furtively to count their pelf.
It was the Purple Robe that had relaxed
Their fibre, narrowing to the well-stocked shelf
Their vile affections.   Last, they were betrayed
By their own Chiefs.   And where was Europe's aid ?

LIX

Then Godfrid wrote : " Come back, and be at peace.
You have done all it befits man to do,—
Fought for the faith that 's in you.   But now, cease.
With Miriam quick recross the waters blue,
And we will back, ere yet the years decrease,
Which once seemed many, that now seem so few,
To our dear island home, and there remain,
Loving the land we bled for not in vain."

LX

But still they came not; though the timid Spring
Grew confident, and all the snows were gone,
Even from the clefts.   Louder the birds did sing,
Louder the streams; the sun more broadly shone,
And life was more like life with everything.
But still they came not; and the weeks went on,
And still they came not: till—afoot,—abed,—
Godfrid began to feel a shapeless dread.

LXI

It was the season of the year when he
Felt Reason's reasons useless, and when most
His heart, suffused with sensibility,
Owned fortitude the unproved stoic's boast.
For 'twas the season when he first did see
The face of Olive, mute unwalking ghost
That slept in Florence, but still came between
His thoughts and peace, like waves that sound unseen.

LXII

But, more than this, than all that e'er had been,
Or e'er could be, it was the season bland
When, flying from a world of noise and sin,
His feet had found Spiaggiascura's strand,
Beheld Madonna's chapel, sought to win
Olympia's love, ta'en with her, hand in hand,
That sweet sad journey, then with speechless pain
Left her betwixt the mountains and the main.

LXIII

Once in the winter, as the time came round
To send his yearly gift of gratitude
To those with whom he life and shelter found
After Mentana dire, he thought he would
Be his own envoy.   Through moist streets he wound,
And soon before the Convent portal stood,
With half-owned hope to find, within, some clue
To her, withal he never must pursue.

LXIV

He rang, and loud through corridor unseen
Echoed the peal; making him wince the while
To think that cloister sheltered and serene
He with unbidden clamour should defile.
But quick a novice peeped through grated screen,
Then opened; saying, with a settled smile,
Not on her lips or lids, but, as it were,
All o'er her face, "How can we serve you, sir?"

LXV

"May I the Mother Abbess see?" he said.
"Will it please you, sir, to enter?"   And she straight
Into a spacious whitewashed chamber led,
Where hung but Christ, and left him there to wait.
And by and by the door was openëd,
And came to him with gravely cheerful gait
That Sister reverend who, when erst did cease
His wounds and weakness, bade him go in peace.

LXVI

After obeisance, " Mother," he began,
"What hitherto I sent I here have brought,
To recognise—repay I never can,—
All that you did for me in days distraught."
" My son," she said, "to succour suffering man
Is our dear duty, and you owe us nought.
I take it for our Lord, to Whom we owe
All things.   And it may soothe some sufferer's woe."

LXVII

Then all seemed said, and he was fain to go,
Though loth ; when, taking courage from his fear,
" Forgive me, Mother ! if it be that so
I 'chance transgress ; but have you sister here
Men call Olympia, whom I once did know ? "
" We have," she said ; " a sister very dear."
" And is she well and happy ?   Tell me true ! "
" She is, my son, and daily prays for you."

LXVIII

And then he knew that he must ask no more,
But go ; and with obeisance fresh he went,
Feeling more lone and restless than before,
And more than ever sundered from content.
And whensoe'er he spied a form that wore
That convent's habit, straight his steps he bent,
And, unobserved, glanced quick, in hopes he should
Find her mourned face beneath the modest hood.

LXIX

But never found he the one face he sought,
Though more than once he seemed to recognise
Those who, when lay he as their guest, had brought
Food to his need and comfort to his sighs.
Had he forgotten how she looked? he thought;
Or was he duped by her austere disguise?
Then would he smile, as men, ta'en unawares,
Smile at a thought they had which was not theirs.

LXX

But as he thus more solitary grew,
And anxious more to learn how it might fare
With Gilbert and with Miriam, rumours new
Began to flock and hover in the air,
That what the wise foresaw was coming true,
And that the harlot city, in despair
At her own degradation, up had leapt,
And turned against herself the arms she kept.

LXXI

Thence, before long, authentic tidings came,
Written with Gilbert's hand, and thus they ran:
"Lo! Paris tolls the knell of human shame,
Knell for which time hath yearned since time began.
Not now for kings, priests, soldiers, country, fame,—
Vampires or vainest shadows,—but for Man,
Man too long gaoler of himself, we shake
The wearied limbs of War, and bid them wake.

LXXII

"Paris hath been cajoled, betrayed, by chiefs
That kept one foot in the foe's camp and held
Parley with kings, for fear the People's griefs
Should by her kingless triumph be dispelled.
Their season now hath vanished like the leaf's,
Their sceptre like the rotten trunk lies felled;
Their sycophantic pomp hath joined the dead,
And every crawling parasite hath fled.

LXXIII

"What! back to Capri now! now that the hour
Of centuries' gestation waits its birth!
When Freedom, born in panoply of power,
With godlike brain shall renovate the earth,
And Light, and Right, and all fair things, shall flower!
No! Godfrid! Burst, yourself, convention's girth,
And shed the tatters worn traditions wind
Around the bareness of your shivering mind!

LXXIV

"You want a Faith. Behold the Faith that feeds
The hunger of the heart all else but starves!
Faith that shall dispossess usurping creeds,
Incense, and train of priests, and fatted calves,
Vain supplications for phantasmal needs!—
Faith in Mankind: not faith that feels by halves,
But faith complete, whose dogmas shall redeem
Humanity from its distempered dream!

LXXV

"Fling off the loose impeding folds of doubt,
Standing, tight-mailed, in arms of confidence,
And put the pale Past's gibbering ghosts to rout
That fool you with their shadowy pretence,
And shut the Future's dawning daylight out!"
More still there was, but ever in this sense;
And just one word from Miriam, which but said:
"Come to us, Godfrid, and no more live dead!"

LXXVI

Still walking, as he read it line by line,
Through undistracting Rome, his feet had strayed,
When it was ended, to the Esquiline,
Where, at its summit, the fair Mother-Maid,
Spouse of the Spirit, hath her chiefest shrine,
And on Corinthian column undecayed,
From fane long vanished, with soft-victor shoon
Stands in the hollow of a crescent moon.

LXXVII

'Twas the last day of March, midway between
Noon and slant eve.   The air, the sky, was bland,
Even as She, Protectress of the scene.
Around, beyond, afar as near at hand,
Lopped arch and jaggëd wall with mantle green,
Calm wrecks of world-wide conquest and command,—
These the dumb comment, as his eyes he raised
From Gilbert's sanguine page, and round him gazed.

LXXVIII

"Mankind! Faith! Future!" mournfully he cried,
Folding the letter; "Who shall build new faith
'Mid ruins such as these! The Gods have died,
The beautiful grand Gods, and but their wraith
Haunts the forsaken spot they sanctified.
Empire, Religion, Truth,—all perisheth.
Cæsar hath gone, and Christ seems following fast :
Only our wants and weak deceptions last."

LXXIX

So musing, toward the marble steps he walked
Of the Basilica, and sate him down ;
Where past his mind the long procession stalked
Of vestals, shepherds, wearers of the Crown,
Tribunes and senators, and consuls baulked
Of regal gewgaws by the People's frown,
Pontiffs, and Emperors that mighty were—
Mere voices wailing in the unechoing air.

LXXX

There sate he, as the sunshine slowly died,
While ever and anon, behind his back,
Some one the heavy curtain thrust aside,
And, past him, down the steps took homeward track :
Happier, that they before the Babe Who cried
In Bethlehem had laid life's heavy pack ;
Monk, peasant, mendicant, the halt, the hale,
But all sad-burthened with some human tale.

S

LXXXI

"I too must go," he murmured.   "Unlike those
Who have passed onward, I can nowhere cast
The burden of my weakness and my woes,
Which I, unhelped, must carry to the last."
Just then, once more the heavy curtain rose
Behind him, and adown the steps there passed,
Slowly, the figure of a nun who wore
The habit dear to him for evermore.

LXXXII

He had not seen her face, her aspect, ought
Men would call hers.   But he had staked his soul
It was Olympia! and, as quick as thought,
Sprang forward, and forgetful of control,
Clutched at her robe.   "O you whom I have sought
Along lone course that seemed to have no goal,
Speak to me!   Let me see your face, and hold,
Your hand in mine once more, ere mine grows cold!"

LXXXIII

"Godfrid!"   And paler than the smooth white hood,
Worn where once gleamed her undulating hair,
Glued to the spot by memory, she stood:
She looked into his face, she murmured prayer,
Quick, then exclaimed, as though 'twas all she could,
"Have you the cross?"   "I have," he said, "'tis there!"
His left hand pressed against his heart, his right
Creeping the while near hers, clenched close and tight.

LXXXIV

"I knew it was your hand, Olympia! placed
The cord and cross around my neck; and hence,
'Mid all beside discarded or effaced,
It ne'er hath been, shall ne'er be lifted thence.
But, tell me: from the lone Campagna's waste,
When I lay reft of sword, and strength, and sense,
How did you move and carry me to Rome,
And how conceal me in your Convent home?"

LXXXV

"Ah! if you knew Madonna, would you ask?
When the day dawned, and still you, breathing, slept,
Then I, by her inspired, began to task
My brain to rescue you; and as I stepped
Into the morning air, upon a cask
Of wine-cart from Correse that slow crept
Along the track of the Nomentan way,
Romeward, a half-waked contadino lay.

LXXXVI

"He murmured a good-morrow, and I prayed
That he would halt a moment; and he did.
Whereat I said he would be only paid
By Heaven in doing the task that I should bid.
There was a wounded man must be conveyed
Straightway to Rome, and in his cart be hid.
I too should go, and on the wain would sit,
And, for the rest, that I would see to it."

LXXXVII

Hereat she paused; and he was mute, for woe,
Gazing upon her with blent love and awe.
Her nun's tale told she simply, even as though
Nun she had ever been. But he,—he saw
The free-born girl, that like the bounding roe
Glanced o'er the down or flitted through the shaw,
Beneath whose garb reserved still lurked the wild
Prompt helpful instinct 'of the mountains' child.

LXXXVIII

"Yes, dear?" he said, to end the pause. "And then?"
"Well, then I got upon the wain, whilst he
Walked by his mules to ease their load, and when
None was in sight, I used to peep and see
If still you slept, nor looked like dying men,
And, when I dared, your head and chest left free,
Lifting the straw and sheepskin; though, for fear,
Oft I replaced them when was no one near.

LXXXIX

"Thus slowly crept we on, the heavy wain
Jolting and swaying on the rough-hewn stones,
Making me wince in terror of your pain,
And fancy that I caught your waking groans.
But you lay hushed; and when to the good swain
Fresh groups of soldiers spoke in cheery tones,
Returning his salute or proffering theirs,
I knew Madonna smiled upon my prayers.

XC

"'See now,' I said to him, 'is nought to fear ;
And you your charity will never rue.'
He answered, 'Mary grant it ! Yet 'tis clear
These harm me not because they reverence you.
Ha ! I can tell you, if you were not here,
I should have had to broach for not a few.
But when we reach the Gate, how then ? For there,
Excise-dogs nose and rummage everywhere.'

XCI

"Thus did he warn me in his homely way,
As we drew nearer, nearer still to Rome,
While I could only quiet sit, and pray.
But when the last ascent of all we clomb
That hides the city, and lo ! there it lay
Before us plain, crowned by Saint Peter's dome,
My heart grew most of me, and I began,
Wavering in faith, to frame some human plan.

XCII

"But ere I could devise one, there we were,
There at the Gate ! and, round, a prying band.
Then prompt the peasant said, 'Look here, good sir !'
Addressing him that seemed to have command,
'What must I pay ? There's nothing, I aver,
Save wine-casks,—you can count them with your hand,—
That pays the tax. I have the money here :
Take it, I beg, and give us passage clear.

XCIII

" ' The sister sitting on the cart is pressed
To reach her home.   To help her on her way,
Who helps us others, I my mules distressed,
That have not had or bite or sup to-day,
And crawl half-dead for want of food and rest.
So pray you let us on without delay.'
The which he said with such a simple air,
I did not think they could refuse his prayer.

XCIV

" Withal, the rest began the cart to scale,
While he addressed came over to my side.
' Is it true, good sister?   And will *you* go bail
For this rough yokel's word ? '   I quick replied,
' Yes, he hath told you, sir, an honest tale.
Upon his wine-cart he hath let me ride
Straight from Mentana ; and his wine 's the whole
Of what it bears on which you levy toll.'

XCV

" Then through the city safe we went.   But see,
My sisters I was waiting for come out
Of the Basilica."   He turned ; and three
Who wore Olympia's garb, demure, devout,
The steps descended, two of whom could he
Recall as being of those who moved about
The room where he had helpless lain for hours,
Brought food, smoothed sheet, and changed his faded
        flowers.

XCVI

"This, sister, is the wounded brother who,
Three years ago, was in our Convent nursed."
"O yes, I well remember, do not you?"
Softly replied the nun addressed the first.
"Yes, perfectly," the second; "he that through
The chest was gashed, and could not sleep for thirst."
Then both put questions tenderly, the while
The third looked on with blandly holy smile.

XCVII

Answering, he strove to thank them; feeling, though,
Helpless the while, as feel we when we strive
To bless Heaven for good things. "You doubtless know,
Although I warrant in your useful hive
You work without much buzzing, that I owe
To this sweet Sister I am still alive.
And, never having seen her since that day,
I had so much to ask, so much to say."

XCVIII

"We love her very dearly," said the nun
Who had as yet been silent. "Yes, and now,
She is to leave us," added quick the one
That first had spoken. "Leave you! Leave you how?"
Godfrid exclaimed. "To work elsewhere, my son,"
Rejoined the third. "She but obeys her vow,
And goes where our dear Lady wants her aid
For suffering man. For her, be not afraid.

XCIX

"They need more help in Paris, now that there
Men fight anew, and many die, 'tis said.
She is the only sister we can spare,
And but awaits an escort.   She had led
Hither our steps, to say one parting prayer
Where Mary's worthiest temple rears its head.
But, sir, we must be going.   In the sky
Ave Maria is fast drawing nigh."

C

So he was fain, though loth, to let them go,
Olympia with them; touching not her hand,
But speeding all alike with reverence low:
Feeling like one who lately thought to stand
Within that Gate where Virgins white as snow
Follow the Lamb through the celestial Land,
And then sits dark without, and sees alone
His sinful self, and hears the silence moan.

CI

But when the morrow flushed the summits topped
With statue or with stone-pine, and in street
The noise grew steadier, swift he sped, nor stopped
Till once more at the Convent paused his feet.
There, the same novice the same curtsey dropped,
Led to the same room with same welcome sweet,
Where, at same interval, there crossed the door
The selfsame reverend figure as before.

CII

"Mother!" he said, "I haply yester-eve
Your daughter saw, whom men Olympia call."
"I know you did, my son, with Heaven's good leave,
As told me she herself, who tells me all.
Your interview was timely; for I grieve—
Though in our life such partings oft befall,—
To think she quits us shortly, and but waits
An escort unto France, to leave our gates."

CIII

"Mother!" he gravely said, "why not let me,
Me be her escort? I have close friends twain
In Paris, whom I fain would go and see,
And, be it not too late, snatch back, insane,
From maelstrom into which, no longer free,
Foolish and wise alike seem swirled amain.
Can I not take her, since our bourne is one,
Leaving her where you will, the journey done?

CIV

"I shall remain your debtor to the end,
And thanks must be my ransom. But intrust
To me this treasure, it will I defend
From hurt, as I would keep my sword from rust.
From morn to eve will I her steps attend
As faithfully yet distantly as must
Some dim meek satellite its unreached star,
Following her orbit fondly, but afar!"

CV

"My son!" she said, "so be it.   Nothing loth,
I will commit this jewel without flaw
To you, to her, to Him Who died for both;
Hoping thereby her heavenly track may draw,
Not by the force of wavering human troth,
But by a steadier and diviner law,
The erratic course of your unguided soul
Into its own, and thence to God, its goal.

CVI

"I know each prayer she breathes, each gift doth make
Of her own will before the Throne of Grace,
Each sacrifice of self, each act, each ache,
Each flood of tears before Christ's wounded face,
She breathes, she makes, she offers for your sake.
For you she works; she puts you in the place
Of her own soul; as though, so linked your lot, ›
She too must perish if she saves you not!"

CVII

He strove to speak, but spake not.   Tears, not words,
Choked up the mortal avenues of sense;
And so he silent stood, as one that girds
Will against weakness.   "Come then, three days hence.
And since our claustral matins, like the birds',
Are chanted early, come betimes; though whence
You start, or which the road you take, content
To you I leave."   "I will," he said, and went.

CVIII

And soon the twain were journeying on the sea,
Hearing no more discordant tongues of men,
But only ocean's plastic melody,
With wave attuned to wave, attuned again
To wave, where every wave withal was free.
And, there, before them zigzagged, full in ken,
The road they traversed, in the final stage,
Long years agone, of their vain pilgrimage.

CIX

Full many a little town they could descry,
Passed through of old, and sometimes catch the peal
Of church-bell ringing between slope and sky.
Lo ! there the spot where took they mid-day meal,
And yonder where they did the first night lie.
But up the hills as dusk began to steal,
They saw no more, though sorely did he long
To note where once she sang her even-song.

CX

But when dawn purpled wave and hill once more,
He found Olympia kneeling on the deck,
With gaze intently fastened on the shore,
Where Spiaggiascura shone, a little speck ;
Which, as the vessel ever westward bore,
Past deep smooth creek, past jutting cape and neck
Laced with white foam, still plainer, larger, grew,
Until it stood, its very self, in view.

CXI

Yes! there the little city, and yes, there
The marble chapel straight afront the sea,
Whither he carried her Spring posies fair,
Had heard the humming of the truant bee,
Pale butterflies seen flickering everywhere,
Before Madonna with her bent the knee,
Brought love and ache where all was peace before,
And given his heart away for evermore.

CXII

Straining his gaze, and with the bodily eye
Coupling perchance fond fancy's quick-fooled ken,
Once, twice—there! there!—he thought he could descry
The very beck, the very mountain glen,
Where, while the lark shrilled loud, he saw her try
To reach the tantalising thorn, and then
Atiptoe tried once more, but only shook
Its snow down on herself and on the brook.

CXIII

Quickly he glanced to see if, like to him,
She recognised the first dear place of old.
But she saw nothing now but misty rim
Of tears that down her cheeks slow-trickling rolled,
And, save to her soul's sight, all else was dim:
While he could only stand by and behold,
Speechless, her speechless pain, nor breathe one throe
Of all he felt, to share or soothe her woe.

CXIV

There knelt she, mute and motionless, until
Again Spiaggiascura fainter grew,—
The vessel through the west waves arrowing still,—
Slow dwindled to a speck, then quick to view
Was lost behind a seaward-jutting hill.
Then up she got, and softly near him drew,
While he, scarce knowing what to say, or how,
Asked her who watched Madonna's chapel now.

CXV

"You must not talk to me of that," she said,
"I cannot bear it.   Let us shred some lint,
Whereof will much be needed; or, instead,
You might, so please you, whittle wood for splint,
And I that simpler task, or ply my thread."
So down they sate, offering or taking hint,
And working busily.   But she no more,
That day, cast look or thought toward the shore.

CXVI

Anon she said, "Pray tell me who are those
That have on Paris this dread carnage brought
Anew, and count their own compatriots foes.
They must be very wicked."   Then he thought:
How shall I make her understand the woes
Of either camp, and why the twain have fought,
When even they who scan the horizon wide
Of human passion can but take a side?

CXVII

"Listen!" he said, "and you yourself shall judge
If one or other merely wicked be,
Or if mischance hath haply wreaked its grudge
On both, and forced this joint extremity.
When conscience sees clear, conscience need not budge :
But there are times it cannot clearly see
This way, or that, and then it strives to stand,
Holding an even balance in its hand.

CXVIII

"No easy task, Olympia! even when
The solitary conscience thus is tried.
When conscience shocks with second conscience, then
Where shall we find third conscience to decide?
This is the last perplexity of men,
For which, you know, the red-robed martyrs died,
Men holy deemed have men deemed holy given
To pain and death, unpitied and unshriven.

CXIX

"I hope you do not think me wicked, dear!
Because my conscience jars your conscience so,
That we have been apart this many a year,
Who might have been together." "O no! no!"
Quick, she rejoined. "That, you need never fear.
I always think of you as good, and know,
Whether your conscience be Christ's foe or friend,
His Precious Blood will save you at the end."

CXX

She ceased.   And he made haste not to reply,
For all his soul was trembling.   When he spake,
'Twas with a quivering voice and filmy·eye.
" Sweet words, Olympia, that much mend my ache ;
And I am glad to hear them ere I die.
I would have given up all things for your sake,
Save what none *can* give, yet themselves remain
A gift worth having,—candour without stain.

CXXI

" Yet what a Human Tragedy is here !
We have not clashed on battlefield, but ours,
Pathos, and pain, and many a wasteful tear,
Dropped silent through the barren-moving hours.
Tragic enough ! when one, that one holds dear,
Buds not, despite love's coaxing sun and showers !
But we, though one, keep two, for conscience' sake,
Not dying sooth, but living at the stake.

CXXII

" There was no help,—there now can be no cure.
Withal, who stanched my wounds and bathed my brow ?
Who, if not you, the pitiful, the pure,
Forgetting all except compassion's vow ?
Yet, as before the Cause that can allure
Service like yours I bow my head, allow,
Allow, Olympia !—for indeed 'tis true—
That they with whom I served were upright too.

CXXIII

"See then, my child, the Tragedy, and see
What feeds it.   Love, Religion, Country, all
That deepest, dearest, most enduring be,
That make us noble, and that hold us thrall,—
Once gone, the beasts were no more gross than we,—
'Tis these for which the victims fastest fall,
Man's self, in days that are as days that were,
Suppliant alike and executioner !

CXXIV

"Now once again this Tragedy, this jar
Of conscience against conscience, hath, meseems,
In Paris struck the lurid light of war.
Haply, they slay for straws, they die for dreams.
But things that seem must still be things that are
To half-experienced man, who perforce deems
He doth not dream, but knows not, nor can know,
Till death brings sleep or waking, is it so.

CXXV

"Another dream, another watchword 'tis,
This strident Commune shrills upon the wind,
Which to it Love, Religion, Country, is,—
Level Equality for all Mankind.
Hence once again the man-made bullets whiz
'Gainst man man-made.   I can but lag behind,
Sceptic, yet see withal the dupes that die
For falsest faith are somewhat more than I !"

CXXVI

Thus mournfully he spoke ; then slowly she :
"I think I understand.   But tell me why
Are not the poor content still poor to be,
Since mainly 'twas for them that Christ did die ?
And equal ?   What is equal ?   Are not we
All equal in the great Superior's eye ?
Are they not blest that weep and suffer wrong ?
And is it not peril to be rich and strong ?"

CXXVII

Out of another world they seemed to come,
These humble words and doctrines obsolete ;
So that their very strangeness made him dumb.
"Alas !" he said at length.   "You but repeat
Saws long rejected by mankind ; though some
Still mumble them, when gasp they toward the seat
Of wealth, or place, or power, as boys bear
Pebbles within their mouth, to faster fare.

CXXVIII

"Yours, dear, the teaching I myself did learn,
When on my upraised gaze my mother's shone.
I find none better wheresoe'er I turn,
None truer, fitter ; but 'tis gone, clean gone.
Men will not have it so.   The candid spurn,
The hypocrite ignore, what children con
Only to find it fable.   'Tis a world,
Where Christ's meek banner longwhile hath been furled.

T

CXXIX

"Man stands upon the hilltops in the dawn,
With veiling mists below him; and he sees
Only the Heaven of Heavens sublimely drawn
Above his ken, and blue immensities.
Slow melt the mists; then, comely breadths of lawn,
Forests, and lakes, and many-pastured leas,
Cities and herds of people, labour, mirth,
He scans, and all the kingdoms of the earth.

CXXX

"O gorgeous vision! dazzling wonderland!
Swift he descends to share it.   Then he hears
Sounds that at first he scarce can understand,
Discord, and taunt, and dismal drip of tears;
Love sobbing with her fresh gift in her hand,
Because none takes; menace, reproaches, jeers;
Greed munching refuse, jealous to repel;
And melancholy toll of funeral bell.

CXXXI

"Then, desolate of heart, he deems it best
To reascend the hilltops; and he goes,
With gaze upon the ground and panting breast.
But, as he mounts, mists round him once more close;
And when he turns to see if from the crest
Earth still looks fair, it blurred and doubtful grows;
While now in heaven glooms something dark afar,
Only, with here and there a flickering star."

CXXXII

He ceased ; and ceased the swishing of the wave,
Which to the end accompanied his speech.
Furled were the sails, and mute the vessel drave,
Through folds of still smooth water, to the beach.
Olympia to the crew blest rosaries gave,
While Godfrid had a word and vail for each,
As stood they, honest sea-folk, cap in hand.
And then the pair were softly rowed to land.

CXXXIII

And soon on roaring lungs through burrows black
They were being swiftly borne ; past towering crags
That seemed to frown on their presumptuous track,
And whither, save the chamois' or the stag's,
No foot hath ever clambered and come back ;
Past gentler cliffs where waved the iris-flags,
And vineyard terraces, that catch the blaze
Of the south sun, with pastures at their base.

CXXXIV

Then imperceptibly the mountains waned
To hills, the gorges unto valleys spread,
The valleys out to plains, and nought remained
Of that fair Italy from which they fled.
Nature grew less, man more, and use profaned
The bare-stripped homes of beauty, as they sped
Past populous cities, level stretch of fields,
Blank as the desert save for what it yields.

CXXXV

Thus all one day they journeyed, all one night,
Halting but seldom, and with brief delay :
Noting at first,—to both familiar sight,—
The kepi-ed umpires of Mentana's fray,
That changed at length to leathern helmets bright.
Whereat Olympia asked him, " Who be they?"
" These are," he said, " who late from France's hand
Struck sword, and now for ransom hold the land."

CXXXVI

Thence onward saw they sentries none but these,
Then scattered groups of comrades, next close files,
Last, armies, bivouacked 'neath boughs of trees,
Along straight road that seemed to stretch for miles.
Then Godfrid said : " That Paris is, one sees
Where lights begin to twinkle in long aisles.
We shall be there ere long." And, just as night
Mastered the day, they halted, to alight.

CXXXVII

Straight to her bourne, through many a dim-lit street,
Her he conducted, till at length they stood
Before its portal. Then for journey sweet
He thanked her, adding that he promptly should
Unto the Convent bend anew his feet,
To see the Mother of the sisterhood.
Then the gate opened ; and she, paler grown,
Passed in, and he was in the street alone.

CXXXVIII

Then quick his steps he bent through narrow ways,
Built in the times when grew up side by side
Palace and hovel, and in all men's gaze
Sleek splendour feasted while lean misery died,
To those famed thoroughfares, with lights ablaze,
Far-stretching, vast, monotonous in pride,
Imperial ædiles framed, to baulk the claws
Of Freedom, and replace its ravished laws.

CXXXIX

But siege, and sordid famine, and the yoke
Of foeman's fork, humiliation, rage
At turncoat Fortune's contumelious stroke,
Iconoclastic group, had swept the stage
Of pasteboard pomp; and erst where harlot folk,
Train-bearing eunuchs to a sensual age,
Pandars, and purple parasites that glut
Their maw with slaver, used to swarm and strut;

CXL

And lustful song and jest obscene passed round,
And sexless things, with faces falsely fresh,
And cold limbs feigning wantonness, were crowned
By senile satyrs, as they wove the mesh
Of palsy premature o'er young and sound,
Ere haggling for the price of rented flesh;
While jingling gold, and sniggering mock, and gird
At God and man, in unison were heard;—

CXLI

Hence now had sneaked the comfortable crew;
Or if one slunk along with eyes askance,
He strove to make him viewless to the view,
And, crawling to his hole, there bide till chance
The days for warm-furred vermin should renew.
There was no light lewd song, no pornic dance.
The streets seemed half-ashamed and half-aghast,
And night's sparse lamps blinked drowsy as he passed.

CXLII

What few here held the ways were those whose tramp
Held it as victors: proletarian hordes,
Wealth in its jealous terror strives to cramp
Within the limits penury affords;
Driving them back to their own barbarous camp
With the unsteady aid of hireling swords,
Or coaxing them with golden bounties lest
They should swarm down, and rudely seize the rest.

CXLIII

But these had broken through the flimsy line
Of strained Civilisation, and now strode,
Grim apparitions,—with its dainties fine
And gauds abandoned making their abode,
And littering all the spot, like bristly swine,
Where lately lay its lapdogs snugly stowed;
And twisting to stern need of force and fear
Its gilded toys, soft beds, and silken gear.

CXLIV

These ever and anon his footsteps stayed,
With short sharp challenge.   Whereupon he told
His simple tale, and asked if they could aid
His search for friends who fought within their fold.
Some bade him pass; some churlish answer made,
Some courteous; none gave tidings that consoled.
And fitful throat afar from sleepless bed
Bellowed, and whistling missile burst o'erhead.

CXLV

Some scanned him with suspicious, hateful eyes,
Since in each lineament, soft-curving jaw,
Lithe gait, fair garb, slow questions, calm replies,
Hands that ne'er grasped or trowel, file, or saw,
A son of those cursed sires they viewed, whose cries
Of need or menace to their sires were law,
In days when these drew water and hewed wood,
And men to men denied their brotherhood.

CXLVI

And some, lest they should smite him, turned on heel,
And spat a curse upon the ground; while some
Pushed him aside with curt retort of steel.
Whereat, for very sadness, he was dumb;
Well knowing in his heart that he could feel
Most wofully for woe, past or to come,
And the sole privilege he prized or sought
Was power to cure the wrongs that others wrought.

CXLVII

At length one,—then another,—then a third,—
Sware to have seen them : a most goodly pair,
She lustrous-dark as plume of ebon bird,
He blond, robust, with grizzled beard and hair.
But nought of either had they seen or heard,
Since Paris, first aroused, had from its lair
Burst out, on myrmidon of priest and king
Leaping, to rend, and—curse on it !—missed its spring.

CXLVIII

Further, none helped him.   But, desisting not,
Still to his search he eachwhere craved reply ;
Till he was greeted by a scowling knot
With "See his Teuton face !   A spy !   A spy !"
Whereat armed rabble shuffled to the spot,
And loud reviled him.   But with quiet eye
And front he scanned them, as in Delian wood
Apollo 'mong the satyrs might have stood.

CXLIX

To base gesticulation, wordy spite,
Mute he remained, and but surveyed them still
From the lone perch of sorrow's fearless height :
Affronting by confronting them, until,
Like hounds that egg each other on to bite
By barking, clamour giving heart to kill,
Closer they hemmed him, and, ferocious made
By their own throats, their hands upon him laid.

CL

Then because blood heats quickly, he, unarmed,
Flashed them aside, and as the foremost fell,
The rest shrank back that lately round him swarmed,
And clear he stood, still ready to repel.
Yet not for long his mien their rage had charmed,
But that more swift than pen or tongue can tell,
One bustled to the front, and ere the crowd
Could set its teeth afresh, exclaimed aloud :

CLI

"Hold, citizens !   This man is Freedom's friend,
Of English stock, no Teuton, and no spy.
I saw him at Mentana rout and rend
The Pope-King's wolves.   You doubt it ?   Well then, try!"
Then turning quick to Godfrid, "Pray, sir, lend
Best confirmation that I do not lie.
Show them your breast !   I know the foeman's steel
There gashed a rent that ne'er will wholly heal."

CLII

"Good comrade !" Godfrid said, "I scarce recall
Your Southern face ; yet what you say is so,
And yours the land I have loved best of all,
After my own.   My breast I need not show.
The thrust you speak of when you saw me fall,
Hath left its brand.   Enough for these to know
I say it ; and what wounds I feel or felt,
Fighting for Freedom, their compatriots dealt."

CLIII

"Not ours!" they loud protested, timely shame
Awaking chivalry; "not Frenchmen those,
No countrymen of ours!   And in the name
Of France we hail you friend and them as foes.
But since for you hath Freedom's mountain flame
Once served for rousing beacon, how is it glows
Its watchfire now in vain, and that you stand,
There, with no answering weapon in your hand?

CLIV

"See! arms here are!   Quick! don them, and come fight
For Cause far purer than you yet have known,
That of Mankind and Universal Right!"
But he forbore to take them, and with tone,
Strange contrast unto theirs, said, "Would I might!
But if I cannot make your thoughts my own,
How can I, honest, share your sword, and strike,
For striking's sake, at foe and friend alike?

CLV

"Forgive me!   I to neither camp belong.
For, brothers mine, I fear you miss your way,
Aiming at too much right through too much wrong."
"Pah! 'tis a casuist," some began to say;
"Wails with the weak, but battens with the strong,
And takes a brief alike from night and day:"
While others sneered, "Do whelps belie their bed?
Look at his smooth white hands and dainty head!"

CLVI

Upon the morrow, fourth day from the eve
He for Olympia had her Convent found,
Thither once more, no longer loth to leave
A plainly bootless quest, he gravely wound.
But now he wore, conspicuous round his sleeve,
A blood-red Cross upon a snow-white ground;
Emblem and shield, through fratricidal fray,
Of those who stanch the blood they cannot stay.

CLVII

There it was ordered he should daily come,
Soon after sunrise, to the Convent yard,
Where, of the sisters, were there always some
Ready to start for rampart, gate, or ward.
And henceforth, every morn, at roll of drum,
With them he sallied forth, a constant guard,
Doing their hests till fire and fight grew slack
At dusk, then led them to their cloister back.

CLVIII

Oftenest Olympia came, and with her one,
Now two, now more, but not unoft alone,
Since that, in pairs, the work could best be done;
And thus, ere long, it had to custom grown
They should together start at rise of sun,
Together find the spot where gash and moan
Craved pity's presence most, together learn
To-morrow's post, together should return.

CLIX

Oftenest their steps were bent—since loudest there
Was heard the awakening cannon's surly sound,—
Along the way presumptuous fribbles dare
To call Elysian, past the boastful ground
Where slaughter's storied Arch confronts the air,
And splendour's palaced alleys radiate round,
That house new wealth's gross pomp and surfeit sleep,
Onward to Neuilly's gate and Maillot's sweep.

CLX

And there, 'mid hiss of shell, and quick hot hail
That was its own unwarning messenger,
Oft minding of Mentana's closing tale,
Godfrid moved active, followed still by her
As by wan shadow; she composed but pale,
He flushed, as one whom curbed-in instincts spur,
And whose majestic port seemed far more fit
To lead to carnage than to wait on it.

CLXI

At times a sullen unexpected lull
On the demoniac din awhile would fall,
Fierce-baying fort growl low, and then wax dull,
And rifle-rattle cease from ditch and wall.
Then Godfrid and Olympia, glad to cull
A passing respite from the thick of brawl,
As in the happier days, their wallet shared
Under some new-leafed tree rage yet had spared.

CLXII

Then, seizing the brief chance, the birds would sing
Their love-song in the branches of young May,
And round the cannon's jaw and cold bright ring,
Grimly reposing, butterflies would play,
Sipping the sun, at peace with everything.
The fume of mortal fury rolled away,
Leaving the blue heaven bare, till half-closed eyes
Might deem the earth as happy as the skies.

CLXIII

And Godfrid, pointing through the shimmering air,
Shimmering and still, would say, " Look, sister mine !
Doth Mont Valérien, perched up peaceful there,
Not mind you often of the Aventine?
One well might deem it, too, a hill of prayer.
Il Priorato's convent wall, the shrine
Of Sant' Alessio, and—there ! leftward, see
Sabina's Church, with Dominic's lemon-tree ! "

CLXIV

But, as he pointed, lo ! quick puff of smoke,
And, in it, for an instant, flash of light,
And loud the claustral-seeming fortress spoke,
Bellowing its summons to renew the fight.
Then straight each dozing throat of war awoke,
And hoarse bayed back ; while muskets' mongrel spite,
At the big war-dogs' signal to begin,
With short sharp yaps accompanied the din.

CLXV

Then Godfrid and Olympia started up,
As May's sweet birds crouched silent, prompt to lend
Once more the helping hand, the timely cup.
But when day's ending brought awhile to end
This daily rage, and, homeward bound to sup,
Would the unwounded in disorder wend,
As each one willed, he oft sought news again
Of Gilbert, questioning knots of armèd men.

CLXVI

One eve when fight had even fiercer been
Than its fierce wont, and vantage had been gained
At point the assailants long had strained to win,
A stripling, with the day's work smoked and stained,
Of Gascon speech, blue eye, and tawny skin,
Hearing him put the question some disdained,
Some could not answer, forward pushed, and said,
" That pair are with the captive or the dead.

CLXVII

" Stalwart, intrepid, fair,—I mind them well,
And saw them with these eyes, that morn accurst,
When, ruin-lured by treachery or by hell,
We from yet open city pell-mell burst
To strangle wrong. Know you where Flourens fell,
Gay, gallant Flourens, of the foremost first ?
There, in the river's bend I saw them both,—
Have seen not since."   Then with a guttural oath,

CLXVIII

Which every throat around took up;—a deep
Chorus of curses,—"You may stay your search,"
He laughed aloud; "they have been drugged to sleep
With leaden dose, their backs against a church."
Then others growled: "Why on your left arm keep
That tame badge, leaving vengeance in the lurch?
Grasp with the right, man! if you want to aid,
Not the smooth scalpel, but the jaggëd blade."

CLXIX

Thereat he turned away, and strode along,
She at his side; both, though perturbed with fear,
Striving with help of silence to be strong.
But when they reached the Convent, and could hear
The nuns within, singing the even-song,
He stopped, and gravely said: "To-morrow, dear,
I cannot come with you. I must pass out
Straight to Versailles, to solve this dreadful doubt."

CLXX

Just then a half-intoxicated band
Trolled by, and mocked her with a gesture foul,
She saw not, seeing would not understand,
And passed within. But Godfrid, with a scowl
Of startled ire and ready-flashing hand,
Rolled two in mire; whose comrades with a growl
Of sottish rage their pieces cocked and raised
Against him and each other, drunk and dazed.

CLXXI

Swift as the lightning leaps from unguessed sheath,
A blade was flashed on high, then swooping down,
Scaring and scattering backward those beneath,
Swept space for Godfrid, while each stumbling clown
Muttered a muzzy curse betwixt his teeth.
"Away, ye sots! ye blots on our renown!
Is this a time to hiccup and carouse?
Hence home! and hide in sleep your shameless brows!"

CLXXII

Cowed, they slunk off; and, before Godfrid, stood
Gilbert and Miriam both! both, quick embraced
In the wide-opening arms of brotherhood:
One closely curved round Miriam's nestling waist,
She the while babbling all the joy she could,
The other upon Gilbert's shoulder placed
With firm fond grip; each gazing upon each,
But all alike yet mendicants for speech.

CLXXIII

But Godfrid first found words to tell his tale,
Quickly as words could say it: how he came
Thither from Italy with prosperous sail,
Olympia's escort, cherishing the aim
To find them, but till then without avail;
How he felt sure, since none had heard their name,
They had gone homeward,—till that eve, he said,
News he had heard, to fear them ta'en or dead.

CLXXIV

" No fabled news !   Your Gascon lad spoke true.
We but an hour ago repassed the wall
From which we sallied forth, a motley crew,
A wasted month since.   We saw Flourens fall.
My turn came next, though I was but struck through
The foot and lamed.   But we contrived to crawl
Among thick river-canes, and, crouched from sight,
There passed a dripping day and famished night.

CLXXV

" Neither upon the morrow might we move ;
For we could hear the foe's feet all around,
Prowling through copse and brushwood-bank, to prove
If living thing still lurked upon the ground :
And oft would bullet cleave a clean straight groove
Through the dense cane-stems with a swishing sound,
We lying close, and praying, scarcely loth,
The ball that found out one would find out both.

CLXXVI

" On the third morning we no more heard steel
Beating the covert ; but we still lay close.
For I was helpless yet with smarting heel,
And with long hunger numb and comatose.
Then Miriam crept along, and scraped a meal
From field hard by, of roots and refuse gross,—
What she could find,—and thus for two days more,
What flesh and blood at bay can bear, we bore.

U

CLXXVII

"But what an endless tale ! as long as were
Those nights and days that came, withal, to end.
Now, thanks once more to Miriam's craft and care,
And subtle help of friend succeeding friend,
I hale am yet again, and here to share
Defence's bitter dregs, or, should Heaven send
New hope to our extreme, with breast as meet
To swim to victory as to stem defeat.

CLXXVIII

" Plague on the long-lost weeks, wherein I lay
At Suresnes, then at Courbevoie, hearing still
The cannon bellow and the bugle bray,
My weakness chafing hourly at my will.
I convalescent days since, but to-day
We slipped the lines, and more by luck than skill ;
For though the bloodhounds failed to do us hurt,
They put their fangs, you see, through Miriam's skirt."

CLXXIX

" A tasteless morsel ! " Miriam laughing said,
Spreading the riddled folds ; as Godfrid drew
Her arm through his, and, Gilbert following, led
Along the pavement, trodden now by few,
To his own hearth.   "Come, I have board and bed
For both, if rough ; not rough perhaps to you,
My dauntless Miriam, and your wounded wight.
Come, Gilbert !   You are mine, at least to-night."

CLXXX

Thus as they strolled, he sought, in leisured walk,
To scan both closely, but the while to hide
His anxious scrutiny with cheerful talk :
Fancying, withal, in Gilbert he descried
A generous plant which, flowering, runs to stalk,
A lavish stream whose bed is wellnigh dried
By its too copious flowing, a quick fire
Burnt by the very wind of its desire.

CLXXXI

He looked a nobler and completer type
Of those one saw around; who, since that he
Was nobler, could more keenly feel the stripe
Of contumelious destiny, and be
For madness and for misery yet more ripe :
Like them, by war, and want, and gloomy glee
Of vain resistance, famine, failure, hate,
Fevered to fiery point prescribed by Fate.

CLXXXII

She was less changed, and change in her had wrought
But summer's growth of loveliness ; for though
Her steps had been with those that frenzied fought,
Hers still was woman's work ; to come or go,
As Gilbert swayed.   And so she had but caught
From this weird hour the purple-crimson glow
That comes upon dark streams when red suns set,
And day and night at twilight tryst have met.

CLXXXIII

Once round his board, them craftily he strove
To lead in thought towards Italy, with speech
Which, momentary theme eschewing, wove,
Far-off but well within affection's reach,
A glowing tale of how the dear land throve,
But hinting how it needed still from each,
Who loved it still, exclusive heart and soul ;—
Keeping it wholesome, having made it whole.

CLXXXIV

Close-watching if their blood were taking fire,
In hers he marked infection wax apace,
And saw her glance at Gilbert to inquire
His thought.   But he, like one that lends his face,
But hath elsewhere his ear and his desire,
Sate cold as listening statue in his place :
Whereat the warm flush faded from her cheek ;
Then Godfrid knew that he in vain would speak.

CLXXXV

So still avoiding discord and distress,
He lured discourse, with subtly-wandering wing,
To ruins softened by the sun's caress ;
Saying at length : "Will you, dear Miriam, sing
One of those songs of love and simpleness,
Such as in happy Capri often ring
Up goat-browsed cleft?"   Whereat, without stringed aid,
In her own tongue she sang this serenade.

1

Sleep ! lady fair !
O but thy couch should be
The fleeciest cloudlet of the summer air,
The softest billow of the summer sea,
Or that unforsaken nest
I keep warm within my breast,
For thee, for thee !

2

Dream, lady sweet !
The moon and planets bright
Now thread thy slumber with unsounding feet,
Now lure thy fancy with unshaped delight :
As my spirit fain would steep
Thine, when only half asleep,
This night, this night !

3

Wake, lady mine !
See ! are awake the flowers,
Their chalices begemmed with dewy wine,
And, buoyed on song, the moist lark trills and towers.
Wake ! If thou must be away,
Nightly, let at least the day
Be ours, be ours !

CLXXXVI

Discordant with the gently closing notes,
A swelling roar of demon music stormed
The night without, growled by a thousand throats,
Hoarse, hirsute, ragged, in armed phalanx formed
Round wain designed for autumn's sickled oats,
Now piled with human forms life lately warmed,
Death-blanched and bloodless, swaying with each jar,
And jolted by each jolt, of the rude car.

CLXXXVII

And, guttering in the smoked air, torches flared
Upon their upturned faces; clotted beard,
Limp necks, dead-weighted arms, and breasts half-bared,
Feet with the blood they fell and died in smeared,
And lidless eyes that saw not but still stared,—
Blind-orbed, mute-mouthed, dull-nostrilled, and deaf-eared:
While, with notes deep as sullen-sounding surge,
The tramping mourners trolled a vengeful dirge.

CLXXXVIII

Thus o'er the stony street the exposed dead,
Dirged by the living, vengeful moved along:
Godfrid with folded arms and downcast head,
Gilbert, stern-hearkening to the chanted wrong,
Miriam, heart-torn 'twixt sympathy and dread,
Each gazing down upon the marching throng.
Which passed, they nothing said, since each one guessed
The other's thought, and straight retired to rest.

CLXXXIX

And ever narrower closed the iron ring
Around the city, stronger, as it shrank ;
To desperation's ever-shortening spring
Presenting stouter barrier, front and flank.
One gap there was : but this the Teuton King
Held for his own, and with the sabre's clank,
Valid as though 'twere waved on high to strike,
Warned off besiegers and besieged alike.

CXC

And Godfrid and Olympia, still close-bound
By their and others' sorrow, moved intent
On lulling anguish wheresoe'er 'twas found,
And finding it, alas ! where'er they went.
For slaughter seemed to spring from out the ground,
And wounds and wailing from some secret vent
Of Heaven down-poured : their wedded help, withal,
Not spent but strengthened by woe's constant call.

CXCI

Now scared no longer by the bellowing quake
Of fulgurating smoke, in gardened street
Bold birds descanted gleeful pipe and shake,
And you could catch their love-notes 'twixt the beat
Of hatred's feverish pulse. Syringa's flake,
Laburnum's golden chains, the lilac's sweet,
Hanging unheeded o'er each vacant bench,
Mingled their perfume with war's sulphurous stench.

CXCII

"O that we were in some moist Alpine valley,"
Loud, once in momentary lull, he sighed,
" Where orchards bloom, and runnels swift that sally
From far-up cleft in sheltering mountain side
Trip smiling past the door of pine-wood châlet ;
Where cattle-bells make music far and wide,
Where pale-blue crocuses the green meads dapple,
And I could build you, dear, another chapel."

CXCIII

"O yes !" she cried.   " Or rather that we were
Back, back at Spiaggiascura !   'Tis, you know,
The Month of Mary, and is no one there
To give her of the round thorn's blossoming snow,
To scour the hill for cyclamens, to bear
Jonquil, and rose, and all sweet things that blow,
To her immaculate feet, and never cease
Importuning her ears for love and peace.

CXCIV

" But this will soon be over, will it not ?"
Gravely she asked.   " Yes, very soon !" he said.
And as he said it, through his heart there shot
The unhallowed thought that when no more the dead
And dying linked his life with hers, his lot
Would be once more his widowed world to tread
Alone, without her ! and it then required
All virtue's will to wish the strife expired.

CXCV

"And those you love?" she added. "What of *them*?"
Meaning thereby, as well he understood,
Gilbert and Miriam. "I as lief might stem,"
He answered sadly, "ocean at its flood,
As them withstand. Yet, let us not condemn.
They think they die for human brotherhood.
So far, their lives seemed charmed." "Heaven grant they may
Still be!" she said. "For both, our Sisters pray."

CXCVI

She face to face with neither had been brought,
Since that he daily studied to evade,
With false male instinct, meeting none had sought,
And, happening, woman's tact had simple made.
Yet kept he closest watch where Gilbert fought
And Miriam followed, by the trusty aid
Of eyes well paid, and bound, by orders curt,
To seek him straight, should either suffer hurt.

CXCVII

Beneath his roof he held them, keeping now
From vain expostulation. But, one night,
Gilbert the moment absent, Miriam's brow,
Temples, and cheek, turned suddenly as white
As dark waves sundered by a surging prow;
And with a cry that stifled seemed by fright,
And hands stretched out to help the eyes that fail,
She swooned upon the ground, and lay there pale.

CXCVIII

By her he knelt, and on her bloodless face
Dashed water, till she opened wide her eyes,
And murmuring it was needless to unlace
Her bodice now, for she should shortly rise,
Vowed, " It is but the strangeness of the place,
Some need of mountain air, of native skies.
Now lift me up; it will be over soon;
And tease not Gilbert with this foolish swoon.

CXCIX

" You will not,—will you?   'Twould but harass more
His heart already harassed overmuch.
Promise me, Godfrid !   Promise, I implore !"
And she besought him so with voice and touch,
And eyes with tearful pathos brimming o'er,
That he, but vulnerable stuff to such,
To give the asked-for pledge was feeling fain,
When a suspicion flashed across his brain.

CC

Why this importunate violence of fear ?
Why thus so anxiously his help discard ?
And whence that swoon, more fit for luxury's sphere,
In one stern-nurtured as the hawk or pard ?
" Miriam !" he said, " you ought not to be here !
For you have now another life to guard.
Answer me straight !   You solitary bear
A sacred secret Gilbert ought to share !"

CCI

Again the paleness of the sky-peaks' snow
Spread o'er her face an instant, ere it took
The crimson flush they wear at sunset's glow;
And she exclaimed, with supplicating look,
"You will not tell him? For he must not know!
Promise me, Godfrid! Oh! I could not brook
To clog his stroke just as we near Fate's shore.
Can you not wait? You see 'twill soon be o'er!"

CCII

That instant Gilbert entered, with a gaze
Which, fixed on far-off anguish, noted not
Pallor and pain in life's familiar ways,
And in the world's woe home distress forgot;
And, ere from horror's dizzying amaze
Godfrid his thoughts could steady, from the spot,
Saying, "Come, Miriam! deepens now the fight;"
Had with her passed into the hurtling night.

CCIII

But when they had gone, and Godfrid nought could hear
Save hungry boom of death, then left alone
With his own self and formless ghosts of fear,
He fancied in each gust of battle blown
Over the roof by echoing atmosphere,
To catch now Gilbert's cry, now Miriam's groan,
Or in the rattling pane and quaking street
To hear the scamper of their flying feet.

CCIV

Outward he rushed, unterrified by such,
For terror in his heart : his one sole thought,
Amid the crackling hurricane, to touch
The barrier where he knew that Gilbert fought ;
To search it, force his way to front, and clutch
The arm that should be sheltering her it brought
Full face to face with death, and shame the sire,
Since deaf the husband, from its jaws of fire.

CCV

But as he reached the point he strained for, lo !
Defence had vanished from it, and it stood
Naked to night, empty of friend and foe,
Horribly silent as some haunted wood.
Aghast he paused ; then, turning quick to go,
Though without thought or purpose whither should
His feet next fly, by something lying prone
Across his path, was tripped, and forward thrown.

CCVI

He fell upon his hands in warm wet slop,
That splashed up in his face and neck, and sprawled
At first he scarce knew where, then lay atop
Of that which threw him ; but, as back he crawled,
Placing one hand upon it for a prop,
Wherewith to raise himself, he felt, appalled,
A human form beneath his touch, whose clothes
Got with his own entangled as he rose.

CCVII

Then, touch befooling sight to see, he thought
That in that tumbled heap he plain could trace
The figure of the combatant he sought,—
The arm, the hand, the head, the hair, the face.
And, fumbling in his pouch, he struck, distraught,
A fearful light, which, fluttered by the pace
At which he lowered it through the air, went out,
Leaving him once again in dark and doubt.

CCVIII

So this time carefully he knelt him down
Hard by the face ere striking light, which then
Flashed suddenly upon the visage brown
Of—no, not Gilbert! but, scanned close again,
Of a poor, low-browed, famished-featured clown,
Lying as he might lie with reaping men
At mid-day meal; a face which, though unknown,
Through death seemed kindred and familiar grown.

CCIX

With thankful gasp he scrambled from his knees,
And, at that moment, the short match burnt out;
Yet not before he saw, quick as one sees
Landscape by lightning, dotted thick about,
Dead shapes of men, like felled but unbarked trees:
Whereat instinctively he gave a shout,
Listening for answer. But came no reply,
Of living groan or dying agony.

CCX

Then he paused silently among the dead,
Transfixed there by the scene which he could see
More plainly for the darkness, and by dread
Stamped on his brain for ever instantly.
When hark ! he thought, he heard a shuffling tread,
Then saw a shifting light that seemed to be
Coming anear him slowly ; so he cried
Aloud once more, and a man's voice replied.

CCXI

And moving toward the light, the light towards him,
He met a wizened thing, blear, hunchback, spare,
One of wealth's pariahs, who, when night grows grim,
In to-day's offal for to-morrow's fare
Grope with a pointed stick and lantern dim.
Him foul, with fairest words, he begged to bear
The link before him, so that one by one
He might the corpses scan, omitting none.

CCXII

Then picking through the dead his way, he bent
Over each body, and with dread renewed
At each fresh trial, while that other lent
Careless his light, the wan blank faces viewed,
Fearfully searching every lineament,
Lest death had chance the well-known look imbued
With its own strangeness ; and, at times, again
Stooping, to make more certain of his ken.

CCXIII

But terror found not what it sought, and thence,
Hastily dropping guerdon, straight he fled,
With horror at his heels, each separate sense
Sharpened to keen acquaintance with the dead.
Nor paused he till he reached the portal whence
His steps had started; mounting, with new dread,
To his own hearth, lest haply he should there
Find waiting summons, to make doubt despair.

CCXIV

There found he line from Miriam, saying, "I send
This line by messenger,—a last farewell;
For we are face to face now with the end.
How yet we live unscathed, I cannot tell;
Brought finally to bay, our ranks defend.
The routed Commune's topmost citadel,
At Belleville, compassed round by foe that gives
Nothing but death to anything that lives.

CCXV

"Seek for our bodies, claim them if you may,
Gilbert's and mine, and for the love you bore
Unto us both, across the bright blue bay
Row them, yourself, back unto Capri's shore,
And within hearing of the murmuring spray
Make us a grave; and see you strew it o'er
Sometimes with flowers from Tuoro Grande's brow.
I never loved you, brother, more than now."

CCXVI

Again he hurried outward, hope and dread
Lending joint wings.   But as into the street,
He passed, he heard his name by some one said,
And, close behind, the sound of hastening feet.
Turning, he saw Olympia!   "Oh! not dead!
Not dead!" she cried, with rapture that was sweet
Unto his ear even in that bitter hour,
Asserting 'mid worst woe love's lasting power!

CCXVII

"Dead?   No, dear love!" he with prompt lips replied,
And arms instinctively outstretched to fold
Her form to his, then sudden to his side
Dropped mindful, empty, reverently cold.
"But why, Olympia! deemed you I had died?"
He asked, in accents tender, but less bold.
"Because you did not come to me," she said,
"And so I thought you must indeed be dead."

CCXVIII

Again love's swift electric current ran
From the heart's battery to the moving hands,
Tingling to fondle.   But, man checked by man,
Flesh paused, the noble serf of soul's commands.
"I did not come to you, because you can
Do nothing more," he said.   "Infuriate bands
Nor see nor spare.   I felt, 'mid rage like theirs,
That you, dear child, were better at your prayers.

CCXIX

"For me there is one office left, and then
I to your Convent will repair.   For see!
Gilbert with Miriam in defeat's last den
Are close shut in, and from it cannot flee,
Even if they would; their comrades desperate men,
Who nor to earth nor Heaven would bend the knee,
And whom their foes, now biding vengeance' tryst,
Would slay, if clung they to the skirt of Christ!"

CCXX

"Then let us go there straight!" she said, "and save!
It was for this Madonna sent me here.
Can we not start at once?"   But he, the brave,
The unshrinking, cried with pallid lips of fear,
"My child! I cannot take you to your grave!
You must not come.   I hold you far too dear."
"Not go where *you* go!" solemnly she said:
"*I* must live safe, *you* perilled,—perhaps dead!

CCXXI

"O Godfrid! I have lived without you long,
And shall live ever thus, while yet I live;
But it was Heaven's promise made me strong,
That when earth's refuse should have run the sieve,
And nought remain but spirit, for the wrong
Love here hath suffered, love beyond would give
Eternal compensation!   If it be
You now face death, you face it must with me!"

X

CCXXII

"Come then!" he said, fear now extinct. "Come quick!
Each step is precious!" Then up streets they wound,
Where slaughter of its own work had grown sick,
And dreadful silence followed dreadful sound.
Men's doors were closed; but now and then the click
Of latch was heard, and head, sly glancing round,
Protruded for a moment, quickly then
Withdrawn, and latch dropped noiselessly again.

CCXXIII

But as they got up higher, barricade,
Empty, except of the unnoticed dead,
Abandoned rifle and unwielded blade,
Grew thicker, and the ways more blocked to tread.
And shortly, trim battalions, on parade,
But with accoutrements splashed foul and red,
As though through blood they had waded, held the place,
By moody cannon flanked that gazed on space.

CCXXIV

And many a hand was lifted in salute,
Returned by Godfrid, though intended less
For him than her, who walked meek-eyed and mute,
Her senses cloistered in her sober dress,
And lips in prayer composedly resolute,
Close at his side; and as the martial press
Waxed denser, one whose garb bespoke command
Stayed them, and said, with deprecating hand:

CCXXV

"'Twere best to go no farther, sir ! You stray
Beyond our lines, and desperadoes hold
What is beyond. At any moment may
The bugles flourish and the drum be rolled.
We shall attack at once. So turn back, pray !"
And others, crowding round, like story told.
But he, " I thank you, gentlemen ! Withal,
You see my badge ; I but obey its call."

CCXXVI

So these, once more saluting, let them pass ;
And by streets staircased, intricate, they came
To where the remnant of the rebel mass
Waited behind last rampart, pledged to shame
Ungenerous Fortune, deaf to shame, alas !
For her desertion, and from juster Fame
Extort the avowal, if unfit to live,
Their brave death makes vindictiveness forgive !

CCXXVII

Just as they reached the very topmost crown
Of the rude citadel, and came in view
Of its defences,—in the lower town,
From which they just had clomb, a bugle blew,
And upward whizzed a shell, then hurtled down.
Swiftly to arms the loitering victims flew,
And Godfrid Gilbert saw, amid the chase,
Hurrying with Miriam o'er the open space.

CCXXVIII

Fast as can foot be lifted from the ground,
Unheeding even Olympia, straight he·ran,
Shouting their names before him.   At the sound
They halted and looked back; while hastening van,
Urged on by hastening rear, of battle, wound
Past them, defiance now its only plan;
Leaving them stranded, as by scudding wind
Are hesitating leaves left loose behind.

CCXXIX

"What do you here?" asked Gilbert.   "This is not
The place, the hour for mercy.   O fly! fly!"
"I fly!" cried Godfrid.   "Man! you have forgot
Your manhood utterly.   'Tis you, not I,
Who must be dragged, if need be, from the spot;
For, by Love's sovran right! she shall not die!
Do you not know she bears within her womb
Its pledge, you now would cradle in the tomb?"

CCXXX

Was it a mortal bullet from the foe,
Or only Godfrid's words, pierced Gilbert's brain?
Pallid he stood, then staggered back as though
He a farewell had made of life and pain.
But propped by Miriam promptly, "Is it so?"
Aghast he murmured.   "Tell me,—tell me plain!"
"It is," she said.   "But what untimely power
Brings you here, Godfrid, in this final hour?"

CCXXXI

" It is not final," he replied.   " Now quick !
Gilbert, be calm, and do as I shall bid !
See you yon curving wall of crumbling brick ?
Turn, when it turns to right, then straightway thrid
A twisting alley where stone stairs stand thick,
Until you reach an archway almost hid
By the contiguous dwellings.   Once when there,
You will be safe.   Then to my roof repair.

CCXXXII

" Here is a pass, the safest you can wear,
'Twill serve for both."   And from his arm he took
The Red Cross brassard rapidly, and ere
Either could speak, the badge began to hook
Round Gilbert's sleeve, who still with horror's stare
Stood as transfixed.   But Miriam cried, " Look ! look !
See what he does.   He helps us both to fly,
And, unprotected, he remains to die !"

CCXXXIII

" Silence !   It is not so," he sternly said,
" And if it were, what then !   I bid you flee !
The unborn shall not be mingled with the dead !"
Then gazing round, he saw and bade them see
A Sister bending by the upraised head
Of dying form.   " She will suffice for *me*:
That is Olympia, and her garb will sue
For both of us, as this for both of you."

CCXXXIV

"Swear you are safe !" said Gilbert.   "'Then, we go !"
" I swear it !   Now, farewell !   One moment more
May prove too late.   For I can hear the foe
Firing more closely, and the rising roar
Of troops advancing.   But first,—see you !—throw
Your arms away ; put on this cloak I wore
Expressly for your need.   There ! now depart ;
Delay, and it may be too late to start."

CCXXXV

But Miriam fought for one embrace, and then
They were gone ! safe passed beyond the shattered wall.
And Godfrid, gazing round with rapid ken,
Beheld Olympia, still to misery's call
Lending her ear, deaf to the yells of men
Maddened with battle, deaf to cannon's brawl,
And murmuring for pale lips, which 'neath her lay,
Prayers long unsaid, prayers now they could not say.

CCXXXVI

He hastened towards her, and below her saw
That timely face which, when they dubbed him spy,
Pleaded against the rabble's lawless law.
" Alas !" she said, "I fear that he must die !
He spoke my tongue."   " In truth, he ne'er will draw
Life's breath again !   He is dead !   Now must we fly ;
For we too should be gone.   In vain to wait,
When upon mercy wrath hath clanged the gate."

CCXXXVII

"And have you saved them?" "Yes! my badge they wear,—
Enough for both.   Now must I cling to you,
My safeguard ever!" "Welcome!   They who spare,
Or slay the one, must spare or slay the two,"
With joy she cried; "so straight hence let us fare,
If nought be left for pity's touch to do.
But lest that any fail to understand
We two are one,—here! Godfrid! take my hand!"

CCXXXVIII

He took it.   "See, Olympia! we must make
To the west corner, for the opening where
Gilbert and Miriam vanished."   As he spake,
Shouts of fierce exultation rent the air,
And swarming in wherever foot could take
Or head force passage to the rebel square,
The storming files of vengeance came apace,
Death in their hands and fury in their face.

CCXXXIX

Too few to guard each passage, and thus ta'en
In rear and flank, the rebel band faced round,
Their sole thought now to slay before being slain,
And with lowered points fired blank across the ground
At ranks that, blind as theirs, flashed deadly rain
Direct on all their level barrels found
Standing erect; both far too fierce to know
Whether their bullets fell on friend or foe.

CCXL

And Godfrid had but time,—at last !—to fling
His arms around the form he had loved so well,
Thinking to save, and she to him to cling,
When, 'twixt the madness of the twain they fell :
He pierced by ball that fought for faith of old,
She by their shaft who 'gainst all faith rebel ;
Albeit so close was this their first, last troth,
One well-aimed bullet would have served for both.

CCXLI

Thus were they found, when, rummaging among
Mixed heaps of slain, the victors came to save
The corpses of their brethren, ere was flung
The refuse in one contumelious grave.
And seeing that one who wore Christ's habit clung,
Even in death, to form so worldly brave,
They touched them not, but prayed that priest or, nun
Would come and say what meet were to be done.

CCXLII

Then quickly from the Convent thither sped
The reverend Mother, with two daughters dear ;
Who, when she saw this bridal of the dead,
Weeping, commanded, " Put them on one bier,
And bear them after me with gentle tread."
And straight she sent for him who many a year
To them had been Heaven's helpmate in that place,
A venerable man, with tranquil face.

CCXLIII

To him, in hearing of them all, she told
The story she herself had learnt when first,
Six brief weeks gone, Olympia joined their fold,
And next, how Godfrid, aiding her, had nursed
The wounded she with deeper balm consoled ;
But from their ears withholding not the worst,—
His strange sad unbelief, which still had kept
The pair apart, till one in death they slept.

CCXLIV

The agëd pastor, thuswise as she spake,
In silence listened, and then slowly said :
" My children ! these two souls, for Truth's pure sake,
Divided were, since Faith, in him, was dead.
Who knows ? perchance it did in death awake :
It was to save the lost Christ breathed and bled.
Doubt watered by such prayer must somewhere bud ;
And see ! he hath the baptism of blood.

CCXLV

" Therefore I dare not say Christ vainly died
Even for him.   And since the twain would lie,
Methinks, at Spiaggiascura side by side,
Heaven will not earth's infirmity deny.
So let us there one grave for both provide,
In consecrated ground beneath the sky.
She needs no epitaph ; so let his plea,
Dilexit multum, sole inscription be !"

CCXLVI

So you who go, half guided by my song,
To Spiaggiascura, there a grave will find,
To which the waves make music all day long,
And wherein sleep the gentlest of their kind,
Sheltered for ever now from hap of wrong.
And, can it be our mortal causes find
Immortal consequence beyond the tomb,
He either shares her bliss, or she his doom.

CCXLVII

Enter the little chapel, as you pass,
That still stands shimmering in the fragrant air,
Though she who loved it is not there, alas !
And, if you can, kneel down and say a prayer.
Then seek, without, a grave amid the grass,
With that inscription carved in marble fair ;
And falling tears will sound, if wept for woe,
Sweeter than summer shower to those below.

CCXLVIII

And should it be the springtime, go at morn
Straight up the dewy dell, until you gain
Spot you will know, and from the blossoming thorn
That on the streamlet showers its snow-white rain,
Pluck branch, and just as from the tree 'twas torn,
Lay it at their feet.   And, lastly, will you deign
Lend one kind thought, be such prayer not too bold,
To him who, stammering, hath their story told.

CCXLIX

Gilbert and Miriam live, and strive to cope
With grief in tutoring a baby mind,
Named after Godfrid, that is taught to hope
For common happiness to all Mankind.
Surely, a blameless creed ; for we must grope
Onward to light, so long as we are blind ;
And, through the deepest night and murkiest air,
Hope still waves torch and beckons to despair.

CCL

But whether the unsetting day shall rise
For which the downcast weep, the sanguine pine,
Or, but as hitherto, in fitful skies,
Dawn must to dark, fair will to foul decline,—
For gentle hearts and steadfast-gazing eyes
Thou, thou at least, wilt never cease to shine
On wreck of things that were, or things that are,
Love ! reconciling Love ! eternal Star !

THE END

Printed by R. & R. CLARK, *Edinburgh*

Now Publishing in Monthly Volumes.
Crown 8vo, Cloth, 5s. each.

A COLLECTED EDITION

OF

THE POETICAL WORKS OF

MR. ALFRED AUSTIN

Vol. I. THE TOWER OF BABEL: A CELESTIAL LOVE STORY.

Vol. II. SAVONAROLA: A TRAGEDY.

Vol. III. PRINCE LUCIFER.

Vol. IV. THE HUMAN TRAGEDY.

Vol. V. NARRATIVE POEMS.

Vol. VI. LYRICAL POEMS.

MACMILLAN AND CO., LONDON.